A MAN FOR EVERY OCCASION

OCCASION

Jimi Goninan

I0544904

Lydian Press

There's always time for love.

The bustling city of Port Davinica is home to many stories of love, lust and more than a few happy endings. Follow the adventures of these men as they find love in all manner of places with an amorous touch of the supernatural thrown in for good measure. You'll soon discover in this collection of romantic tales that no matter the festive occasion – Halloween, Christmas, and especially Valentine's Day - there's always time for love.

CONTENTS

All previously published as individual eBooks by Lydian Press

To My Beloved Husband Antoine

LUST AFTER DEATH

Timothy Waters had the distinct impression that he was being watched. His hand hovered just over the page with a blood-red pencil gripped tightly between his fingers. He was preparing to turn around and confront the intruder when he was startled by a flying blur of blackness. Timothy jumped in fright, as his sketchbooks scattered and pencils went tumbling off onto the polished floorboards joined shortly afterward by his Superman figurine.

"Mikey!" exclaimed Timothy, as he bent over and began to pick up the mess.

Timothy turned to face the bed and looked at the thoroughly unrepentant kitty, who was now sitting amongst the pillows, cleaning his silky, midnight-black fur and purring contentedly. He wasn't truly cross with the frisky feline but he would've preferred that Mikey – whose full name was Michelangelo – refrain from the almost daily high-speed circuits of his room. Mikey was rather an affectionate thing and usually came in for snuggles every morning, even though Timothy would have preferred an entirely different wild creature in his bed.

Beggars can't be choosers.

Technically, Mikey wasn't actually his, but belonged to the apartment that Timothy had moved into a month beforehand – well as much as a cat would consent to belonging to anything. The owner of the apartment, Miles, in addition to being a strapping specimen with a swarthy complexion, was also his roommate. He was around Timothy's age with a head of dark curls, crystal-blue eyes and a dusting of short dark hair on his arms and legs that drove Timothy to distraction. Sadly – well in Timothy's opinion at any rate – Miles was decidedly straight…if the female squeals and shrieks of pleasure that he'd heard regularly ringing through the bedroom walls were any indication.

Timothy turned back to the desk, tucked a wayward lock of hair behind his ear and picked up his pencil to recommence his drawing. His eyes focused intently on the page before him as a figure slowly took shape. He was a graphic artist by trade and thanks to the wonders of the modern age was able to work from home. Timothy worked mostly with an agency that handled corporate clients, designing logos and the like. His reliability and professionalism had stood him in good staid and the agency kept him busy with a steady stream of projects. While it paid the bills, Timothy didn't find it overly stimulating, as he was often quite limited in his designs by the conservative briefs dictated by the clients. To maintain his creativity, Timothy took on the occasional freelance job drawing for graphic novels. Comic books had been a passion of his from childhood, although these days he preferred those of a more adult nature. From time to time he would tinker with his own characters, but hadn't ever really managed to put them together into an interesting story – apart from placing muscle-bound men in all sorts of compromising positions that is.

Timothy had only recently moved back home to Port Davinica, after spending the last five years in Europe… mostly in Paris. When he'd first returned, Timothy had been staying with his parents but they'd soon lapsed back into treating him as if he was thirteen instead of thirty-three – as is often the case when adult offspring return to the nest – and he'd had to escape before he was tempted into a spot of double homicide. He had searched through the classifieds for a month, encountering all sorts of dumps and dubious characters, until he had finally met Miles through a friend of a friend.

Initially, Timothy had thought it all too good to be true. Not only was his new roommate handsome and friendly, but the apartment itself was practically luxurious. It was located one floor down from the penthouses in Graywood Gardens, in one of the trendiest areas of the city. His room was almost the size of his parents' lounge room, with a large en suite and had stunning views over the city. The rest of the apartment was spacious, light and airy, and tastefully decorated with an eclectic mix of modern and Art Deco pieces. Admittedly, he probably would have lived in a hovel if he'd been able to share it with Miles.

What had aroused Timothy's suspicions, however, was how low the rent was given the location and the size. Before he'd agreed to move in, Timothy had tentatively broached the subject with Miles.

"I don't really need the money and I like the companionship," Miles had explained. "Although, I was starting to think I'd have to give it away."

"What do you mean?"

"Well, to be honest, you'd be the third new roommate in as many months."

"Really? What happened?"

"No idea. Both only lasted a few weeks before giving notice but not really explaining why, just that it wasn't working out."

"Can't imagine why. The place is great!"

"I know. I'm starting to get a complex that it's me."

Even though Miles laughed when he said it, Timothy thought there might be a kernel of truth in his words. His curiosity was piqued but Timothy didn't want to push the matter any further. He liked Miles and loved the apartment and didn't particularly want to lose either of them, so he pushed his concerns to the side and moved in.

Three weeks passed without incident and Timothy had settled into a routine of sleeping in late – he was in by no means a morning person – and spending the afternoons working at the big oak desk in his bedroom. Timothy's worry about the high turnover of previous roommates had all but faded away…and then the dreams began.

* * *

They all featured the same man and while they were extremely realistic, Timothy found them more unsettling than threatening. Unlike previous dreams of a similar nature, these were set in his bedroom instead of some exotic locale and always began the same way with Timothy turning over to find the man in the bed with him – naked and ready. The man wasn't anyone he'd seen before but was certainly handsome and wonderfully in proportion. He looked to be in his early thirties with olive skin, curly blue-black hair and the most striking bright-green eyes. His right eyebrow was broken by a small, faded, scar, which only added to his allure.

The first dream had been so vivid that Timothy surprised, and a little disappointed, to find himself alone in bed afterwards. He had woken up with a start, his crotch a sticky mess…something that hadn't happened since he was a teen.

In the dream, the man had smiled shyly and without saying a word moved forward to kiss Timothy softly on the mouth. His tongue darted between Timothy's lips, tasting of vanilla, before slowing down to a languid pace, swirling between their mouths. The mysterious man had then moved on top of him, the weight of his muscular build pressing Timothy against the mattress. His dark skin was smooth, almost silky, to the touch and contrasted beautifully against Timothy's pale white hue. They lay kissing, writhing together, their erections rubbing between each other.

Timothy moaned gently as the man slowly began to move downwards, teasing and taunting him with his tongue. The stranger seemed content to take his time, lightly nibbling on Timothy's dime-sized, light-pink nipples, while his strong hands ran the length of the lean body beneath him.

He gasped as the man slid further down, licking and biting as he went. Timothy grabbed the back of the man's head; his fingers ran through the soft dark curls, pulling him in closer. He could feel the man's breath warming his skin, sending waves of pleasure through his crotch, as the mouth worked its way around, along the inside of his left thigh, back up under his balls and onto the other side. He ached for the stranger to feast on his cock, which was now dribbling precum all over itself.

Still in no apparent rush, the man continued to torment Timothy, by running his nails ever-so-slowly down Timothy's sides, while his mouth explored the warm, sweaty crotch. Timothy shuddered as he felt the man's tongue lapping at his cockhead, licking away the salty-sweet juice before it ran up and down the length of his engorged manhood.

Suddenly, the stranger plunged his face forward, taking Timothy's member deep into his throat. Timothy cried out in pleasure as he felt the heat of the man's mouth engulf his member…it was almost enough to make him blow right then and there. The man then began to bob his head up and down, as his tongue expertly snaked its way around Timothy's shaft. Timothy felt one hand gently tugging on his ball sack, as the other hand moved underneath, its fingers circling around his rosebud, pressing against it, trying to make their way inside.

The stimulation soon had Timothy at the brink of ejaculation, his breathing grew more rapid and his body tensed in anticipation. All it took was the sensation of a thick finger finally breaching his tight hole and Timothy erupted into the waiting mouth of the stranger, who in turn greedily gobbled all the cream down.

The strength of the orgasm ripped Timothy out of his slumber, leaving him confused but strangely satisfied. He grabbed a crumpled t-shirt from the floor and cleaned himself up then he rolled over and went back to sleep, this time without any erotic intruders.

He'd thought no more of it until midway through the following week when the man once more made an appearance, just as hungry and full of lust as before. Again, Timothy woke up expecting someone to still be in bed with him and was a little saddened to find that he was alone. He'd been single for over a year now, ever since Marco and he had parted back in Paris and he was more than ready for a fresh start…although he had been hoping for a man somewhat less imaginary.

His dreamland trysts continued, usually a week apart and always with a happy ending, although his comely companion never spoke a word. Even though Timothy found it odd that he kept dreaming of the same man, it wasn't the dreams that were cause for concern. What had started to trouble Timothy was the sense that something wasn't quite right in the apartment. It was nothing to do with Miles, who was practically the perfect roommate and wonderfully easy to live with. Rather, the problem was that Timothy felt like he was being followed – and not just by the predatory pussycat. There were times that he could have sworn Miles was home but when he had called out there was no response. Timothy never saw any evidence that anyone else had been there but he began to wonder if this strange sensation was what had caused the previous renters to leave so quickly.

Not that Timothy was inclined to leave, mind you. In fact, he and Miles had started to grow quite close over the weeks, often spending evenings eating dinner together and then chatting on the balcony, admiring the twinkling lights of the city below them. Timothy had learnt quite a deal about his roommate, such as that he'd actually been born in Sri Lanka – his mother's homeland – only moving to the States when he was eight and consequently spoke Sinhala as well as English. He also discovered that they shared a love of drawing, although Miles had turned his talents towards architectural endeavors.

For the most part, Timothy put down his unease as simply a product of an over-active imagination.

But still…

* * *

Nearly two months after he had moved in with Miles, Timothy was sitting on the sun-soaked terrace of One Happy Piggy – a popular eatery in the heart of the gayborhood, not far from his apartment. It was a beautiful clear-skied day and there was a light breeze, which helped to temper the summer heat. Timothy's mouth watered, and his stomach rumbled, as the delicious smell of freshly fried bacon wafted over from the café kitchen. He hadn't yet ordered, as he was patiently waiting for his best friend Lukas, who, as usual, was running late. They had a standing brunch date every Saturday, and while they had tried a few of the other cafés in the area, this was by far their favorite. The friendly service, generous portions and tasty menu kept them coming back for more – the copious amount of eye candy to be seen from the terrace was also undoubtedly a contributing factor.

Timothy had first met Lukas three years beforehand, during a drunken night out in the Marais when they'd both been living in Paris. There had been an instant attraction, which was completely understandable given Lukas' friendly nature and boyish good looks. Indeed, his friend had been somewhat blessed in the genetics department. Not only did he have the rare, and thoroughly striking, combination of auburn hair, startling blue eyes, and golden olive skin, but he also had been with gifted with nine, juicy, uncut inches that had capably pleased many a man.

Naturally, they had gone home together and had a wonderful night of drunken, messy sex. This was followed by several other similarly satisfying encounters, during which time they discovered that they enjoyed each other's company and actually had a lot in common. The sexual side of their relationship had petered out after a few months but the friendship had continued to grow and survived the separation of Lukas moving back to the States a year or so before Timothy. Lukas had originally been from San Francisco but after all the tales he'd heard about Port Davinica he decided to check it out for himself and evidently loved it so much he'd ended up relocating there.

Timothy had been waiting a good fifteen minutes before he spied his friend parking his secondhand, bright-red Jeep Wrangler in a spot across the road and then rushing across to the terrace.

"So sorry, I'm late."

"That's fine, I've just been watching the gays go by. Trouble kicking out last night's conquest?"

"Ha! I'll have you know that my bed was empty last night except for me and my trusty hand…although I may have stopped by ManHole on the way home from work."

"I knew it. Dirty dog!"

"Jealous much? So have you lured Miles into yours yet?"

Lukas had encountered Miles when he'd helped Timothy move in and had nearly tripped over his jaw in lust.

"I wish!" Timothy hesitated a moment before continuing, unsure whether or not to bring up his dreams. "But, I haven't been alone exactly."

"What does that mean?"

"Well, I've been having these really intense dreams."

Timothy went on to describe the dreams in great detail, careful to keep his voice low so as to not traumatize the other diners. He didn't, however, mention his feelings of being watched.

I don't want to sound like a nutter!

"So lucky! All I've been dreaming about is being trapped at work with an unending pile of paperwork and a drag queen dressed as a nun giggling in the corner."

"You have problems!"

Lukas playfully smacked Timothy on the hand.

"So what do you think it means?" asked Timothy, keen for a fresh perspective.

"That you're in desperate need of a cocking from Miles."

"Very funny."

"OK, he's not a possibility, but you should put yourself out there. When was the last time you hooked up with a handsome stranger?"

"I don't know…a while I guess."

"There you go then. We'll go out tonight and see if we can't get you laid. I bet those dreams will stop right away."

"Not sure I want them to."

"Now who's the one with problems?"

The twosome broke into laughter, as their regular buxom, raven-haired waitress, Gloria, came up to their table.

"Glad to see you boys enjoying yourselves. What can I get for ya?" she drawled in a strong Southern accent, which stood out amongst the flatter coastal accents of the native Port Davinicans.

"You ready?" asked Timothy.

"No, I haven't had a chance to decide."

"Sorry we've been chatting," said Timothy apologetically to Gloria.

"Well, if you hadn't been so obsessed with your dream lover," teased Lukas.

Timothy was mortified and shot Lukas a harsh look across the table. He loved his friend's cheeky nature but sometimes he could happily strangle him.

"Sounds saucy! Take your time and I'll be back in a bit," said Gloria, giving them a sly wink before she sashayed away.

"I can't believe you said that!" Timothy admonished Lukas.

"What? She doesn't care."

"Hurry up and choose, I'm starving!"

"We'll get you a nice juicy piece of meat tonight then."

"That's great but right now I'd rather have French Raisin Toast with crispy bacon."

"Fine, fine."

The boys ordered a few minutes later and then spent an agreeable hour eating and enjoying the array of barely-clad beauties that passed by the terrace.

* * *

The following morning, Timothy arose even later than normal as he'd been out with Lukas to some wonderfully ungodly hour. They had gone to Sanctuary – a deconsecrated church and the hottest gay club in the city – and while they had had a fabulous evening of drinking and dancing, Timothy had returned alone. He was pleased to see that Mikey was curled up on the pillow next to him, purring away.

At least someone's happy to be in my bed.

After giving Mikey a good belly rub, Timothy slipped on his loose blue running shorts and stumbled to the kitchen to brew himself a pot of industrial-strength coffee. He then poured the piping hot caffeine into his over-sized Bugs Bunny mug, added a fair splash of milk and headed back to his bedroom. After taking a few sips of his faithful wake up juice, Timothy opened his blinds and let the afternoon sunshine flood into the room. He sat down at his desk and was about to start work on his newest assignment when he was disturbed by a loud shriek emanating from the balcony.

Startled, Timothy jumped up and ran to the lounge room where he saw Miles standing on his weights bench at the far end of the balcony looking absolutely terrified. Timothy was completely confounded until he spotted the source of the trouble – a small Daddy Longlegs scuttling along the doorway to the balcony.

"Please, get rid of it!" begged Miles, seemingly close to tears. His voice was quite shrill in comparison to his normal dulcet tones.

It came as a complete surprise to Timothy that Miles was deathly afraid of spiders. As much as it shouldn't, it amused him to see his strong, masculine roommate turned into a frightened little boy by such a small – and in this case totally harmless – creature.

Timothy sprang into action, grabbed a nearby newspaper and promptly scooped the offending beast onto it. He carefully carried it to the garbage chute in the hallway outside. When he returned to the apartment, Timothy could see that his roommate had calmed down again.

"Thanks so much!" said a clearly grateful Miles.

"You're welcome."

"My hero," said Miles, apparently trying to lighten the situation and make fun of himself before Timothy could.

"Happy to be of service."

Timothy resisted the urge to tease Miles about it, although he had several ideas of how Miles could reward him for his chivalrous behavior if he'd been so inclined. Besides he knew firsthand that phobias weren't a laughing matter. Indeed, if it had been a clown instead of a spider he would have run screaming back to his room and barricaded the door.

If anything, Timothy found the whole situation quite endearing and it made Miles even more attractive to him, not that he particularly needed help in that regard. His roommate was far from the first straight man that Timothy had had an unrequited crush on, but he was the first that he seemed to be having more than a little trouble moving on from.

I need someone else to drool over.

Sadly, he hadn't met anyone since his return that'd taken his fancy – besides Miles that is. Not that the city wasn't full to bursting with gorgeous, available men but at this stage in his life he was searching for something more than a pretty facade. His ex, Marco, had fitted the bill perfectly and he'd considered a long-term future with him but the fates had had different ideas.

"Let me know if you need me to battle any more ferocious beasts."

"Will do, my good Sir."

His words sent a glow from Timothy's heart to his groin and back again. It didn't help that Miles was only wearing a pair of skimpy light-green shorts and a white singlet that barely covered his dark-brown nipples – he'd apparently been in the middle of a workout when the spider had appeared.

Stop it! He's straight, he's straight, he's straight!

Timothy smiled and retreated to his bedroom to dive into his work and hopefully distract himself away from his increasingly naughty thoughts.

* * *

The following weekend, Timothy was lying naked in bed when he suddenly felt that he wasn't alone. Without even needing to look, he knew that the mystery man would be there again. He turned his head to the right and sure enough there he was. This time, however, instead of simply moving towards him, and beginning their usually wordless erotic encounter, the man spoke to him.

"Hi Timothy, it's good to see you again," said the man.

"How do you know my name?" asked Timothy, surprised.

That's a stupid question. He's obviously a manifestation of my subconscious so of course he knows my name. Duh!

"It's written on the cover of your sketch pad," replied the man, matter-of-factly. "I like your drawings."

"Thanks," said Timothy, feeling flattered.

I'm complimenting myself now?

Timothy decided to ignore his inner voice and just enjoy the dream; it was the only action he was getting of late, after all.

"What's your name then?" asked Timothy.

"Giovanni…but my friends called me Gio."

"Pleased to meet you."

"And you too, my handsome friend," said Gio, with a cheeky grin.

Instead of letting Gio take the lead, Timothy moved forward and kissed him passionately, their tongues wrestling one another.

God damn this feels so real…and so good!

"Someone's keen today," commented Gio, when they broke for air.

Timothy pulled Gio in even closer to him, determined to enjoy his dream lover fully. Gio seemed to be equally enthused and their hands grabbed at one another in a frenzied fashion, light moans escaping their lips. Timothy was possessed by an urgent hunger, causing him to bite all up and down Gio's body, loving the way his companion squirmed in pleasure.

In the previous dreams they hadn't yet made it past oral, as Timothy had gotten too excited each time and blown before the main event. To be honest, Timothy was impressed and a little frightened by the length and girth of his companion's manhood – a good solid, ten inches. Even so, he was determined that today he would be man enough to try and take it.

"I wish you were real."

"Doesn't this feel real?" said Gio as his left ring finger pushed its way inside Timothy's tight rosebud.

Timothy gasped as it probed inside him working its way to his sweet spot, while Gio gently nibbled on his neck.

"Oh fuck, yes!"

The finger was joined by a second, and then a third pushing roughly inside; swirling around his hole, touching his prostate and sending shivers up and down his body. Timothy was writhing on the bed, moaning as the digits moved as one. The fingers suddenly withdrew and Timothy was disappointed for a second until they were replaced by Gio's warm mouth, the tongue snaking its way inside following the same path as the fingers.

Suddenly, Gio moved back and roughly flipped Timothy over onto his stomach and lavished attention on the ass while his right hand slowly wanked Timothy's erection, as the precum dripped from the slick cockhead and onto the white cotton sheets below. Gio spit onto Timothy's exposed hole and used the saliva to work his fingers back inside, preparing Timothy for what was to come.

"Please, I need it," pleaded Timothy.

Even though he knew he was dreaming Timothy didn't feel as if he was in control of himself. In answer to his pleas he soon felt Gio's fingers replaced with a bare cockhead. It felt heavenly just sitting there pressed against his opening. Gio started to move it around in slow circles, barely breaching the opening. Timothy ached to have it inside him but was also enjoying being so exquisitely tortured. He pushed his hips back, opening himself further hoping to encourage Gio to venture deeper inside.

Apparently it was the sign Gio had been waiting for and he began to push more forcefully, his cock slowly sliding further inside the moist tunnel with each rotation. Timothy's breath quickened as he felt Gio penetrating deeper and deeper. There was a slight discomfort as his passage struggled to accommodate to the thick inches forcing their way inside. The pain was fleeting and it was shortly overcome by small bursts of pleasure.

Timothy soon felt Gio's hips pressed flush up against his buttocks and was grateful his companion had paused to give him time to adjust. He couldn't remember the last time he had taken such a big cock but it felt damn good.

Gio slowly started to work his manhood in and out of Timothy's snug tunnel. Each time he slid in, it pressed straight into Timothy's prostate making him grunt and groan at the sensation. As Gio started to lick and bite the back of his neck, Timothy arched his back and contracted his ass around the intruder.

The slow pumping soon built up to a heavy pounding. Timothy never wanted it to end. He buried his face in his pillow to try and muffle his moans. Even though he was dreaming he had no idea what sounds he was making in the real world and he didn't want to wake up Miles. He was thoughtful to a fault.

Gio slammed to a halt, and gently maneuvered Timothy around onto his back. The sensation of the cock spinning inside him almost caused Timothy to blow. His cock was leaking a veritable stream of precum. Timothy daren't touch himself, as he knew that with all the stimulation he'd likely explode after the first stroke.

Timothy looked up into Gio's eyes, and saw nothing but burning desire. It sent a thrill through his body to be so earnestly wanted. Gio leaned forward and gave Timothy a long, lazy kiss as he ground his crotch into Timothy's buttocks. Once more Gio started off slowly but before too long his battering had returned to its previous rapid speed. Sweat dripped down his face and chest, and onto Timothy's slick alabaster skin.

Timothy saw Gio's body begin tense up, which was followed quickly by a cry of release. He felt every creamy spurt coating his insides, filling him with warmth. This marvelous sensation sent him over the edge and he sprayed his own thick load onto his chest. Gio laid down on Timothy his cock still firmly inside. They lay there gently kissing as their bodies began to cool down after their exertions.

"Pity I didn't meet you before," said Gio, his voice tinged with sadness.

"Before what?"

Gio only smiled ruefully and then leant back down to resume their gentle kissing. Timothy wasn't surprised, and didn't mind in the slightest, when Gio started pumping again – his cock was still admirably rock-hard. This time was even faster than before and Timothy soon felt a second load building up for release. Timothy took himself in hand and jacked furiously, desperate for another ejaculation. With the constant stimulation of his prostate he was soon granted his desire and he spurted his seed all over himself once more.

Gio stopped his ferocious assault, pulled out and straddled Timothy's hips. After only a handful of strokes he added his creamy goodness to Timothy's already sticky chest. A drop hit Timothy on the lips and he greedily ran his tongue across them to taste his lover.

Timothy suddenly woke up with a start. This was by far the most intense of the dreams he'd had, so much so that he was sure that he could still taste Gio's salty-sweet cream in his mouth. The room was still dark, but felt humid and stuffy, almost as if he'd really been having sex. Running his hands over his chest he felt that he was a sweaty, sticky mess so he decided to have a shower before trying to go back to sleep.

As Timothy got up to go to the bathroom he realized that he was moving a little gingerly as he still had the phantom cock sensation inside him.

How is that even possible?

He reached his hand between his ass cheeks and half expected it to be sticky with Gio's seed but there was nothing but a little sweat. He was half-worried and half-comforted. Timothy switched on the bathroom light and climbed into the shower. The hot water soon cleansed his body of the effects of the dream, although his mind was still muddled.

What's happening to me? Could it be the cheese I ate before bed? Am I going crazy?

When he was done, he toweled off and made his way back into bed. Timothy felt exhausted and soon drifted off, his thoughts still very much on his dream lover.

Well at least he has a name, now!

* * *

When Timothy emerged from his bedroom late the following morning, he found Miles lazing on the terrace, soaking up the sun in a pair of snug, sky-blue Speedos, which showed off his sizable package to perfection. His roommate's deliciously, dark skin glistened with sun tan lotion. The sunlight caught on Miles' ever-present silver necklace, with its half-moon pendant nestled just above his solid pecs. Despite his satisfying, slumber-time shenanigans Timothy's cock couldn't help but stir in his boxers at the arousing sight.

Given how pumped up his muscles were looking, Timothy guessed that Miles had not long finished a workout with the mini-gym that was permanently set up on the left side of the balcony.

Damn, why does he have to be straight!

Timothy immediately admonished himself, as it was the same thing he hated hearing from girls in reference to hot homosexuals. Timothy fetched himself a tall glass of fresh orange juice and joined his roommate in the sun.

"Morning," said Timothy.

Miles turned over and gave Timothy a welcoming, white smile.

"Hey Timmy, it's a glorious day isn't it?"

It was an abbreviation that Miles had used from the first day they met and Timothy had never bothered to correct him. Normally, he hated it cause it reminded him of being a little boy but he made an exception for Miles.

He can call me whatever he wants. Stop that! What? You know what. Leave the straight boy alone. Fine!

Sometimes the little voices in his head could be tiring to listen to. Timothy saw them as his very own guardian angels – one innocent and the other somewhat fallen. Unfortunately, it was the side of purity that seemed to win most of the time of late.

"That it is," Timothy answered, as he resisted the urge to leap right on top of Miles and ravish him right there and then. "I might just join you in a…"

Jump on him!

Timothy jerked in surprise and dropped the glass. It smashed on the red tiles of the terrace floor. Miles hopped up quickly to avoid the mess of shattered glass and juice.

"Hey, you OK?" asked Miles, his voice full of concern.

"Yeah…sorry it just slipped out of my hand," replied Timothy, reluctant to admit the truth. "I'll get some paper towel and the dustpan to clean it up. Sorry."

"No use crying over spilt….juice," said Miles, smiling.

As Timothy walked back to the kitchen, he was concerned about the real reason he dropped the glass.

That wasn't my voice!

Timothy was used to hearing his own thoughts urging him to mischief but this new insistent voice had sounded like it was coming from next to him. And the oddest thing of all, he could have sworn that it sounded a lot like the deep, sultry voice of Gio.

What's wrong with me?

Disturbed by events, he grabbed the necessarily supplies and hurried back to the terrace to clean up the mess he'd made. In a few minutes, all that was left was a small damp patch, which would quickly dry off in the sun.

"Sorry, again," said Timothy regretfully.

"Don't be silly, it was just a glass. Now go get changed and get some color on that pasty skin of yours," teased Miles.

"Blame my Irish ancestry!" Timothy retorted.

"Excuses, excuses."

Timothy enjoyed the habit of light-hearted banter that had grown between them.

If only I could banter him into bed. Stop it!

Timothy silently berated himself for his thoughts but was glad they were his alone this time. He quickly changed into his swimwear and joined Miles on the terrace.

"Want me to cream you?" asked Miles, shaking the bottle at Timothy.

Do I ever! Calm down!

"Yeah that'd be great."

Timothy shuddered as the cold cream splattered onto his back and tried his best to think of anything but Miles' strong hands, as they slowly rubbed the lotion deep into his back. It was all to no avail, however, as his erection threatened to poke right through the sun lounge. Timothy was proud of himself for at least resisting the urge to moan.

"There you go all done."

"Thanks!"

Timothy stayed lying face down until he was able to turn over without shame. The pair spent the rest of the day together chatting about nothing in particular and enjoying each other's company, as they looked out towards the harbor with the air shimmering over the city in the heat of the summer's day.

* * *

Halfway through the next week, Timothy had just gotten home after one of his regular runs with Lukas, in the park just across the road from his apartment building, when he received a quiet unexpected phone call.

"Hey Casper!"

It was his ex-boyfriend Marco. The nickname always made Timothy smile. To be fair, in comparison to Marco's swarthy, olive skin Timothy did resemble a ghost. They were both from Port Davinica originally and had moved to Europe together five years ago, after they'd already been an item for two. The pair had broken up when Marco had received a job offer in Iceland that he couldn't refuse. He was a marine biologist and the opportunity to head up a study on the declining walrus populations was too good to pass up. Sadly, Timothy had no desire to live there and neither of them believed in the viability of a long distance relationship. They had parted amicably enough and had kept in sporadic constant ever since.

"Hi Polo. How you been? Still in Reykjavik?"

"No, I'm actually a little closer than that. Do you know the Grand Babylon Hotel?"

"The five-star place by the harbor in Port Davinica?"

"Guess who's their newest lifeguard?"

"What?"

"Well my contract ended and I wanted to take the summer off and head somewhere warm, so I came home."

"Why didn't you tell me?"

"I wanted to surprise you."

"Aren't you slightly overqualified to be a lifeguard?"

"Yeah, but it's only temporary and I just wanted something not too demanding until I figured out where I wanted to go next. So, I'm working this afternoon, why don't you swing by around 5pm, I'll be finishing up and we can catch up over cocktails."

"Sure, that sounds great."

Timothy was beaming when he got off the phone. He was looking forward to seeing his former beau and was glad to have him back in town.

And it will help get my mind off both Miles and Gio.

A few hours later, Timothy walked out on to the large terrace of the outside pool at the rear of the Grand Babylon Hotel, sporting a pair of baby-blue shorts and a tight-fitting white t-shirt. Even though they weren't together anymore, Timothy still wanted to look good for their first meeting in more than a year, and judging from the looks he was getting from some of the poolside guests he had chosen well.

Timothy scanned the pool area and caught side of Marco by the base of the small lifeguard tower, a whistle around his neck and dressed only in a pair of bright yellow Speedos – that left little to the imagination – with LIFEGUARD emblazoned across his buttocks in big black letters. His body glistened from the water, he'd obviously just been in for a dip and his body was even better than Timothy had remembered, although he was a little paler; unsurprising given how long he'd been in Iceland. Timothy's crotch involuntarily swelled at the sight, and at the many, many pleasant memories that came rushing back.

It was then that Timothy noticed the man his ex was talking to. He was darker than Marco, his skin almost coffee-colored, tall with a lean build and handsome features. The man was dressed in a white polo with the name of the hotel across his right pec and a pair of red shorts that showed off a wonderfully curved ass and not inconsiderable package in front. The hotel was well frequented by gentlemen of a certain persuasion and the staffing choices clearly reflected it.

They certainly know how to cater their guests.

Timothy made his way over to the pair, doing his best to keep his eyes at head level.

"Casper, you made it!"

Marco broke away from his companion and swept Timothy up in a big bear hug. Timothy felt warm and tingly from the familiar sensation of Marco's strong arms wrapped around him as their bodies pressed tightly together. To be honest, he was a little disappointed when Marco released his grip and turned back to the man he'd been chatting to.

"Lorenzo this is Timothy, my…Timothy, and Lorenzo is the head Cabana boy here at the hotel."

"Pleased to meet you," said Lorenzo, offering his hand.

"Likewise."

Timothy appreciated the firmness of the handshake and briefly wondered how the hand might feel wrapped around another part of his anatomy.

"Well, I've got to get back to it. Have fun, guys, and I hope to see you around, Timothy."

"Definitely."

As Lorenzo walked away, Timothy couldn't but admire his spectacular derriere.

"I see why you like working here," teased Timothy.

"What? Lorenzo? Yeah he's a great guy and very *friendly*, if the hotel grapevine is anything to go by."

"So have you and he?"

"Nah…well, not yet," said Marco, a cheeky grin on lips.

"It's so good to see you."

"You too, Casper. I've missed you a lot."

"The walruses weren't enough company?"

"They were but you gave better head."

"You're gross."

"That's why you love me."

From there their conversation fell straight back into their easy pattern of light-hearted teasing. Not bothering to change, Marco led Timothy over to the bar and ordered two Cuban Mojitos – Timothy's favorite cocktail.

"Ahh, you remembered."

"Of course, how could I forget anything about you?"

Timothy blushed, he hadn't expected Marco to be so flirty – not that he minded.

Maybe the spark is still there?

Cocktail followed cocktail and they chatted away as if they'd never been parted. Before they knew it, night had fallen and the pool area became deserted, which they only noticed when the barman – a ruggedly handsome Brazilian with dark piercing eyes – interrupted them.

"Sorry Marco, but I really need to pack up."

"No problem, João. We'll get out of your hair." Marco turned back to Timothy. "Walk me back to my locker, kind Sir?"

"It would be an honor, my dear."

Timothy was rather tipsy by this point and had to lean on Marco slightly as they made their way to the far left side of the pool where the staff locker room was located. Once inside, Marco went to his locker and began to change. In his inebriated state, Timothy openly ogled his ex-boyfriend and a whole series of wicked thoughts flashed across his mind.

Marco was soon dressed and they exited the locker room without Timothy giving in to his baser urges. He didn't want to make things awkward, even though he was fairly certain that Marco wouldn't have put up a fight.

"Can I give you a ride home?" asked Marco.

Hell yes, I want to ride you!

"Sure, that'd be great! But haven't you drunk too much?"

"Nah, my last two were non-alcoholic cause I knew had to drive."

"So you were trying to get me drunk to take of advantage of me?" joked Timothy.

"Drat! You discovered my secret plan!"

They laughed together and then walked downstairs to the parking garage and hopped into Marco's small, white hatchback – a relic from his college days. It reminded Timothy of the many road trips they'd taken…and the shenanigans they'd gotten up to on the way. His crotch bulged uncomfortably, as his growing manhood tried to escape.

The traffic was quite light and they pulled up outside Graywood Gardens only fifteen minutes later.

"It's been fun, we should this again soon," said Timothy, as he leaned forward to give Marco a kiss goodbye.

"Yes, we most definitely should," agreed Marco, in a rather seductive tone.

Timothy pecked Marco innocently on the lips but when he pulled back he saw desire in Marco's eyes. Before Timothy had time to say anything Marco moved forward and planted a far more passionate kiss on his lips. Timothy responded in kind and they stayed locked in their passionate embrace for a good few minutes.

Eventually, they broke for air and Timothy made to get out. He needed time to think.

"I should get going."

"See you soon, Casper."

Timothy watched as Marco drove away, his mind abuzz with possibilities. It was all so unexpected. He had thought that part of their relationship was well and truly over but now he was not so sure. Timothy found his old feelings beginning to resurface; whether it was just nostalgia or the start of a new chapter he couldn't say.

At least he's not straight!

* * *

Timothy spent the next few days mulling over his predicament – his growing attraction to Miles, his strange experiences in the apartment and the reappearance of his former flame. Needless to say, he wasn't being productive with his work and was in danger of missing a deadline.

Fortunately, he was due for his weekly brunch with Lukas and he was currently sitting in the café at the base of his building – Perk Up. Timothy was a regular in there, often dropping in for a caffeine boost mid-afternoon. He liked the comfy couches and their brain-zappingly strong coffees. Timothy had also developed a friendly rapport with one of the baristas, Prudence, a fine-featured lass with blonde dreadlocks and a lip piercing.

He was sipping on a double shot Speculatté when Lukas waltzed in the door, surprisingly only five minutes late.

"Did you think we were meeting earlier?" teased Timothy.

"You're hilarious."

They went to the counter and placed their orders, Timothy took the Buckwheat pancakes, while Lukas settled on the Spanish omelet. Once they sat back down Timothy launched into the story of Marcus' return and their consequent lip-locking.

"So you're getting back together?" asked Lukas.

"I have absolutely no idea."

"Why not? It only ended because of the whale thing right?"

"Walruses, and yes."

"And he's even hotter than before?"

"Yes…but I'm just not sure. Plus there's the whole Miles thing."

"Erghh, don't be such a cliché!"

"Look who's talking, lusting after your boss."

"Touché."

Timothy had often patiently listened to Lukas gushing about his boss at Babylon Enterprises – the unhappily married, and smoking hot, Mr. Daniels.

"You need to get a real cock in you instead of a dream one, no matter how good it feels," insisted Lukas.

"I know."

"Then why don't you stop pining over your straight roommate and your dream lover?"

"It's not just that though. Lately, it feels like I'm being watched in the apartment when Miles isn't there. "

"Maybe it's haunted!" joked Lukas. "You did say that the other tenants all moved out suddenly without a reason."

"I don't know and I don't want to talk to Miles about it in case he thinks I'm some sort of freak. I really do love the apartment."

"We can have an exorcism. Splash some holy water about the place and shout some Latin."

"So funny, you're such a big help."

"Any time my friend, any time."

Just then Prudence arrived with their meals. The smell of the pancakes made Timothy salivate in anticipation.

"Enjoy, guys!" she said, before hurrying away to serve a frantically gesturing customer in the corner.

As they munched away in companionable silence, Timothy wondered if he should give things with Marco another chance.

He's still the man I fell in love with. But do I still love him?

* * *

Timothy sighed as he leant back in his chair and rubbed his tired, bloodshot eyes. He had just pressed SEND on what he hoped to be the final draft of his latest project. The client – an established hardware chain seeking to update their image – had been exceedingly difficult, frequently changing their minds on what they wanted and rejecting just about every idea he'd presented to them. He'd been at it all week and had barely had time to do anything else.

The one bright spot was that it hadn't given him time to dwell excessively on the men in his life. Timothy had messaged back and forth with Marco but they hadn't met up again since that steamy kiss goodbye the previous week. Miles was also apparently rather busy with his own work and so they had barely seen each other either – except in Timothy's daydreams where they were often fucking hard on the balcony with the hot midday sun beating down on their slippery skin.

His right hand softly stroked Mikey, who was purring happily in Timothy's lap. Absentmindedly, Timothy picked up one of the chewed pencils on his desk – a bad habit he'd had since childhood – and started to doodle on the nearby sketchbook.

Timothy's eyes were half-closed and his breathing started to become heavier as the stress of the past week took its toll on his tired body. He might have fallen asleep right there on the desk if Mikey hadn't chosen that moment to suddenly leap from Timothy's lap without warning and race out of the room, causing Timothy to jerk upright.

When he recovered from the sudden fright, Timothy looked down at the page and saw that he had drawn a muscular vigilante-type, clad in black leather, with a mask over the eyes – one needs to maintain one's secret identity, after all. The figure looked familiar and it took him a minute before it clicked who he'd drawn.

It's Gio!

Timothy picked up his blue pencil – equally as chewed – and added some piping up the legs and arms and to the mask.

My very own superhero!

"What should I call you?" Timothy said to the page.

He didn't want it to sound too corny or too much like a porn star but it was somewhat difficult, as all the good names already seemed to be taken. He quite liked the blue of the outfit and wanted to incorporate it somehow.

"Blue Justice…Blue Vengeance…Blue Velvet Cake… and now I'm hungry…"

Blue Hunter.

Timothy jumped up and turned around to see an empty room. It was that damn strange voice in his head again, the voice that was definitely not his…the voice that still sounded like Gio.

"It's actually not a bad name though."

He sat back down, picked up a pencil, flipped to a new page and started drawing. It was as if his creative juices had been uncorked and he couldn't stop the flow. Timothy started to fill page after page with his new action hero. By the time he stopped two hours later, his left hand was cramping and his head was pounding. He sat back and slowly flipped through the pages, amazed with how much he'd drawn in such a little time. Timothy thought he was on to something. Normally, he just drew images to match the stories he had been given by the various writers of the graphic novels, but laid before him was his very own creation, which already seemed to have a life of its very own. He decided to have a good night's rest before deciding what to do with it.

Even though it was his hand that had done the drawings, Timothy couldn't help but wonder if his dream lover was perhaps the driving influence of his recent bout of creativity.

Maybe I am being haunted?

* * *

Timothy was panting, perspiration dripping from his body, the muscles in his legs burning from exertion. He turned to look at Lukas who was in a similar state by his side.

"I'm exhausted! You want to finish up?" asked Timothy, between gasps.

"Yeah, I'm beat too."

The pair turned the corner and headed for the big patch of grass by the gate closest to Timothy's apartment building. They were just coming to the end of their third lap of Janeway Park, each circuit being roughly three miles…it was the biggest park in the city, after all. Normally, they did five laps and even though it was early evening, the humidity of the day had sapped their strength.

Timothy adored running outside. He loved being out in the fresh air, his heart thumping in time with his feet, as he pounded away. Timothy had tried other forms of exercise but nothing else gave him the same sense of exhilaration. A few years beforehand, Lukas had tried to introduce him to the benefits of adding dance classes to his fitness regime but they soon discovered that Timothy had two left feet and sometimes a random right one. Lukas, on the other hand, was quite adept at tap, street jazz and hip hop…much to Timothy's chagrin. Timothy had also tried the gym on a few separate occasions but had always been put off by the muscle-bound wildebeests loudly grunting and banging about their weights in an obvious attempt to be noticed.

The duo collapsed on the grass, to catch their breath before starting on their habitual alternating sets of pushups and crunches. The air was heavy with the sweet scent of jasmine, which grew in abundance in the gardens bordering the grass. It reminded Timothy of the small rooftop terrace of the apartment he'd shared with Marco before they'd moved to Europe, which had been similarly filled with the vine.

In the distance, Timothy saw another runner approaching them with bright red shoes, and a matching cap worn backwards. For a brief moment, he thought it was Miles, due to the man's build and coloring, but as the runner came closer Timothy realized his mistake. He wasn't too disappointed though, as the man was still quite the strapping specimen. The runner was hairier than Miles with a trimmed beard and copious chest hair poking out of a white singlet, which clung to his body with perspiration. What really caught his attention, however, was the man's light gray track pants and his obvious lack of underwear. The man was unquestionably well endowed and the way his unrestrained manhood swung back and forth under the material was truly mesmerizing.

The man came to a halt about ten feet away from the pair and gave them a broad, dazzling white smile, as he stopped on the grass to stretch. The boys were then treated to a most marvelous display as the man spread his legs wide and bent over in front of them, causing the track pants to cling to the round orbs of his ass, highlighting it to perfection.

"Fucking hell," muttered Timothy, under his breath.

"Tell me about it."

They happily watched the man stretch for a good five minutes before he turned, gave them another cheeky smile and wandered out of the park. Once he was gone the boys quickly finished off their own exercises.

"Do you want to come back to mine for a shower?" asked Timothy.

"Nah, it's OK. I'll be home soon enough."

"See you Saturday."

"It's a date."

Timothy headed across the road to his apartment. A short elevator ride later he was in his en suite bathroom, naked, with his sweaty clothes in a messy pile on the floor. He turned the water on full and waited till the steam began to fill the room before he hopped through the glass doors and into the large shower cubicle. It was big enough that he could sit down on the tiled floor with his legs stretched out, which is exactly what he'd done on nights when he'd gotten home after a few too many cocktails with Lukas.

He rested his head against the tiled wall and closed his eyes. The hot water felt so soothing, as it pounded down on his back and legs. In fact, it was almost as if someone was massaging him, their strong hands slowly working their way down his body, releasing the tension. The sensation of phantom hands seemed to be moving down his back and towards his ass. All of a sudden Timothy felt an unexpected pressure against his rosebud, rather like a finger was trying to push its way inside. He spun around wildly and almost lost his balance on the slippery floor. Fortunately, he righted himself in time but his heart was racing. Timothy was positive that somebody had been in the shower with him, but he could plainly see that it was only him and the steam.

"Gio?"

There was no response.

Now I'm talking to the air! I must be cracking up. It's only my imagination.

Feeling foolish, Timothy decided it was time to finish up. He squeezed a generous dollop of citron-scented body wash and lathered up his body. As he was washing himself Timothy's thoughts turned back to the swarthy stranger from the park…and the contents of his track pants. He slowly jacked himself, and pulled on his balls with his free hand. The water tickled at his neck, very much like someone was nibbling on it.

He was so caught up pleasuring himself that it took him a moment to realize that the sensation of something prodding at his hole was back. Timothy turned his head and saw that he was still alone in the shower. He relaxed back into the wank and when he felt the pressure there again he pushed back against it and felt his sphincter stretch for an invisible intruder. He then had the impression that hands were running all over his torso so he closed his eyes and gave into the feeling.

Maybe I'm dreaming.

Timothy found the situation scary and exciting. He moaned as the pressure inside his tunnel increased and expanded, if he didn't know better he'd think he was being fucked. It only took a few minutes before his ragged breathing and tensed body gave way to a glorious release; wad after creamy wad splattered up against the tiled wall and trickled down towards the floor. After he was spent, Timothy felt as if he was now alone. He washed away the remnants of his orgasm, turned off the water and toweled himself off. When he wandered back into his bedroom he saw that his bedroom door was wide open.

I'm sure I closed it.

Timothy was suddenly embarrassed, as he could hear Miles rattling pots and pans in the kitchen.

Was he in the room watching?

As exciting as that prospect as that would be, Timothy instantly dismissed it as pure fantasy on his behalf. He threw on a t-shirt and shorts and went to the kitchen to see if he could help Miles with the preparations for dinner.

* * *

Several days later, Timothy was downstairs in the basement of Graywood Gardens, rummaging through the storage area, trying to make space for his boxes, when he made a surprising discovery.

His parents had recently cleaned out his old room, in preparation for turning it into a sewing room for his mother, and had insisted that he come over and save anything he didn't want sent to the trash. After first overcoming the indignation that his parents would dare throw out any memento of his childhood, he'd traipsed over with Lukas, who'd generously offered the use of his jeep, and went through his things.

Memories flooded through his brain as he rediscovered all sorts or relics from his early youth – toys, comics and his very first gay magazine. He even unearthed the first Valentine's card he'd received from Marco, which gave him a very warm and fuzzy feeling inside as he remembered the night of deliciously debauched passion that had followed.

He was always such a sweetheart.

After two hours of sorting and reminiscing, Timothy ended up with about ten boxes of items he just couldn't part with – especially the magazine – which he and Lukas then transported back to his apartment.

It was only after they'd carried all the boxes into Timothy's room that he saw there wasn't close to being enough space to fit everything – well not if he wanted to move about at any rate. Lukas had left shortly afterwards, as he had a hot date with a guy he'd met online, leaving Timothy alone to work out what he was going to do. He was still there an hour later, surrounded by open boxes with their contents spread throughout his room.

"Did your room explode?" inquired Miles lightheartedly, upon passing by Timothy's door and seeing the mess.

"Nah. It's stuff from my parent's place. Can you believe they threatened to throw out my treasured possessions?"

"Heartless!" exclaimed a smirking Miles. "We have a space downstairs if you need to store some things. I haven't been down there in a while but there should be enough room for a few boxes at least."

"That would be awesome. Thanks, so much."

"No problem. You live here after all. Do you need help carrying it down?"

"Nah, I still need to decide what I want to keep in my room."

"OK. Let me know if you change your mind."

"Will do."

Timothy managed to fit all but three boxes of his keepsakes into his room, without it looking too untidy. He'd then carried the remaining boxes downstairs and was in the process of rearranging things when he tripped over a large mahogany chest and accidentally knocked it open. Inside it was full of paintings, brushes and a dried up palette. He was quite surprised, as he hadn't known that Miles was a painter…or had been one in the past given the layer of dust that had been on the trunk. He wondered why Miles had stopped, as some of the paintings were really rather good, especially the third one he'd found…a dark, abstract piece with a face taking up the foreground. It looked familiar but Timothy couldn't place where he'd seen it before.

Or something very much like it.

After another half hour of shuffling he managed to get everything back into some semblance of order and returned upstairs, dusty and more than a little sweaty. He had brought the painting upstairs, as he was curious to ask Miles about it. Timothy was thirsty after his efforts, so he went to the kitchen to get a big glass of cold water, which he promptly gulped down. He was on his way back to his bedroom, carrying the painting under his left arm, when he ran into Miles in the hallway.

"How did you go?" asked Miles.

"I got it all in. Why didn't you tell me you used to paint?"

"What do you mean?"

Timothy held the painting up.

"I found this when I was moving stuff about. It's very g..."

Miles lunged forward and practically ripped it from Timothy's hands.

"Why do you have that?"

"I really liked it and I…"

"You should have left it down there."

"Sorry, I didn't realize."

"Just leave my things alone alright?"

"Sure."

Miles stormed off to his bedroom and slammed the door, leaving a very bewildered Timothy in his wake.

"Sorry," he said to the empty hallway.

Timothy didn't understand why Miles had acted in such a rough manner. He'd never seen him angry like that before. He went to his room feeling upset and somewhat perplexed. To make himself feel better, and to wash away the grime and perspiration, Timothy took a long, hot shower.

When he was done he decided to get stuck into some work in order to distract himself. Luckily, Timothy had just received a new project and was able to bury himself in a pile of paperwork to help him forget his troubles. Before he knew it was 1am. He switched off his lamp and climbed into bed, but as soon as he closed his eyes all he could see was Miles' angry face.

Have I fucked everything up?

* * *

The next day dawned clear and bright and Timothy awakened to brilliant blue skies. He wandered into the kitchen and turned on the coffee machine, a little afraid of running into Miles after the incident the previous night.

"Hi," said a sheepish voice behind him.

Timothy jumped as he hadn't heard Miles come in over the noise of the machine. He turned around to face his roommate, who looked more than a little forlorn.

"Hey, I'm sorry for yesterday. The paintings were by a close friend who died suddenly and it just brought it all up again for me."

"No problem. I totally understand. Besides, you were right I shouldn't have gone through your things."

"Nah, it's fine. I overreacted. I hope I didn't offend you."

"Not at all." Timothy was overjoyed that things were still good between him and Miles but felt bad about his part in dredging up painful memories. "Your friend was talented."

"Yeah he was."

Timothy could see tears starting to well up in Miles' eyes making him appear ever so vulnerable, so he tactfully changed the subject.

"Wanna go to the beach with me and Lukas? I hear it's going to be our last spot of good weather for a while?"

"That sounds good, but I have plans unfortunately. Murdoch Beach I'm guessing?"

"We hadn't decided but probably."

"It's a pity, I love it down there!"

"Really? I just didn't figure it was your kind of place."

"Yeah, I like to get my kit off on occasion. And it's not like I have much in the way of competition for the lovely uninhibited lasses that go there," said Miles, smirking. "Plus I don't mind giving the guys something to look at, " he added with a wink.

"Cheeky monkey."

"Yeah that's why you love me."

Timothy panicked for a second before he realized that Miles was joking.

If only you knew.

While Timothy was ecstatic that Miles was no longer angry with him, he was a little embarrassed that his crush seemed to be getting worse, not to mention a little disappointed that he wasn't going to see his roommate bare ass naked on the beach.

In an apparent effort to make up for his behavior, Miles made them both a scrumptious breakfast of fresh fruit, muesli and yogurt, which they ate together on the balcony. They chatted away for a good hour until Timothy received a message from Lukas, saying that he was parked outside. Timothy bid adieu to his roommate, grabbed his beach bag and headed downstairs. He climbed into the jeep and the friends headed off for an afternoon of sun, sand, surf and boy-watching.

* * *

"Oh God, yes, yes, yes!"

Timothy was at his desk trying to concentrate but the noises coming echoing across the hallway and into his room weren't helping.

Seems like another satisfied customer.

Miles was going through even more women than usual of late. His bedroom had been fairly busy before but it seemed in the last week or so that he'd upped his game. Timothy wondered if it was connected to his finding the painting and reminding Miles of his friend's death, prompting his roommate to seize life…or at least as much sex as he could find.

Strangely, he hadn't appeared to see the same girl twice, not that Timothy had met all of Miles' recent conquests but the noises seemed to be a little different each time – ranging from meek mice to veritable screamers. Timothy found it more amusing than irritating and knew that if became too distracting then he could always pop downstairs to work in Perk Up or in the park.

It was safe to say that Timothy was a little jealous, partly because it wasn't him being pounded senseless by Miles but also because it was making him feel a bit like a monk, seeing the most action he was getting was from a figment of his own imagination… his dreams of Gio had increased in frequency to almost every night.

Of course, Timothy realized that it was completely his own fault. Timothy knew he probably could have been having copious amounts of sex with Marco if he wished but there was still something holding him back. They had caught up twice in the past week, for coffee and then a dinner, and each time their goodbye kiss was definitely leagues away from being platonic.

Why am I fixated on what I can't have?

"Pound me, Daddy!"

Timothy burst out laughing at the latest outburst from his roommate's bedroom. He decided he needed to leave and give them their privacy, as he didn't want to ruin their fun by giggling like a schoolboy, no matter how amusing he may find their erotic outbursts. Timothy shoved his sketchbook and a few pencils into his brown leather satchel and headed downstairs to do some drawing in the park while the light was still good.

Maybe I'll bump into that runner.

* * *

The delicious smell of frying onions filled the kitchen and wafted throughout the apartment. Timothy was busy preparing burritos for a movie night with Lukas.

"Mmm…smells great," said Miles, upon entering the kitchen.

"Thanks. You're always welcome to have some."

"Might just take you up on that."

"You're home late. Another long day?"

"Long and not particularly thrilling."

"You don't like your current project?"

"No, not really…but I haven't enjoyed the last few either."

"Why don't you quit?"

"I'd love to but no one seems to be hiring at the moment. Believe me, I've been looking."

"I'm sorry, I didn't realize it was that bad. Could you start your own firm?"

"Again, I'd love to, but it'd be a struggle financially and it would mean scrambling for clients."

"I'm sure there's heaps of people who'd love to have you erect something for them."

What did I just say!

"Oh really?"

Miles' eyes were sparkling with mischief.

"I mean…"

Just then the intercom buzzed and Timothy was grateful for the distraction. He went and pushed the button to let Lukas in. Shortly afterwards there was a knock at the door and Timothy let his handsome redheaded friend into the apartment. They went back into the kitchen to return to the cooking. Timothy was relieved to see that Miles had disappeared off to his room.

"What did you need me to do?"

"You can chop up the rest of the vegetables, while I grate the cheese."

"Sounds good. So how's Gio?" teased Lukas.

"What did you say?" asked Miles, who'd just walked back into the room, looking confused.

"Gio. It's the man of his dreams," mocked Lukas.

"Shut up," said Timothy, slowly dying from embarrassment.

"What do you mean?" asked Miles, his face awash with emotion – fear the most prominent.

Reluctantly, Timothy explained about his dream lover, not going into too much detail. Miles nervously fiddled with the pendant on his necklace, appearing more and more upset. He then left the kitchen abruptly without saying a word. Then they heard the front door open and bang shut.

"What did I say?" asked Timothy, completely confounded.

"Too gay for him, maybe?"

41

"I don't think so. He's one of the most open and accepting straight guys I know."

"It certainly was strange."

They were interrupted by the smell of burning onions. Timothy raced over the stove and lifted the fry pan off the hotplate.

"Dammit! Dammit! Dammit!"

He scraped the burnt remains into the bin and started over again. The conversation then turned to other more pressing matters as they finished preparing dinner – such as fact that Lukas' boss was getting a divorce and how long would be considered appropriate before trying to seduce him.

A short while later they settled down in the lounge room with a substantial Mexican feast spread out before them. Timothy flicked through the movies on offer and he and Lukas settled upon a Hollywood action blockbuster, with a good-looking actor in the lead, known more for his body than his acting ability – neither of them minded, of course.

They tucked into their food and were soon treated to a mess of explosions and hammy dialogue. Timothy tried to switch off his brain and enjoy the film but in the background he kept thinking about Miles, replaying his odd behavior over and over again.

I'm missing something.

* * *

A week of awkwardness followed, with Timothy and Miles barely speaking to one another, except about mundane things like the broken cupboard that the building super was coming by to fix that week. Sadly, he was a portly grandfather rather than the type of handyman that porn portrays as the norm.

It seemed that their camaraderie of the previous months had vanished overnight. Several times, Timothy tried to broach the subject of their newly strained relationship but on each occasion Miles had simply brushed him off.

It didn't help that Miles was hardly ever home. Timothy suspected that his roommate was purposely avoiding him but he couldn't for the life of him work out why. To help escape the tension, Timothy had been seeing more of Marco, not that he'd decided what he wanted on that front, though. He certainly enjoyed the company of his former flame but he wasn't sure that getting back together was for the best, especially as there were no guarantees that Marco wouldn't accept another far-flung post and force them to go through the annoyance and heartache of breaking up again.

What wasn't in question, however, was the obvious sexual attraction between them, as their goodbye kisses had begun to border on indecent with much groping and grinding. It was their third catch-up of that week – Timothy was still reluctant to call them dates – where things came to a head. Marco had walked Timothy back to his apartment building after seeing the latest Ryan Reynolds film, which had understandably gotten both of them quiet worked up.

Feeling emboldened, and more than a little horny, Timothy decided to forgo their goodbye kiss.

"Do you want to come upstairs?" he asked; his meaning quite clear.

"I thought you'd never ask!"

The pair raced inside and began making out as soon as the elevator doors shut behind him. Tongues teased and wrestled together, while their hands roamed freely. Timothy's cock sprang to life against the fabric of his jeans and he could feel Marco pressing into him in a similar state of excitement, both of them evidently eager for release. The chime dinged for Timothy's floor and they pulled away from one another long enough to get inside the apartment. Timothy didn't see Miles' keys in the dish by the door so assumed that his roommate wasn't home. Not that he was too worried if he had been, seeing he'd had to listen to enough of Miles' conquests over the past weeks.

Clothes were hastily discarded and the excited exes were soon rolling around naked on Timothy's bed. It felt strange, yet thrilling, to be back with Marco like this. Their bodies moved together like dance partners rediscovering a familiar rhythm. Despite their obvious arousal, neither seemed in the mood to rush things, content to simply kiss and grind together. Timothy adored the weight of Marco's tanned body pressing down on him as their mouths were locked in a passionate embrace. He ran his fingers down Marco's back, with just a little hint of his nails, causing Marco to groan in appreciation.

I've missed this.

Marco had started kissing down Timothy's writhing body when he suddenly jumped up off the bed and cried out in pain, in conjunction with a hiss and a growl.

"Fucking hell!" he cried out.

"What happened?" asked Timothy, more than a little confused.

"The damn cat!"

Marco turned around and Timothy saw that he had several deep scratches with blood beginning to seep through.

"Oh my god! I'm so sorry. Don't move; I'll get bandages and rubbing alcohol from the bathroom."

As he entered the bathroom he saw Mikey sitting contently on the sink.

"Mikey what have you done. Bad cat!"

44

Timothy shooed Mikey out of the room and shut the door firmly behind him. He then got the supplies from his bathroom and returned to his injured companion. Marco winced in pain as Timothy began to clean the wounds.

"Sorry. I'll be done soon," said Timothy, mortified.

"Is your cat normally possessive?"

"He's not really my cat but I've never seen him attack someone like that."

With the wounds all cleaned, Timothy put some light bandages on to help stop the bleeding.

"There, all better," said Timothy, kissing Marco softly on the shoulder.

"Thanks."

"Well, that kinda killed the mood."

"Yeah I'm going to go home, I think. I've got an early shift tomorrow anyway."

"You sure?" asked Timothy, feeling an unpleasant mixture of guilt and disappointment.

"I think I need a little time to recover from the vicious attack!" joked Marco. "Next time at my place?"

"It will probably be safer."

Damn cat!

Timothy was frustrated but understood. He saw Marco to the door, where they shared a long, lingering kiss goodbye, which only served to send blood rushing back to his nether regions.

"Take care, Polo."

"You too, Casper. I look forward to picking back up where we left off."

Does he mean the sex or the relationship? Do I really want things to progress?

After closing the door, Timothy retreated to his bedroom where he found Mikey curled up on his bed, looking far too smug.

"Why did you do that for, you silly kitty? If I didn't know better I'd think you were jealous of Marco."

Once more Timothy shooed the frisky feline from his room, amid a great protest of meowing and wriggling. He climbed into bed and took himself in hand, determined to have the ending he'd been denied. With his other hand, Timothy tweaked his right nipple before moving down to take a firm grip of his full balls that were aching for release. To start with his thoughts were filled of Marco but as his hand moved faster and faster along his shaft the face of his fantasy changed. As he tensed up and started to shake it was Miles that his body was crying out for. Seconds later, Timothy threw his head back and he gasped in pleasure as his seed sprayed up into the air and splattered back down over his heaving chest. He lay there happy in the warm afterglow, as his heartbeat slowed back to normal and his breathing calmed.

Timothy stirred back to life a few minutes later and headed to the bathroom. A quick hot shower washed away his stickiness and he was soon back in bed feeling fresh and clean. He switched off the light and as he made the slow descent into slumber he questioned why Miles had replaced Marco in his imagination.

Why can't I get him out of my system?

* * *

Dr. Evelyn Waters sat across the table from her grandson, a friendly smile played on her lips as she sipped on her Mango Lassi. Timothy could sense her sharp blue eyes examining him. His beloved nana was a successful therapist with a thriving practice and couldn't seem to stop herself from applying her skills to everyone she met – family members most definitely included. They had always been close and it would be fair to say that they were each other's favorite family member…not that they'd ever formally acknowledged it.

The small Indian restaurant – Bombay Dreams – was filled with the contented chatter of their fellow diners, as the pair enjoyed their fortnightly lunch date. They both adored Indian food and this was one of Port Davinica's most raved about restaurants.

Timothy had always turned to her in times of need as she invariably gave good advice – unsurprising given her vocation. Indeed, it was to her that he'd first turned when he realized that he was attracted to guys not girls, which had vexed him greatly at the time. She had helped him to accept himself and realize that his sexuality was only a part of him – a natural one at that – and not something by which he needed to define himself, for which he'd ever be grateful.

Today, however, he was a tad reluctant to go into his troubles with his grandmother. If it was just his confusion over his romantic life he wouldn't mind but Timothy had begun to consider the very real possibility that the strangeness of the apartment was actually all in his head. He wasn't in the mood to deal with that possibility today and just wanted to have a nice lunch.

After twenty minutes of pleasant conversation his grandmother asked the question he'd been dreading.

"So are you going to tell me what's bothering you?" she inquired in her usual forthright fashion.

Why does she always have to be so damn perceptive?

"What do you mean?" said Timothy, feigning ignorance.

"Man trouble?"

"What? No, I mean…I don't know."

Despite his reservations, Timothy soon found himself pouring out the entire story – his confusion over Marco, the complicated relationship between him and Miles, and finally his encounters with Gio and his fears for his sanity. In the torrent of words that flowed from his mouth he admitted things that he'd been scared to tell even Lukas – like the voices in his head and the incident in the shower.

"What do you think?" asked Timothy, half-afraid she'd want to have him committed.

"Dear oh deary me, my poor little mouse! Now doesn't that feel better to get that all out?"

"Yes, Nana."

"First off, I don't believe for a second that you're in danger of losing your mind. I do, however, think you're placing a lot of stress on yourself and that is manifesting itself in different ways. You're scared of resuming your relationship with Marco and feeling rejected by Miles, so you've invented a perfect dream lover. It's really not that uncommon."

"Well, that's comforting at least."

"My only worry would be if you start to prefer the relationship with your fantasy man to having one with a real live person."

"I don't think I'm quite that bad."

Not yet.

"Good to hear. As for Miles' behavior, grief affects people in different ways. The best thing you can do is encourage open communication and let him know that you're there to support him if he needs it."

"If he even wants me to be there anymore. Sometimes I think he'd be happier if I just moved out."

"From what you tell me the two of you had become good friends, so I doubt that he would want to throw that away.

Besides I think you're fabulous to have around…although I may be a tad biased," she said, laughing lightly. "In terms of your feelings for him, I won't tell you what to do but I'm not sure if longing after him is particularly healthy…unless you think it may lead somewhere."

"Oh no, I doubt it."

No matter how much I want it!

"One never knows in affairs of the heart, my dear. Even so I wouldn't discount Marco, I always found him such a charming lad."

"Thanks, Nana."

Feeling much lighter after his confession, Timothy heartily tucked into the last of his Cheese Naan and Tandori Chicken. He vowed to try and get Miles to open up to him that very evening.

* * *

Timothy returned from lunch ready to get stuck into his latest project – illustrations for a new gay graphic novel. The story was quite good, with good helpings of sex and violence, and he was toying with asking the writer to see if he wanted to team up on his Blue Hunter comic. He walked into the lounge room and was surprised to see that Miles was already home.

Maybe I should talk to him now?

"You're home early. Everything OK?"

It was then that Timothy noticed that Miles was holding the sketchbook with the Blue Hunter drawings and that his face held a darkly furious expression.

"Why did you draw Gio?"

Miles' voice was level but there was a clear anger behind it. Timothy felt his own anger building in response.

"What are you doing going through my stuff?"

"Answer my question," spat Miles, ignoring Timothy's query. "How do you know about Gio?"

"I told you it's the guy I've been dreaming about. Now, why were you going through my stuff?"

"I wasn't, the book was lying open in the lounge room when I got home," said Miles, sounding almost aggressively defensive.

"I left it in my room!"

"Well, that's not where I found it."

"I know where I left it," said Timothy through gritted teeth, feeling his face flushing red with anger.

"Are you calling me a liar?"

"Well if the shoe fits!"

Both their voices began to rise in volume and the tension between them was explosive. Timothy's pulse was racing and he had a growing fear that their confrontation would turn physical.

"How dare you! Don't think I don't know what you're up to."

"What the hell are you talking about?"

Timothy's head was spinning. He felt completely lost and couldn't understand how things between them had degenerated so quickly. They were standing so close together they were practically shouting in one another's faces.

"I don't know what you want but I'll be damned if you're going to ruin his memory. I'd rather throw you from the balcony."

"What?"

"Don't test me, faggot!"

Suddenly there was a huge crash as one of the shelves on the bookcase by the far wall collapsed, sending books and photo albums sprawling all over the floor. They both jumped at the unexpected noise and it stopped their fight…for the moment at least.

One of the albums had fallen open right by their feet. There on the page were several photos of Miles, smiling with his arm around another man. Timothy was astonished. The man in the photo looked exactly like the man from his dreams. He also noticed that the man was wearing Miles' necklace with the half moon pendant.

"Who is this?" demanded Timothy.

"Gio," replied Miles, in a small voice choked with tears.

Then Miles collapsed to the floor and broke down sobbing, all the anger seeming to flow from his body with the tears. Timothy sunk to the ground as well and held Miles in his arms, thinking only to comfort his friend. The animosity of the past few minutes was completely gone; the only sound in the apartment was of Miles crying.

After a few minutes the tears began to ease and Miles slowly sat back and slid free of Timothy's embrace. Timothy patiently waited while Miles gathered himself together before he asked the question he'd been dying to since he saw the photo.

"Who is Gio?"

"Gio was my best friend. We'd known each other since we were just little kids. We were inseparable...he was always there for me..."

Miles was clearly struggling to hold back another torrent of tears. Timothy reached forward and placed his hand on Miles' shoulder and gave it a reassuring squeeze. Miles regained his composure once more and continued with his story.

"He came out to me in high school but it didn't matter to me. Nothing could have made me love him less."

"You were a good friend."

"Thanks." Miles managed the tiniest of smiles. "After college, we saved up and bought this place together, it was the only way we could afford it. Some people thought we were a couple because we were so close but I didn't care. Everything was great, until…until…"

Timothy's heart ached for his friend in pain.

"It's OK, take your time."

"About a year ago, Gio was out drinking with a friend. They were cutting through the back alleys to get home when…when they were mugged by a guy with a knife. Apparently they fought back. His friend was hit in the head but Gio…he…he was stabbed."

"Oh God."

Tears began to silently roll down Miles' face.

"He died on the way to the hospital."

"I'm so sorry."

"But it's all my fault! I was supposed to be out with him that night but I was too tired and now he's dead."

"You can't blame yourself."

"I should have protected him! Why didn't I go with him?"

Miles seemed to deflate and Timothy moved forward to hold him once more. The pair sat on the lounge room floor as the grief and tears poured out of Miles in an apparently unstoppable torrent.

The minutes ticked by and calm slowly returned to the room.

"I'm sorry for being such a mess" sniffled Miles. "And I should never have called you that word, it was hateful. I'm so sorry."

"It's fine. You're obviously going through a lot."

"I didn't tell you before because I just didn't know what to think about your dreams and the drawings. I never believed in ghosts before."

"Well, I don't either but how else can you explain it?"

"I can't. But if it is him why would he appear to you and not to me?"

"The dreams are all very erotic and you're straight so…"

Timothy noticed a strange look flutter across Miles' face but then it was gone.

What was that about?

"What should we do?" asked Timothy, pleased to have a problem to solve and happy that he wasn't going crazy…and that Miles no longer appeared to hate him.

"I don't know."

"Maybe we could contact a priest?"

"And say what? I don't think they'll come running cause you're having sex dreams about my dead friend."

"I see your point but we have to do something."

"I can't deal with this now. I need to think."

The boys slowly got to their feet, both a tad awkward after what had happened.

"Are we OK now?" asked Timothy timidly.

"Yeah, we are, but I really need to process all this."

"Understandable, just remember I'm here to talk whenever you need me."

"Thanks."

Miles gave Timothy a warm smile and headed to his bedroom. As emotional as it had all been, Timothy was glad that everything was out in the open. He was still trying to come to grips with the discovery that he was indeed being haunted.

At least it's better than going mad…maybe?

Timothy surveyed the mess on the floor and decided that Miles had enough on his mind without worrying about cleaning. He moved over to examine the fallen shelf. It didn't appear to be broken from the weight of what had been sitting on it, as he'd originally thought. Rather it looked as if someone had yanked it loose. Timothy had a sneaking suspicion that there may have been a spot of spiritual assistance.

"What are you up to, Gio?" asked Timothy, addressing the empty air.

He fitted the shelf back into position and restacked the books and albums. When he was done he went to his room, changed into his running gear and headed downstairs to clear his head.

How does one deal with a playful ghost?

* * *

Over the course of the next few weeks a sense of normality returned to the apartment. The tension between the roommates was gone and Miles appeared back to his chipper old self, except that his dance card was a lot emptier these days. The stream of anonymous women through his bedroom had slowed down to barely a trickle. It would be a lie to say this didn't please Timothy – much as he tried to hide it – as it meant that he got to spend more time with the attractive architect. Indeed, most evenings the pair could be found on the balcony, eating dinner and chatting away. It made Timothy much happier than it ought to.

Just like a couple. Except you're not! I know, I know.

Timothy was well aware that he should move on to someone who could actually return his romantic interest, like Marco, but he couldn't seem to let go of his attachment to Miles. It didn't help that there was an extra level of closeness between them since the revelation about Gio. Timothy had yet to mention the discovery to anyone, not even Lukas. It just felt too personal and on a purely selfish level, Timothy liked the fact that he and Miles shared a secret.

Out of respect to Miles, Timothy had also decided to shelve his Blue Hunter idea. He could have redrawn the figure with a different face but he felt it was better to concentrate on something completely new. Unfortunately, his inspiration had somewhat dried up in that regard. Ever since the incident in the lounge room, Gio had been notably absent from Timothy's dreams and he found that his new drawings were lacking the same spark. On the plus side, Timothy no longer had the sensation of being watched, although he wasn't convinced that things had really come to an end.

Has he really gone?

* * *

Midway through the next week, Timothy was seated in his usual chesterfield armchair in the far corner of Perk Up, reading quietly. Autumn had well and truly arrived and the afternoon was wet and windy. The café was deserted apart from him and the barista Prudence, who was behind the counter cleaning up after the lunch rush. On days like this Timothy loved nothing more than to curl up with a good book and a big mug of hot chocolate – although he wasn't opposed to replacing the book with a man and the chocolate with whipped cream when the opportunity arose. Not that it had of late. Since the misadventure with the cat, Marco had been working double shifts at the hotel due to two lifeguards quitting unexpectedly, so they'd yet to have another try. And with the disappearance of Gio back into the ether, Timothy had been left with only his imagination and his hand. So literature and chocolate it was.

For now, at least.

Timothy was so engrossed by the well-written period detective story in his lap that it took him a minute to realize that there was someone standing over him. When he looked up he was surprised to see a bird-like woman, with unkempt, frizzy brown hair and wide brown eyes that were studying him intently. Timothy hadn't noticed her approach and felt slightly uncomfortable by the intrusion into his personal space.

"Can I help you?" asked Timothy.

"He only wanted to help the two of you, Timothy."

"Excuse me? How do you know my name?"

"Gio told me. Lovely lad. Very handsome, I must say."

Timothy felt a chill run up and down his spine and a sense of unease in his stomach.

I must have misheard her.

"What did you say?"

"Gio. He's been a very naughty boy from what he tells me. The dreams and whatnot… quite a mischievous scamp," the lady said with a little chuckle.

A million questions raced through Timothy's brain, a few of which then attempted to escape his lips at the same time.

"How do you…who are…what do you...is he…"

"It's OK, dear. People are often confused at first. May I sit down?"

Timothy nodded dumbly, still suffering from a slight shock.

"My name is Gabriella and I'm a medium. Sometimes I get messages, sometimes visions, it's a little bit different each time, really."

Before he'd moved in with Miles, Timothy had had no interest in the supernatural and thought that psychics were just a bunch of fraudsters. Yet now, he no longer knew what to think.

"Has he…is he still here?"

"Here? No. But he is around. He's not finished yet."

"What do you mean?"

"Well, the way the poor thing died was so traumatic that it left him trapped, unable to move on."

"But why the dreams?"

"You can't blame him from wanting to have a little fun after what he's been through now can you?"

"I guess not."

The conversation seemed more and more surreal. Part of Timothy wanted to get up and ran away but he also had a burning desire to know more.

"Do you know what else he's planning?"

"No, sorry dear. But I can tell that you and Matthew will make a lovely couple."

"Matthew? Who's Matthew?"

"Or was it Martin? No, Mitchell…no, that it isn't right either. Definitely something starting with an M. Anyway, I must be off, my dear."

"Wait! Is there anything we can do to help him?"

"I'm not sure dear, but I'm certain he'll be in touch with you again. Toodle-oo!"

Timothy sat there with the book lying forgotten in his lap, his mind buzzing from the encounter. He was still in a bit of a daze when Prudence came up a few minutes later to take away his empty cup. Prudence looked at him quizzically.

"Everything, OK? You look even paler than normal. You're practically a ghost!" she said lightheartedly.

"Something like that," mumbled Timothy.

"Sorry, what was that?"

"No, I'm fine. Can I grab another hot chocolate?"

"Sure, coming right up."

As she moved away Timothy struggled to focus. He had so many questions.

What does Gio want? Why doesn't he appear to Miles? Will I dream about him again?

And the perhaps the most important of all:

Did Gabriella mean Marco or Miles?

* * *

Later that afternoon it seemed the universe was trying to give him an answer. Timothy was at his desk scanning through the requirements of his latest assignment when his phone buzzed with a message. He looked and saw that it was from Marco inviting him over for dinner. It was a wonderfully tempting proposition, as he hadn't seen him in nearly a month…not to mention that his ex was just as wonderfully talented in the kitchen as he was in the bedroom.

Marco was staying in the apartment they'd lived in before moving to Europe. It belonged to his parents and it had been empty when Marco came back to town. Timothy knew that the apartment would bring back a lot of happy memories and he ran the risk of his judgment being clouded by nostalgia.

Maybe this a sign?

Throwing caution to the wind, Timothy accepted the invitation. He dressed fairly casually in blue jeans, a red t-shirt and black jacket. Handily, the apartment was within walking distance so he soon set out on foot, although he was glad of the jacket to combat the chill in the night air.

Thirty minutes, and five flights of stairs, later he arrived at his old front door. It felt odd to ring the buzzer instead of using a key. Marco opened the door looking edible as always in a tight, fitted shirt open to his chest and a pair of light-blue jeans that seemed almost painted on.

"Come in, handsome."

"A small contribution," said Timothy, offering a bottle of rosé that he'd picked up on the way.

"I've set everything up on the terrace. But we can move inside if it's too cold for you."

"Nah, I'm sure it'll be fine."

Timothy walked onto the terrace and smiled as the strong scent of jasmine flooded his nostrils. He'd forgotten just how pretty the view was from there. Granted, it wasn't as grand as from his current apartment, as they were much lower, but the city still seemed to sparkle around them in the autumn evening. It was then that Timothy noticed the inordinate amount of candles that Marco had set up, lending the evening a thoroughly romantic ambiance.

Marco opened the bottle that Timothy had brought and soon handed his guest a glass of wine and proposed a toast.

"To old times and new beginnings."

They clinked and sipped the sweet rosé. There was something in Marco's tone, however, that caught Timothy's attention.

Does he want to get back together?

Timothy sat down at the small candlelit table and couldn't help but remember all the similar evenings they had spent like this and he felt familiar longings begin to rise. Marco then brought out the garlic-stuffed mushrooms entrees – one of Timothy's favorites. The trend continued throughout the evening with each course turning up dishes that Timothy adored, which confirmed to him that he was indeed on a proper date with his ex.

To be honest, Timothy wasn't sure how to feel about it. He was certainly enjoying the easy conversation and the good food. Indeed, at certain points during the evening it felt as if they'd never left Port Davinica and the past few years had just been a figment of his imagination. That aside, he knew that there was a very real possibility that Marco would take off again once his lifeguard job finished up, which should be any time now given the change of season. It was one of the reasons that Timothy had avoided getting too close to Marco, as he didn't wish to be left again.

Just after they'd finished dessert, Marco's face had a touch of seriousness about it.

"Is everything OK?" asked Timothy, noticing the change.

"I've had some fantastic news and I was hoping that it might be great for you too."

"Well don't keep me suspense, Polo!"

"You know that I've been looking for my next project."

"Yes. Don't tell me…you're going back to the walruses!" said Timothy.

He hoped his air of mock-exasperation hid his dismay that Marco was most likely being whisked away again.

"No. I'm not actually going anywhere. I've been offered a teaching position at Port Davinica University and I've accepted."

"That's fantastic news! Congratulations."

"So, it means I'm going to be here in the city for at least the next two years and I was wondering…I mean, I was hoping…would you want to give *us* another try?"

Timothy didn't know what to say. A year ago he wouldn't have hesitated to give a resounding 'YES', but there was something holding him back. He could see the expectation in Marco's eyes and didn't wish to hurt his ex-boyfriend but he just wasn't sure.

"I don't…"

"You don't have to decide now," said Marco cutting him off, obviously hoping to put off a negative response. "I know it's a big step, so take as much time as you need."

"Thanks. I appreciate that."

As much as they both tried to ignore it, it was obvious that the evening had become rather awkward. Timothy only stayed for one more glass of wine, and then pleaded tiredness to make his escape.

They stood at the doorway saying their goodbyes when Marco took Timothy by the hand and looked him directly in the eyes.

"I never stopped loving you, you know."

Timothy's heart did a little summersault in his chest.

"I love you too, but I…I should go. Goodnight, Polo."

"Goodnight, Casper."

Their goodbye kiss was almost chaste compared to their previous efforts. Timothy rushed off home, his brain overcrowded with what-ifs.

What am I going to do?

* * *

As luck would have it, the dreams restarted that very night, as vibrant and erotic as ever. There was, however, one major difference – Gio was no longer his playmate. To his surprise, and great delight, his ghostly companion had been replaced with Miles, although, as with his first experiences with Gio there was no talking, only pure carnality. The one strange thing, well slightly more odd than the whole situation was to begin with, were the kisses – their taste to be precise. Like Gio before him, the dream version of Miles had a hint of vanilla whenever they locked lips. Timothy hadn't the faintest idea why that flavor and no clue as to what it might mean…if anything.

The day following the first dream, Timothy could barely meet Mile's eyes. He'd often daydreamed about Miles but to suddenly experience him in such a vivid manner was almost overwhelming. Timothy told himself that it was just a reaction to Marco's declaration of love and his uncertainty of recommitting to his former flame, although part of him knew that he had real feelings for Miles that weren't going away, no matter how unrequited they may be.

After his initial embarrassment, Timothy began to enjoy the dreams, where they did all sorts of debauched things to one another. As before, he often woke to find himself awash with his own seed and an empty bed. Timothy wasn't sure if it was the dreams were a reward or punishment.

Why must I want what I can't have?

As much as Timothy enjoyed his nightly fantasy encounters they were not helping him decide about Marco. Timothy didn't doubt that he and Marco had worked well together as a couple but he wasn't sure if he could just slip into what they had before. He liked the relationship they had now and he didn't know if it was willing to commit to something more serious again.

What if he leaves me again?

To add to matters, Timothy sensed a change in the relationship between him and Miles. It wasn't as strained as it had been a month ago but it wasn't quite the same as it was before that either. It could have been his imagination, or guilt about the dreams, but Timothy had the impression that Miles had become distant of late. At first, he was paranoid that his roommate knew that Timothy was dreaming of him but he'd soon realized that was impossible.

Timothy had spoken to both Lukas and his grandmother at length about his dilemma but for all their words of wisdom he was still no closer to making a decision. He knew that Marco wouldn't wait forever and that Miles wasn't suddenly going to switch teams and confess his undying love either but Timothy just couldn't see which path to take. He was as overwrought as a schoolboy trying to decide upon his favorite band boy member.

Damn this pesky free will!

* * *

Lukas and Timothy were rifling through the racks and clothing bins of Grandma's Closet – a vintage clothing store not far from the docks. Timothy was glad of the distraction. It had been three weeks since his dinner date with Marco and he still hadn't given him an answer.

"What do you think?" asked Lukas, holding up a long checkered trench coat.

Timothy turned around and immediately wrinkled up his nose in aversion to the gaudy garment.

"You're going for pervert chic?"

"Maybe not then."

Lukas put the coat back on the rack and the lads recommenced their search.

"Need a hand guys?" said a smooth baritone voice from behind them.

They turned around to face the tall, blond shop assistant with pleasing features.

"Yes, actually we do," drawled Lukas in full-flirt mode. "We're searching for outfits for a Halloween party."

The Halloween party was being held in the penthouse apartment above Timothy's, although it had been Lukas who'd told him about it first. Apparently, it was one of the most popular house parties of the season, with a reputation for being packed with ridiculously hot men in all sorts of revealing costumes. It was hosted by the four strapping specimens of manhood who lived there – two were even underwear models. Timothy had often encountered them in the elevator and had always found them to be friendly neighbors...and rather obliging in his occasional daydreams.

When Timothy had mentioned the party, his roommate surprised him by saying that he was already going.

"I used to go with Gio every year. It was his favorite holiday, he loved dressing up and..." A look of sadness crossed his face but was soon brushed away. "Last year was too painful, but I decided that Gio wouldn't want me to be miserable."

"That's great! We can go together."

"Sounds good to me."

Timothy was keen to see what outfit Miles would wear and had had quite a few illicit ideas on the subject. As for himself, he still hadn't decided, and it was only a week away, hence the shopping expedition.

"Did you want to go scary or sexy?" asked the blond shop assistant.

"Sexy!" replied Lukas without a moment's hesitation.

"Couple costume?" asked the assistant, in a not so subtle attempt to find out the relationship between the boys.

"We were thinking the same theme but we aren't a couple," stated Lukas to the obvious relief of the assistant.

Timothy rolled his eyes and moved about the shop leaving Lukas and the blond to continue flirting. He was rifling through one of the bargain bins by the front door when he came across a blue and black leather mask.

That looks just like the one in my drawing of Gio!

He turned back to tell Lukas what he'd found but saw that the two of them were standing so close they were practically conjoined.

I wish I could pick up so easily.

Timothy continued to search through the bins but didn't find anything else of interest. He began to wander through the racks in the far corner of the shop, the musty odor of old clothes washing over him. The racks were cluttered with a veritable forest of fur coats, which absorbed the sound around him, and he could no longer hear Lukas giggling with boyish glee with the shop assistant. Above him the fluorescent light flickered, making the clothes appear to move in a jerky fashion. Timothy knew rationally that it was just a trick of the light but when he suddenly felt a hand on his shoulder he let out a yelp and span around wildly.

"What's gotten into you?" laughed Lukas. "Come on, Valentine has found us the perfect outfits!"

"Who has?"

"The shop assistant…well the owner actually. He's so hot! Anyway, I'm sure you're going to love them!"

Lukas led Timothy back over to the curtained off cubicles for changing. There spread out on the floor was an assortment of army paraphernalia – black leather boots, khaki shirts, shorts and trousers, bandanas and even some dog tags.

"Army boys! What do you think?" asked Lukas, an expectant look upon his face.

"Sure, sounds good."

Timothy knew it was pointless to argue with Lukas once he got an idea in his head. And, truthfully, Timothy wasn't particularly opposed to dressing up as a slutty soldier. They spent the next twenty minutes trying on different combinations with Valentine giving them some styling advice to help show off their assets to their best advantage. There hadn't been any other customers so he'd been giving them his full attention – well more to Lukas but Timothy wasn't too fussed, he had enough men to worry about.

As they were finalizing their purchases, Lukas saw the mask that Timothy had put into the pile.

"I don't think that it will go with the theme," he said, disapprovingly. "Looks like a superhero mask."

"It's not for that. It's inspiration for my drawing."

"Well, that does make more sense. I didn't think you were *that* stylistically challenged."

"You're such a charmer."

"I know."

Valentine handed them their bags and popped a business card into the one Lukas was holding.

"Call me if you need any help at all," he said, innuendo dripping from his words.

"Oh, I will."

Timothy was a little jealous at the attention and wished – not for the first time – that he were as outgoing as Lukas, who brazenly went after, and often got, what he wanted.

They walked out of the store and into the late afternoon sunshine, and headed off to have a coffee to celebrate the success of their expedition…and gossip about Valentine, of course.

* * *

Timothy was standing by the table next to the pool, his hands within easy reach of the punchbowl. He had lost sight of Lukas half an hour beforehand and was feeling rather buzzed from his several helpings of punch, which had been liberally dosed with alcohol. Despite the season, the evening was rather warm and Timothy was enjoying the passing parade of skimpily-attired ghouls, monsters and miscellaneous sexy characters – basically most people used it as an excuse to dress like a whore, not that Timothy objected. Truth be told, he'd chosen this spot so he could people watch, although it had had the added advantage of being able to see the front door.

He was expecting both Marco and Miles to arrive and didn't want to miss either of their entrances – which one he wanted to see more was up for debate. Miles had had a last minute crisis with his project and Marco had family commitments, although both had promised to do their best to make it. Timothy had vowed that he would make a decision that night, as to whether or not he'd accept Marco's proposal.

Timothy turned around, intending on going for a quick lap of the penthouse to see if he could find Lukas when he ran smack bang into a heavenly creature – a white angel to be precise. The lad in question had broad white wings with a feathered codpiece and matching knee-high boots. His spiky black hair had vibrant bright blue streaks, which complimented his preternaturally blue, almond shaped, eyes. His darkly golden skin proclaimed his Japanese heritage and sparkled with white glitter. The outfit was made even more stunning by the perfectly ripped body beneath it, with nary an ounce of fat to be seen. Timothy was practically drooling at the sheer beauty before him.

"Having a good night?" asked the white angel.

"I am, thank you. I love your outfit!"

"Thanks. I'm rather a fan of the military myself."

The two continued to flirt for another ten minutes or so until the white angel excused himself to go to the bathroom. Timothy was pondering whether to stay and wait for the angel or go find Lukas when he spied the angel walking along the far side of the pool towards him.

"Hi, again!"

"Again?" questioned the angel, looking somewhat confused.

It was then that Timothy noticed that something was different. The alcohol had clouded his mind so it took a few moments to register what had changed.

He isn't white anymore!

The style of the costume was exactly the same, but now the feathers were all black and instead of blue eyes and hair, they were now a fluorescent green, even the glitter was a darker shade.

"How did you change so fast?" asked Timothy, in awe of the man's apparent dedication to his art.

"What do you mean?"

Timothy was beginning to think that the punch was spiked with more than just alcohol when the white angel walked up to them. His mind reeled for a moment until it stopped on the only logical solution.

Twins!

"I thought you were the same person. I'm so sorry!" exclaimed Timothy, upon realizing his mistake.

"That's OK, it happens all the time," said the white angel, with a bemused expression. "I'm Haruki and this is my brother Masaki."

"Pleased to meet you," said Timothy, flushed with embarrassment and alcohol.

Standing between the two devilishly handsome angels, Timothy had a very wicked thought but then instantly dismissed it. He doubted his new friends would appreciate such an incestuous suggestion – no matter how hot the idea looked in his mischievous mind.

"There you are!" said a familiar voice from behind Timothy.

He turned to find Lukas in a rather inebriated state.

"Damn I'd like to have you two fight over my soul!" exclaimed Lukas.

Haruki and Masaki just smiled, clearly used to hearing such comments. They did make quite the striking pair, after all.

The foursome chatted for a while until Timothy caught a glimpse of black and blue leather out of the corner of his eye.

It can't be!

Without a word, he left Lukas with the twins and started after the figure he'd just seen. He made his way into the lounge room where the mass of partygoers hampered his view. Timothy frantically scanned the crowd and finally saw the mystery man heading towards the balcony on the other side and went after him in hot pursuit.

By the time he reached the balcony the man had seemingly vanished again. Timothy was about to go back inside when he noticed that the balcony curved around the side of the building where it ended in darkness. When he moved closer he could that the man was standing in the shadows just staring at him.

"Gio?" he asked timidly.

The figure moved slowly towards him. As he moved into the light, Timothy could see that he'd been right, the man was dressed exactly like Blue Hunter, even down to the mask. Timothy was a mess of emotions – excitement, confusion and just a little fear. The man was now close enough to touch; he offered his hand to Timothy, which he warily accepted. Unexpectedly, the man roughly pulled Timothy towards him and back into the shadows. He spun Timothy around and pushed him hard against the wall. Timothy's heart threatened to pound out of his chest.

The man moved forward and planted a fiery kiss upon his lips, grinding his body against Timothy's. It felt familiar but Timothy didn't think it was what he remembered of Gio. As they kissed Timothy lost all sense of time. The noise of the party and partygoers faded away and he was swept into the moment, aware only of their bodies pressing together and the vanilla taste of his kiss.

Vanilla?

And with that, the spell was broken. Timothy broke away from the kiss and pushed the man back.

"Miles?"

Just then a dashing Dracula stumbled around the corner.

"Ooops, sorry guys," he apologized as he disappeared back from where he came.

The mystery man stared deeply into Timothy's eyes, with a look of yearning, before his lips softly grazed against Timothy's. He gave Timothy one last gentle kiss before he abruptly fled the balcony.

"Wait!" Timothy called out to him but he was gone just as suddenly as he had arrived.

Timothy tried to follow him back through the lounge room but there were still too many people in the way. He couldn't understand why the guy had left and he couldn't shake the feeling that it was Miles.

Wishful thinking...stop being a stereotype and lusting after the straight man...but that kiss!

Disappointed, and more confused than ever, Timothy returned to the pool to find Lukas. The party had reached that stage where inhibitions had been pretty much forgotten and all sorts of high jinks ensue. The pool itself was now filled with partygoers who'd discarded their costumes to swim in just their underwear…and some not even that.

Timothy soon found Lukas in a passionate embrace with Masaki, apparently he shared his brother's passion for the military. He didn't want to disturb them so went back and helped himself some more punch.

He took a seat by the edge of the balcony, slightly away from the drunken revelers. A few attractively attired men came up and chatted to him but Timothy rebuffed their advances. After his strange encounter he just wasn't in the mood, so he spent the next few hours drunkenly sulking and quietly wondering.

Eventually, Timothy stumbled his way back downstairs, around the same time Lukas and his angel had flown off to become even better acquainted. As he entered the apartment, Timothy tripped over the hall table and sent the wooden bowl that held the keys flying. Timothy prepared for Miles to come out of his bedroom and complain about the noise but there was nothing.

Must be dead to the world. Or off being a superhero. Who knows anymore?

Timothy stumbled the rest of the way to his bedroom. Despite his blurry vision, Timothy noticed that the mask he'd bought at the vintage shop wasn't sitting on the shelf where he'd left it. He made a mental note to look for it the following day but the alcohol dissolved it almost instantaneously. Timothy moved towards his bed and collapsed on top of it, still fully dressed and fell into a deep drunken slumber.

* * *

Timothy finally crawled out of bed around 4pm the following afternoon. His head throbbed in retribution for his excessive alcohol consumption – only fair given the amount of brain cells he had undoubtedly massacred. Bleary-eyed, he made his way to the kitchen for some coffee and something greasy. Timothy saw Miles working out on the balcony, dressed in sweats. The weather outside was looking decidedly more autumnal than the previous evening. He wearily waved through the glass door and Miles came inside.

"You look like hell," teased Miles.

"Shhh."

His voice sounded like a sledgehammer.

"Someone drink a little too much?"

"Yes, someone did, but it was a great party. What happened to you last night?"

"Yeah, I got home late but wanted to have a little nap before heading up. The next thing I knew it was morning and I'd missed it all. Did you have fun?"

"Yeah I met some interesting people."

"Anyone special?"

"Well, there was a mysterious masked man that I shared a moment with, but he disappeared on me without giving me his name."

Timothy hoped that Miles would bravely pronounce that he was that very man, but was disappointed, although not particularly surprised, when such a declaration was not forthcoming.

"Like Cinderella?"

"Yeah and he didn't even have the decency to leave one of his boots behind so I could go from door to door searching for him," joked Timothy.

"You poor thing. Sit down and I'll make you something to eat. Bacon and eggs?"

"Yes, please. And a coffee would be lovely."

"Of course, my liege," said Miles, bowing in a show of mock respect.

"Good lad."

Timothy was touched at Miles' kindness and sat down on the couch. He closed his eyes, listening to the sounds of Miles pottering about in the kitchen, followed shortly afterwards by the scrumptious aroma of fried food.

I could get used to this.

* * *

It was about a week later when Timothy's world was turned completely upside down. He was looking for some flannel sheets in the linen cupboard when he came across something that stopped him dead. On the top shelf, shoved behind a pile of towels was the costume from the party, with the mask wrapped inside.

It was Miles!

Timothy didn't know what to do. His head was spinning with questions.

Why would he lie? Is he secretly gay? What game is he playing?

He spent the rest of the day running through conversations in his head, trying to figure out the best way to calmly and rationally confront Miles about the mask.

"What the fuck are you up to?" demanded Timothy, flinging the mask at Miles as soon as he walked through the door.

So much for staying Zen!

Confusion clouded Miles' face, which was slowly replaced with a look of complete despair.

"It was you at the Halloween party!" yelled Timothy.

"I'm so sorry."

"Why did you lie to me? Doesn't our friendship mean anything to you?"

"I didn't think it was real. I thought it was just another dream."

His answer infuriated Timothy even more.

"Bullshit! That has to be the lamest excuse I've ever heard!"

"It's true, I swear."

"Well you can't be that straight if you're dreaming about me."

"I know."

The answer hit Timothy like a slap across the face. His rage suddenly felt halved, as shock and curiosity struggled for supremacy.

"What?"

"I haven't been completely honest with you."

Miles went and sat on the couch, Timothy followed suit but left some distance between them…his anger hadn't quite cooled.

"Go on," said Timothy, his level tone disguising his whirlwind of conflicting emotions.

"Gio was more than just my best friend. I loved him…I was in love with him."

It was obvious that it was hard for Miles to admit and Timothy felt the last of his anger gradually give way to sympathy.

"So you're bi?"

"I don't know. Gio was the only man that I'd felt that way about. The only time we had sex was the night before he died. No one knew and I couldn't say anything to anyone. I didn't know what to do. He was everything to me and after he was gone, it was…just too painful to think about."

"I'm sorry."

Timothy felt like an idiot and was ashamed of his earlier actions, realizing how hard it must have been to have not only your best friend, but your newly discovered lover as well, so cruelly ripped away.

"I thought that it was maybe a one-off thing and just went back to seeing women...until I started dreaming about you. Except, it didn't feel like me, it felt like I was watching me with you, the same as it was with the party."

"Hold on. How many dreams have you had?"

"About five or six over the last few weeks."

"I don't think they were just dreams."

"What do you mean?"

"I've been dreaming about you too."

"You mean we've been fucking in our sleep?"

"Yes, but I don't think it was just *us*. I think that Gio was behind it."

It sounded ludicrous to say out loud but it was the only explanation that made sense of their nocturnal adventures.

"So you're saying that Gio has been using us as like what? Porn puppets?" exclaimed Miles, the disdain evident in his voice.

"I don't know if I'd put it quite like that but...yeah."

"This is all just too much," said Miles as he stood up and started to pace back and forth. "How could he do this to me? To us? How could be so cruel?"

"I honestly don't know."

Miles stopped moving, apparently having come to a decision.

"I think I should just go somewhere for a few days. I need to be by myself to clear my head and I can't do that here. Not if *he* is still lurking about."

"If you think that's best?"

"I do...I just can't deal with it here."

"OK, well I'm here if you need to talk."

Miles simply nodded and retreated to his room. Ten minutes later, he headed out the door with a small suitcase, barely acknowledging Timothy as he left.

Timothy was sad to see Miles leave but he understood his need to get away. He didn't know how he'd react in the same situation. The pleasure he'd had from the dreams was tainted now that he knew that Miles hadn't been a conscious participant. Timothy began to question his own longings and wondered if he could be certain of anything that had happened since he'd moved in.

Do I only have feelings for Miles because of a ghost?

* * *

Timothy was miserable. He couldn't work, he had no desire to run or even see his friends. The days dragged on and soon Miles had been gone for over a week without any word as to his whereabouts and when he was coming back. Every time his phone buzzed or rang Timothy practically jumped on it, but it was never his missing friend. Timothy was starting to worry that something had happened to him but he was unsure of what to do. He couldn't very well call the police but he felt like he needed to do something…anything was better than just waiting.

His only real comfort came in the form of Mikey who rarely left his side.

"At least you love me," Timothy often whispered to his furry companion, in his darker moments.

I'm going to end up a deranged old cat lady!

Timothy had confessed all to Lukas, a few days after Miles had left. At first his best friend had been rather skeptical but when he'd showed Lukas the drawings and the photos of Gio he'd been convinced…if not particularly helpful.

"Damn! I wish a hot ghost would use me to bang straight boys!" Lukas had exclaimed.

"Yeah, not as fun as it sounds."

"So you say. Did you want to stay with me? So you're not alone with the ghostly one."

Timothy appreciated the offer but didn't want to impose on Lukas, especially since he and Masaki had become something of an item…their one night stand having turned into a regular fling.

The apartment seemed so empty with Miles gone and Gio yet to make a reappearance. The one bright spot was that it had given Timothy the chance to think without distraction and he'd finally decided what he wanted to do about Marco. So, near the end of his second week without Miles, Timothy once again visited his old apartment to give Marco an answer to his question.

He had gone over without calling, which Timothy was starting to think had been a mistake seeing he'd buzzed twice with no answer. Just as Timothy was preparing to go back down the stairs again, he heard the sound of someone unlatching the door chain. To his surprise the person who opened the door was not Marco. Rather it was Lorenzo – the cabana boy he'd met at the Grand Babylon Hotel – only wearing a short navy-blue silk robe that Timothy recognized as one he'd given to Marco some years before. His hair was wet and slicked back, obviously not long having left a shower.

"Oh hi! Timothy isn't it?"

"Yeah…is Marco home?

"Is it the pizza?" called Marco from inside.

"No, it's your friend."

He stood back to allow Timothy in and he could see Marco coming into the lounge room with a towel wrapped around his waist, his hair still wet. It didn't take a genius to work out what was going on. The look on Marco's face confirmed his suspicion.

"Sorry, it's not a good time. I'll come back later," said Timothy, wanting to exit the awkward situation as quickly as possible.

"No, wait!" Marco cried out.

"I'll leave you two alone," said Lorenzo retreating to the bedroom.

"Casper, I'm sorry about…"

"It's fine. I've kept you waiting for ages…and it's not like we were committed."

"It's nothing serious, just a bit of fun."

"I know, but it doesn't change anything. I came by tonight to tell you that I think we're best as friends." Timothy felt a weight lift from his mind. "I'll always love you, but I think our time has passed."

"I kinda thought that might be your answer by how long you were taking."

"I'm sorry about that but I needed to sort out my feelings and it took far longer than I thought. Besides, I think you and Lorenzo make quite a cute couple."

"I don't know about that."

"Well you have my blessing regardless."

"Why thank you, kind Sir."

Timothy was pleasantly surprised by how mature and civilized they were being about it all. Not that he's expected tantrums and wailing but it was comforting that their relationship had gotten to such a point. Timothy didn't want to disturb Marco's evening further so he said his goodbyes and headed on his way back home. He didn't envy facing the emptiness that awaited him but he didn't feel there was anywhere else he could go.

Not until Miles comes home.

* * *

As Timothy walked, he could see ominous-looking storm clouds building in the sky above him, with the occasional flash of lightning accompanied by the distant crash of thunder. The air felt heavy and he hurried to make it back home before the rain, as he hadn't thought to bring an umbrella and didn't fancy getting caught in the coming downpour.

Sadly, luck was not on his side. By the time Timothy reached the apartment he was sopping wet. The heavens had opened when he was less than a block from home but he was drenched nevertheless. Timothy squelched to his way into bedroom and stripped off his soggy clothes and had a refreshing hot shower. He was just drying off when he heard keys in the front door. Wearing just a towel he practically ran to the lounge room.

"Miles?"

"Hi," said Miles in a sheepish fashion.

"Where have you been?"

"I just went to my grandparents' cabin in the mountains. I told you I needed time to think."

"Why didn't you message? I thought something had happened to you!"

Timothy's concern over his roommate's whereabouts had turned quickly into annoyance at being abandoned. The storm began to rage in earnest outside with the lighting and thunder happening almost in sync. The wind had increased in intensity and sheets of rain buffeted the glass doors of the balcony, causing them to shudder in their frames.

"I'm sorry, alright!" Miles' tone was bordering on belligerent.

"No, it's not good enough. I've been sitting here miserable."

"I never said you had to wait for me."

"That's not what I meant."

The mood inside the lounge room began to feel as volatile as the weather outside. Thunder boomed close by and the lights flickered for a moment before coming back to full power. Mikey was circling the arguing pair, his ears pulled back in attack mode.

"What did you mean then?"

"I'm not just some poor desperate gay boy that you can play with to work out your issues."

"It wasn't my fault!"

"That's right, blame Gio."

The boys were so caught up in their fight they didn't notice that the keys in the dish by the door were rattling together or that the static electricity in the room had caused the hair on their arms to stand on end.

"I wasn't blaming him. You don't know what it's like!"

"Then why didn't you talk to me?"

"I'm beginning to wish I'd never met you!"

The lights started to flicker wildly and objects started falling from the bookshelves. Suddenly the apartment was plunged into darkness. Mikey let out an unearthly howl and practically flew from the room in fright.

"What the…" Timothy began before there was a brilliant flash of light.

This was accompanied by an almighty bang, which shattered the balcony door. The force of the explosion knocked the boys to the ground and sent shards of glass flying into the apartment.

"Are you OK?" said Miles, as he frantically rushed over to Timothy.

"Yeah, are you?"

"I think so."

Miraculously, the glass had cut neither of them. It was then that Timothy noticed that instead of blackness there was a light blue glow illuminating the room. He turned around towards the source of the light and squealed in fright. There, standing in the hallway as plain as day, was a glowing Gio. Timothy turned to Miles who was also looking directly at the apparition… well for the few seconds before he fainted dead away and fell to the floor.

Timothy dropped down and quickly cradled Miles' head in his lap. He was luckily able to revive him with only a few gentle taps to the face.

"What's going on?" Miles asked groggily upon regaining consciousness.

"We have a visitor," said Timothy, a lot more calmly than he felt.

Seeing a ghost in your dreams was far different to seeing one in the flesh…so to speak.

"Sorry to be so dramatic but you guys were driving me nuts," said Gio, clearly exasperated.

"Were you the reason the other renters left?" asked Miles, apparently having regained his senses and moving to a sitting position.

"Yes, but in my defense they weren't right for you."

"Who said you get to decide that?"

"I love you and I just wanted to see that you were happy."

"So you played with us?" asked Timothy, joining the conversation.

"I admit, I could probably have done things better but this whole ghost thing is new for me too."

There was an awkward tension as Timothy and Miles stared at Gio, neither of them quiet believing the situation in which they'd found themselves. Eventually, it was Miles who broke the silence.

"I miss you," said Miles, his voice small and child-like, tears forming in his eyes.

"I miss you too, my love. But you have to move on."

"I don't know how."

"That's what I've been trying to help you do."

Timothy was feeling very much the third wheel and was reluctant to interrupt the emotional reunion but he needed answers.

"Why me?" asked Timothy.

"I just had a feeling about you. I'm sorry for using you both the way I did but I think you two will be great for one another. Just give it a chance. I'll be going away to leave you to sort things out."

"Don't go!" cried Miles.

"It's OK. I'll never be far."

Gio moved to Miles and gave him a gentle kiss on the lips before he faded away.

Miles began to cry, softly at first, then harsh sobbing which shook his entire body. Timothy's nurturing instinct took over and he moved forward to Miles and held him in a tight bear hug. His roommate didn't resist and relaxed into Timothy's arms. They stayed locked in this position for what seemed like an eternity but was in reality barely ten minutes. In due course, Miles appeared to have temporarily run out of tears and broke away from Timothy.

"What now?" he asked, his inner turmoil clearly reflected in his sad face.

"I have absolutely no idea."

* * *

It only took a few days to return the apartment back to normal – physically at least. They had cleaned up the glass and the broken door had been replaced but the atmosphere was still thick with tension like another storm about to break. The roommates hadn't discussed their experience since that night and it was taking a toll on their relationship. Even Mikey was far from his usual affectionate self, hissing at the slightest provocation.

Things came to a head a week later, when Timothy decided it was time to deal with the pink elephant in the room.

"We need to work this out. We can't just pretend it never happened."

"I know…I think there's only one thing we *can* do."

"And what's that?

"We should sleep together."

Timothy was speechless it wasn't even vaguely what he'd expected Miles to say at all.

"Are you sure?"

"It's not like we haven't already, even if I was under Gio's influence. I need to do this. I need to see if my feelings for you are my own."

"But what if doesn't work out?"

"Then we will deal with it. I just can't go on how we are."

"OK. When did you want to?"

"How about right now?"

"Seriously?"

"Yes. You don't want to?"

"Of course I do. It's all I've wanted to do for months but…I'm scared that it might be the end of everything."

83

"Yeah, but it might be the beginning. Besides, it can't be any worse than what we have now."

"I just…"

Miles moved forward and put his hand up to Timothy's face, slowly running his fingers down his cheek and to his chin which he then used to pull Timothy in closer for a soft kiss. Their lips lightly pressed together and Timothy thought he might explode from the sheer joy he was feeling. He soon felt Miles' tongue probe between his lips so he opened them slightly to let him in. Soon their tongues were swirling about together, wrestling gently between their mouths. Their bodies came together as well and Timothy could feel Miles' erection pressing into him. Timothy breathed in Miles' scent, a heady mixture of his natural masculine musk and the mint from the body wash he used.

Timothy moved his hands slowly down Miles' back pulling against the material of the t-shirt. His hands soon reached Miles' plump ass and he began to lightly massage the buttocks. Their kissing increased in intensity and light moaning escaped from both their lips. Timothy could feel Miles pulling him in even tighter and sense the urgency in his kisses.

Miles moved back slightly, breaking their embrace, causing Timothy to look questioningly at him. In response, Miles simply took Timothy by the hand and led him to his bedroom. Timothy had fantasized many, many times of this very thing but now the moment had arrived it felt as if he had butterflies, bees, and a whole host of insects fluttering around inside his stomach.

Once inside the room Miles shut the door firmly behind them and pushed Timothy to the bed. He slowly stripped off his t-shirt, revealing his dark, muscular torso. Miles then unbuckled his belt and slipped his jeans down to his ankles and kicked them to the side, leaving him standing there in just his bright-red briefs, which struggled to cover his erect member.

Timothy was very much enjoying the show, his own cock straining, almost painfully, against the button fly of his jeans. He beckoned Miles to join him on the bed.

Apparently not needing a second invitation, Miles jumped on the bed and straight on top of Timothy.

They started to kiss again, growing more and more passionate as they fully gave into their carnal longings. Miles pulled enthusiastically at Timothy's clothing and soon he too was left clad only in underwear. Timothy looked down and could see a wet spot forming on the fronts of both his and Miles' jocks where their barely contained erections were oozing with excitement.

Miles flipped Timothy over onto his back and started to his kiss his way down Timothy's writing body. Timothy felt teeth grazing across his sensitive nipples as Miles gently nibbled on them. He then gasped at the delicious sensation a tongue tracing its way down his abs and towards his crotch. His ran his hands through Miles' silky black hair, massaging the scalp. Timothy felt Miles bypass his cock and go straight for his balls, taking them into his mouth with one big gulp.

Timothy cried out as Miles rolled them around with his tongue, sending sparks of pleasure up and down his spine. Miles then released them unhurriedly, allowing only one to escape at a time, before running his tongue along the shaft of Timothy's rock-hard manhood. When he reached the cockhead Miles hungrily slurped up the sticky-sweet precum, licking it dry before lowering his mouth ever so slowly over the head and down towards the base. He gagged a little at first but his movements soon became more fluid and he was able to take Timothy deeper into his throat with each bob of his head.

A desperate desire to taste Miles at the same time overtook Timothy, so he maneuvered himself around into a sixty-nine position, and eagerly feasted upon Miles' throbbing erection. The room was filled with the sounds of slurping and their contented moans as they hungrily attacked each other's crotches. Timothy was in heaven as Miles' precum swished about his mouth and down his throat.

Timothy felt Miles' fingers slipping underneath his ball sack to probe at his rosebud. He relaxed and pushed back, keen to let the digits continue with their exploration. The gentle penetration fueled Timothy's hunger and he moved further down away from Miles' delicious uncut meat to taste his hidden recesses. His tongue squeezed into the tight, almost virginal hole and heard Miles groan loudly in response. Timothy expertly worked the hole, widening it and forcing his way deeper inside. It only took a few minutes of this tantalizing tongue-work to have the desired effect.

"Please fuck me," Miles asked, the need evident in his voice.

"My pleasure!"

Miles reached over to his bedside table and grabbed a bunch of condoms and a big bottle of lube from the top drawer.

"Just be gentle, no one has been there since Gio."

"I will," promised Timothy, giving Miles a long, lazy kiss.

Timothy sheathed his weapon and lubricated it well, before positioning Miles on his back with his legs spread wide. He wanted to look Miles in the eyes as he entered him. Timothy pressed his cockhead against the exposed entrance and started to push ever so gently, slowly widening the sphincter, not wanting to cause Miles any pain.

Miles gasped as the cock breached his entrance but the discomfort was soon outweighed by the pleasurable feeling of being opened up by the rigid cock inside him. His breathing quickened as Timothy slowly slid inside with little thrusts, allowing the snug passage to accommodate him.

The sight of his manhood sinking deeper inside Miles and the look of pleasure on his roommate's face drove Timothy wild. It was all he could do to stop himself from pounding away. With great restraint, Timothy took his time penetrating Miles and it was a good five minutes before he felt his hips pressed flat against Miles' body. He rested there, kissing Miles whilst slowly grinding together. Timothy could feel Miles' strong hands pulling at his buttocks dragging him in even deeper.

Timothy started to long-dick Miles, slowly driving fully in and then pulling nearly all the way out so that just the bulbous head remained inside. Each time Timothy pushed fully back inside, Miles' eyes rolled back in pleasure and he let out a series of low moans. Timothy adored the look of satisfaction on Miles' face and was so happy that he was the one causing it. He felt Miles' nails raking down his back, clawing at him, and knew that he'd have a mess of marks to commemorate the encounter. Timothy kept up the divine torture of his roommate's tender passage for a good while, enjoying the almost continuous sounds of pleasure emanating from Miles.

They switched positions many times over the coming hour – on their sides, over the edge of the bed, up against the wall and back to the bed. Finally, it was with Miles on his hands and knees and Timothy pumping away behind him that their passions came to a natural release. Timothy had a firm grip on Miles' hips and was slamming into him over and over again. Miles was almost screaming in pleasure as each thrust struck against his prostate, which sent electric shocks throughout his poor, abused body. Only after a few minutes of the relentless pounding, Miles ejaculated without touching himself, spurting his cream all over the white cotton sheets underneath him.

Timothy stopped his assault, gently pulled out and ripped off his condom. He barely started jacking himself before his load exploded from his manhood and rained down all over Miles' back. After the last spurt, Timothy collapsed down on his roommate and kissed him gently on the back of his neck, as their ragged breathing calmed back down to normal.

"That was…" gasped Miles, his head apparently still swimming from the orgasm.

"Yeah, it was!" agreed Timothy.

They lay there together, half-dozing, as the semen and sweat dried on their cooling bodies. Twenty minutes later Timothy felt Miles wriggling his butt under him, which caused his member to rise once more.

"Ready for round two?" asked Miles.

"You bet!"

The pair played on and off for the rest of the day, dozing in between rounds and grabbing the occasional refreshment from the kitchen to keep up their strength. It was late that night when, exhausted and totally drained of cum, the duo finally drifted off into a peaceful slumber, happily entwined in each other's arms.

* * *

The next morning Timothy rolled over and saw that Miles was lying there beside him.

Thank goodness it wasn't all just another dream.

Timothy lay there just staring at his roommate, taking in his beauty. He reached over and lightly stroked Miles' sleeping face. A wave of love flooded through his body, although he was little frightened that Miles would wake up and not feel the same way.

Timothy was so nervous. He didn't know how to proceed. The sex the night before had been awesome but he wasn't sure it would be so easy for Miles to embrace a gay romance.

Miles stirred and his beautiful blue eyes began to open.

"Good morning." Miles said with a sleepy smile.

"Right back at you."

"So, how does this work?"

"I don't know I've never been in a situation like this before."

Timothy was relieved that Miles seemed to be as uncertain as he was about the whole thing.

"Are we boyfriends now?" asked Miles sweetly.

"I'd like to be, but I understand if it's all a bit too much and if you need time to work things out." Timothy could feel himself babbling but couldn't seem to stop. "I don't expect you to just turn gay. After all there's so much to consider…"

Miles silenced Timothy with a firm kiss.

"It may be new to me but I know what I want," said Miles confidently. "I want you."

Happiness flooded through Timothy making him smile so wide he thought his face might break.

"It's funny, your kisses don't taste of vanilla anymore," Timothy said to his newfound boyfriend.

"Vanilla? No one has ever…oh."

"What?"

"Gio's kisses did. It was the flavor of his favorite chewing gum…I'd almost forgotten."

Miles looked a little forlorn and Timothy regretted that he'd said anything. Fortunately, the mood was broken by a new arrival.

"You guys have made me so happy," said a voice from the end of the bed.

The boys looked down and weren't too surprised to see that Gio had returned, even if he was naked and climbing into bed with them. They moved apart and Gio wriggled in between the two of them. It was the first time that all three of them had been together in such an intimate position but it didn't seem odd or uncomfortable for either Timothy or Miles. In fact, it was downright cozy.

"Speak of the devil. At least you're not glowing this time," said Miles, apparently relieved to see a more normal-looking version of his dead friend.

"Hope you don't mind. I wanted to pop back for a visit."

"Not at all," said Miles, the sorrow having disappeared from his face. "Thank you for bringing us together."

"That goes double from me," added Timothy. "Now that you've settled your unfinished business will you be moving on?"

"Not just yet…I want to see how things go besides there's a ghost in the apartment upstairs who's been giving me the eye."

"You're incorrigible," remarked Miles with unmistakable fondness in his voice.

"And I wouldn't mind one last time with the both of you," purred Gio, his eyes sparkling with mischief.

He put his arms around Timothy and Miles, drawing them into a steamy three-way kiss. Neither of the boys resisted as Gio proceeded to have his wicked way with them once again.

Timothy and Miles suddenly sat bolt upright in bed.

"Did we just have the same dream?" asked Timothy, suddenly afraid that his heartfelt conversation had only been wishful thinking.

"Yes, and I still want you. Ghost or no ghost."

To prove his point, Miles moved forward and gave Timothy a slow, gentle kiss. Timothy melted back down to the bed as

Miles moved on top of him and the two began to make sweet, tender love.

* * *

Many moons later on a dreadfully stormy night, the lads were almost finished getting dressed into their festive outfits. Lightning flashed through the sky, illuminating the room in a stark white light. A clap of thunder echoed through the apartment.

"Perfect night for it," said Timothy, as he fastened the last button on Miles' costume and gave him a light peck on the lips.

"That it is."

Loud music thumped through the ceiling above them. The Halloween party was apparently already in full swing. Mikey was circling around them, rubbing himself up against their leather-clad legs and purring his approval.

"Ready my naughty vigilante?" asked Timothy, his eyes full of impishness.

"As I'll ever be, my faithful sidekick."

The loved-up lads were dressed as the main characters from Timothy's graphic novel – Blue Hunter and Polestar. It had been published two months before, with Miles' full blessing. They both thought it was the perfect tribute to the memory of the man who'd brought them together. The initial sales had been promising, especially in Japan for some reason…strange since there wasn't a tentacle in sight.

Over the past year their relationship had gone from strength to strength. Admittedly, it had been difficult at first with issues on both sides. Miles had lost some friends and his relationship with his parents had been strained for a few months in the wake of his surprise coming out. On Timothy's side, more than a few friends had expressed concern that Miles would go back to a "traditional lifestyle", once he'd had his fun. It had been trying but they came through it stronger as a couple and remained firmly devoted to one another.

Timothy slapped his boyfriend playfully on his pert buttocks. He was so turned on simply looking at Miles' muscles bulging against his tight-fitting costume and was having all manner of wayward thoughts.

"We could just stay home and *rescue* each other," suggested Miles, after seeing the lustful look in his boyfriend's eyes.

As much as Timothy wanted to he decided against it. Lukas, Marco and their boyfriends were already upstairs and waiting for them.

"Later, my hero."

"OK, but I'll be ripping that outfit off you."

"Sounds good to me."

They stopped by the kitchen on the way to grab a few bottles of wine and headed upstairs to join in with the festivities. As the front door shut behind them a contented chuckle echoed through the apartment and a soft blue glow passed through the lounge room and disappeared into the blackness of the hallway…Gio did so love Halloween.

ON THE NAUGHTY LIST

Lucien Noir was something of an unabashed bastard. Indeed, he often gave others the impression that he was only capable of seeing the misery of the world…and rather reveled in it. It was almost as if he was living under a perpetual dark cloud, with nary a ray of sunshine in sight.

This was particularly true at Christmas, where the crass commercialism only served to rile him up further. It was barely mid-October and the gaudy decorations had already begun to go up about the city putting him into an even blacker mood than usual.

It's not even Halloween yet, for fuck's sake!

The one consolation about the festive season was that he didn't have to work at Christmas and could happily spend the day locked securely away in his apartment safe from all the incessant false cheer and forced family togetherness.

It wasn't that Lucien was an inherently bad person, mind you. It was more that he didn't really care a great deal about anyone apart from himself, often coming across as lacking in empathy and about as emotionally available as a refrigerator.

He wasn't exactly heartless, per se, rather he made damn sure his heart was kept well out of sight and protected from the world.

From an early age, life had taught Lucien repeatedly – and with quiet some force – that the only person who he could truly depend on was himself. His parents hadn't been fit to raise a pet rock, let alone a child, and the succession of lackluster foster families that had followed had only cemented his abysmal view of humanity.

Lucien had been in and out of juvenile detention centers since he was ten years of age. The caliber of acquaintances he'd made in that time hadn't been particularly conducive to keeping him on the straight and narrow. If anything, it made Lucien more unruly and resentful of any type of authority figure whatsoever, which in turn contributed to his high turnover in the foster system, causing him to act out even further. It was a painfully vicious cycle that gnawed at his spirit and stripped away any hope he may have once possessed.

His bi-racial heritage also hadn't helped matters, as he'd been constantly treated as an outcast and never had the feeling that he truly belonged. He'd been teased, harassed and beaten simply for the color of his skin, which was either too dark or not dark enough, depending on the preferences of his tormenters. Lucien had soon discovered that it was a battle that he would never be able to win, so he had eventually given up trying.

Unsurprisingly, Lucien developed a hard outer shell and uncaring attitude as a defense mechanism that had served him well throughout the years. It was perhaps because of this aura of aloofness that he was one of the most popular attractions at Seventh Circle – a fetish club located down by the docks. While he had kept his first name, Lucien had taken a new last name for his stage persona – and to wipe away the last trace of his abusive parents. As Master Noir he put on several delightfully debauched shows a week and had a whole host of eager private clients on the side, all quite desperate for his special brand of discipline. His tall, muscular build, shaved black hair, bright green eyes and smooth mahogany skin also undoubtedly contributed to his appeal.

To say that Lucien enjoyed his job as a Dom would be an understatement. He had taken to his new profession with a malicious glee, deriving great pleasure in inflicting pain and punishing all those in his path.

Everyone is guilty of something.

Despite this, there was one person who had managed to penetrate his armor and cause Lucien to feel a small semblance of affection – well, as much as his heart could muster at any rate – his former foster brother, Oliver. Lucien had come to Oliver's parents, the Walkers, when he was seventeen years of age. They were lovely people but by that point he was too far too damaged, by his years in and out of juvenile detention, to appreciate their kindness. Lucien did, however, get along with their son, Oliver, who was only two years younger in age. Oliver had been far more welcoming than any of the other foster siblings Lucien had encountered during his time in the system.

Not rebuffed by Lucien's tough guy persona, Oliver had happily shared his life with him – freely lending him clothes, his beloved computer games, or whatever else Lucien had taken an interest in.

Naturally, Lucien had been mistrustful at first, unwilling to believe that someone could genuinely care for him and ask for nothing but friendship in return. He'd thought that Oliver simply saw him as another of the many stray animals he was constantly bringing home to look after – it was lucky Oliver's mother was a vet. As the months passed, however, Lucien had slowly let his guard down and begun to let Oliver in.

Sadly, this friendship wasn't enough of a stabilizing influence and his self-destructive tendencies eventually resurfaced. After he'd been with the Walkers for just over six months – the longest placement he'd ever had – Lucien reconnected with some of his less savory friends and was soon back to his delinquent ways – petty theft and vandalism being his rebellious acts of choice. It wasn't long before the police turned up on the Walkers doorstep, threatening Lucien with the possibility of doing real jail time. Lucien felt he had no option but to leave. He ran away to New York shortly afterwards, just before Christmas in fact, without a backward glance. Not to say he didn't have a twinge of regret at leaving Oliver, and his earnest friendship, behind.

Lucien's plan of fading into the anonymity of the big city went swimmingly for about five years. It was then that his past unexpectedly caught up with him in a gay bar in Hell's Kitchen.

"You're so fucking hot!" murmured Lucien.

He'd been making out with the handsome stranger against a wall in the barely lit back corner of the bar for a good twenty minutes.

"Thanks Luc," the boy whispered back.

"Have we met?"

"Well, you were my brother," the stranger teased.

"Oli? Fucking hell!"

Lucien was shocked, although that hadn't diminished the size of his erection that was still pushing up against Oliver, where one of equal excitement was pressing back. To be fair, it was unlikely Lucien would ever have recognized Oliver; such was the difference in appearance. Gone was the clean-cut boy he had known and in his place was a stunning man with punkish blue/black hair, tattoos and a dirty attitude.

"Why didn't you say anything?"

"More fun this way," replied Oliver cheekily, before diving back in for another passionate kiss.

Their kissing led back to Lucien's place where they spent several very pleasurable days together before Oliver returned home to his veterinary studies – following in his mother's footsteps. They kept in touch afterwards and a renewed bond of friendship developed between the pair – a rare thing for Lucien who was in the habit of casting men aside without a second thought as soon as he was done with them.

It had been Oliver who'd convinced Lucien to move back to their hometown of Port Davinica two years beforehand, when a spot opened up at Seventh Circle. Oliver had been working there since he'd left high school, his proclivities obliviously just as impious as Lucien's own. Oliver's former partner, Master Vic, had left to go work in a new club in London, paving the way for a new dimension to be added to his and Lucien's friendship. The duo now regularly worked together, with Oliver helping Lucien to bring all their shows to a rousing finish.

Lucien reached the back entrance of the club and knocked firmly on the graffiti-covered metal door. The bouncer, Sid, a wall of muscle, whose intimidating appearance belied his puppy-dog interior, soon let Lucien into the club to begin preparing for the evening ahead.

No rest for the wicked.

* * *

Several hours later, Lucien was trudging along the dark and deserted city streets. The night had been long and he was tired and slightly grumpy, although the few hundred dollars he'd made in tips had slightly improved his mood.

Now I can buy the rest of the set.

Lucien was a great fan of graphic novels – the more violent and sex-filled the better. A psychologist would have had a field day with Lucien's possible attempt to recapture his lost childhood through his interest in what were basically comic books for adults, but Lucien himself wasn't one for introspection. Lucien planned on going to Geek HQ – the premier purveyor of such things in the city – the next day. He had wanted to buy the remaining issues of his favorite series, Blue Hunter, for the last few weeks. He'd been drawn to the story of the vigilante crime fighter and his faithful sidekick, Polestar…and the copious amounts of sex that was packed into each issue. Not that Lucien felt inspired to put on tights and zip around the city saving people, mind you.

Too much effort for something I wouldn't get paid for!

With his thoughts dwelling on the antics of his favorite fictional characters, Lucien increased his pace, trying to warm himself up on the walk to the metro. To protect against the bitterly, cold night air, he'd wrapped a thick red woolen scarf tightly around his neck and the lower half of his face and shoved his hands firmly in his coat pockets but it was a losing battle. Lucien regretted not wearing his thicker winter coat and was very much looking forward to being home and getting some sleep.

As he approached the entrance of the metro, Lucien could hear a soulful masculine voice echoing out of the tunnel. The tune sounded familiar but he couldn't quite place it. He turned the corner and there on the ground with a guitar case opened before him was one of the most beautiful men Lucien had ever seen. The busker had china-white skin, and chestnut-brown hair cascading down past his shoulders. Lucien wasn't usually a fan of buskers but there was something about the man that drew him in.

Lucien came to a complete stop before the man. Normally, when he spied such a specimen, Lucien's thoughts were of a purely carnal nature, but this certainly wasn't the case now. His mind seemed to be filled with the song, which called to him and kept him fixed in place before the man.

The busker was dressed somewhat lightly, considering the weather, in faded blue jeans with a white t-shirt, a thin black coat and a bright blue scarf wrapped around his neck.

Surely he must be cold.

Apparently noticing Lucien for the first time, the man looked up, stared directly at him, capturing Lucien with his bright hazel gaze, and smiled. Lucien had a sensation of lightness in his chest and felt his irritability beginning to fade away. He'd never experienced anything like it before; it was almost as if he was being warmed from the inside.

Lucien was disrupted from his trance-like state by the buzzing of his phone. Annoyed by the interruption, he looked down to see that it was from one of his regular clients and sent the call to voicemail.

He can wait.

Unfortunately, the spell was broken and Lucien found himself standing there awkwardly before the soulful singer. Unsettled by these strange feelings, Lucien had a sudden urge to escape. He quickly resumed his former brisk pace and entered the silver turnstiles for the metro. Behind him the busker continued singing the moving ballad that was at once familiar and comforting. Strangely, the sense of lightness remained with

Lucien, even as he boarded the metro and continued the journey home.

What the hell was that?

* * *

This odd new lighter feeling stayed with Lucien until the following afternoon, keeping him in a surprisingly good mood. He'd even caught himself smiling at his reflection in the mirror, something he never normally would have done.

Why am I so happy?

Unfortunately, it all came to an abrupt end when Lucien arrived home after doing his weekly grocery shop to find that the elevator was out of service. Living on the tenth floor, he was less than impressed at being forced to climb to the top with his bags. Lucien started climbing the stairs, laden with his groceries, and passed other similarly disgruntled tenants. Granted, they didn't live in luxury, serviced apartments, but it was the third time the elevator had broken down in as many weeks – the Art Deco building had definitely seen better days.

As Lucien reached his floor, cranky and sweating from the exertion, he saw that the elevator doors were wide open and there was a scruffy-looking man with a jumble of wires in his hand working on a switch inside. The repairman was wearing grease-stained overalls and looked to be in his late thirties, with unkempt brown hair, dark eyes and a solid build. His unshaven face was dirty with sweat and grime but that only served to enhance his rugged features.

Lucien sat his groceries down by his front door and walked back towards the elevator.

"How long until it's fixed this time?" asked Lucien in a gruff, antagonistic tone.

It wasn't that he truly blamed the repairman for the problems, he just happened to be a handy target.

"I don't know," answered the repairman, just as brusquely.

Lucien bristled at the man's attitude.

"It's broken more often than it works."

"Not my problem, buddy. Look, I just get called to patch them up as cheaply as I can. It's not like the owners want to spend a lot of money on the place, so take it up with them. Now, why don't you fuck off and leave me alone to finish."

Lucien wasn't used to people standing up to him in such a manner, his foreboding appearance usually had people playing safe around him. A fact Lucien quite liked and often used to his advantage.

"What did you say to me?"

"You heard me."

Lucien moved forward into the elevator and shoved the man against the back of the wall.

"Show some respect."

"Make me, faggot!" said the repairman, before he forcefully pushed Lucien right back.

Lucien became enraged at the comment – any slur against his sexuality or race was guaranteed to rile his inner demons. The shoving match rapidly increased in intensity with the men banging up against the side of the elevator walls. In the struggle they hit the control panel, which caused the doors to close, leaving them to tussle in the dim glow of the red emergency light. Their grip on each other was slippery as the scuffle and the enclosed space had made both men sweat profusely.

With a great burst of strength, Lucien pinned the repairman against the back wall of the elevator. Their faces were barely an inch apart and Lucien recognized the look in the repairman's eyes – it was one he had seen many times before. So he did what came naturally when he saw such an expression and kissed the man violently.

The man protested briefly before eagerly succumbing to Lucien's advances. Seconds later, the pair were ripping at each other's clothes with a hate-filled lust. The repairman's overalls fell down to his ankles revealing a solid, hairy build and an impressive erection glistening with precum. Lucien's jeans and underwear soon followed suit and then he ripped off his t-shirt and flung it to the floor. Their naked bodies pressed hard together, as they hands clawed at one another in a desperate show of need.

After a few minutes of this frantic activity, Lucien forced the man down on his knees and shoved his cock deep into the man's throat. Lucien relished every gag and grunt of protest the repairman made, as he punished the man for his insolence. His muscular legs were tensed as he pounded the repairman's mouth, while his hands gripped the back of the man's head keeping it in place during the assault.

The repairman's noises soon turned to that of enjoyment and Lucien was pleased to see that he was now enthusiastically taking to the task at hand – or rather in mouth. Lucien sincerely doubted that this was the first manhood he had serviced…or would be the last.

Mindful of the perishables rapidly thawing on his doorstep, Lucien roughly pulled the man to his feet and kissed him hard once more, before spinning him around to face the wall. Lucien reached down into his jeans pocket and grabbed his emergency kit – a small sachet of lubricant and an extra-large condom. His experienced hand quickly rolled the latex down his rock hard erection. He then ripped open the sachet and liberally applied lubricant to himself and the tight opening of his companion. Lucien forced his slick digits inside the rosebud, fingering the man roughly, who struggled in a very halfhearted manner.

"Please go slow," begged the man in a harsh whisper.

"Sure," agreed Lucien.

Lucien lined up his sheathed weapon with the target and, disregarding his promise, shoved himself violently inside.

The repairman tensed up in pain and cried out loudly.

"Fucking hell, I said slow!"

"Shut up and enjoy it, bitch," Lucien said in a menacing tone.

He then grabbed a rag from the floor and shoved it in his companion's mouth to keep him quiet, lest they attract the unwanted attention of his neighbors. Lucien had the man pinned against the wall and began to slam in repeatedly not giving the repairman any time to adjust to the manhood violating his hairy ass, pounding him into submission. The sound of his hips smacking up against the firm, round buttocks, coupled with Lucien's grunts of exertion and the repairman's whimpers, reverberated in the small, enclosed space.

The repairman's resistance was short-lived and he was soon moving his hips back to meet Lucien's thrusts, evidently eager to have the manhood deeper inside him. Lucien was keen to oblige and fucked even harder.

Lucien's released his grip of his captive's arms and moved his hands down to the man's solid hips to gain a tighter hold, while he continued to plow him hard up against the cold, silver metal of the elevator wall.

The man then moved his hand down and started to feverishly jerk his cock, his hand practically a blur of frantic motion. His other hand grabbed back, latching onto the thrusting hips behind him and holding on tight. His nails began to mark red indents into Lucien's slippery skin.

It wasn't long before Lucien could feel the load building in his balls, such hate-filled sex often lasted a short time once the initial burst of anger began to fade. He hammered away, enjoying the feel of the muscular repairman as his body tensed and writhed in front of him.

Lucien gave one final thrust and began to shoot hard into his protective sheath. He leaned forward and bit the back of the repairman's neck, which was obviously enough to send to the other man over the edge as he shuddered and groaned even louder through the rag. Lucien roughly pulled out, whipped his condom off and threw it to the floor. The repairman slowly turned around and Lucien could see cum splattered on the wall of the elevator, slowly trickling its way down to the floor.

"Clean that up," commanded Lucien, as he pulled up his crumpled jeans.

"Yes, Sir."

The fucking had apparently done wonders for his attitude.

The elevator reeked of their manly play, a familiar aroma of spent seed and sweat that Lucien never tired of inhaling.

They should bottle it!

Lucien grinned and gave the man one last forceful kiss before grabbing his t-shirt and pressing the release button for the doors, which slowly trundled open. He returned to his front door and carried his bags inside, a puckish smile still on his face and a satisfied glow in his crotch.

It was exactly the purely physical play Lucien liked with not a hint of tender emotion in sight. He didn't know why people insisted on complicating it. For him sex was merely a means to a sticky, satisfying end.

Oli will be jealous when I tell him tomorrow.

* * *

A few days later, Lucien was on his way to the gym when a familiar flash of color up ahead attracted his attention. It was a bright blue scarf. There, sitting on the steps of the post office was the beautiful busker, dressed exactly the same as he had been on the previous occasion.

Guess busking doesn't pay too well.

Lucien planned to walk straight past but once more he found himself irresistibly drawn to the voice. He didn't understand why no one else seemed to be similarly affected by the singing. Indeed, even though the street was bustling with people, they hurried right past, not seeming to take any notice of the man at all.

Lucien slowed down and came to a halt in front of the man. The man turned his head towards Lucien and gave a wide, welcoming smile. The strange feeling of warmth and lightness returned to Lucien's chest and began to spread through his body. Lucien quickly looked away and was about to move off when the man finished singing and spoke to him.

"I'm glad you liked my song," he said in a melodic voice.

"You're talented."

"Thanks. I'm Skye Frost," said the busker, offering his hand.

He shook Skye's hand, which felt icy-cold even through the thick navy-blue wool of Lucien's glove.

"Any relation to Jack?" joked Lucien.

"He's my grandfather, actually."

Lucien started to laugh in response but the look on Skye's face was so sincere, the sound died on his lips.

OK, that's a little odd.

"Anyway, I'm Lucien."

"I know."

"What? How?"

Lucien had a sudden sense of panic.

Is this guy a stalker?

"It's on your coffee cup."

Lucien looked down at the Starbucks cup in his hand with his name scrawled across the side and felt rather foolish. He didn't know what it as about Skye that made him feel so out of his element. It was disconcerting, as Lucien wasn't used to a loss of control in his emotions.

"I'd better get going."

"See you around, Lucien," said Skye with a friendly grin.

As Lucien reached the end of the block he turned back to look at Skye, who had starting singing again.

What is it about him?

* * *

Later that evening, after a strenuous workout – that had included vigorously servicing an enthusiastic twink in the steam room – Lucien made his way down to Seventh Circle. As soon as he walked through the back door he was accosted by Bertha – the owner of the club. A short, rotund woman in her sixties, she had a mess of flaming red hair, quick blue-green eyes and an even quicker temper. According to rumor she had quite the colorful history, full of scandal, mischief and possibly a little murder thrown in for good measure. Not that Bertha ever did anything to quell such tales; it was good for business, after all.

"Thank goodness you're here! Why haven't you been answering your phone?" exclaimed Bertha.

Her voice had a certain drag queen-esque quality that was undoubtedly due to her decades-long pack-a-day habit.

"I had it switched off at the gym. What's the matter? I'm not due to go on for another two hours."

"Chad and Sally were in a little car accident. They're a bit battered and bruised and they could be off for the rest of the week."

Lucien could understand Bertha's panic. Chad and Sally – a.k.a Master Adam and Mistress Eve – were another of the club's most popular acts and any canceled shows could put a serious dent in audience numbers and alcohol sales.

"What do you want me to do about it?" asked Lucien.

There was a trace of annoyance in his voice, as he was sure he wasn't going to like the answer.

"Well, you and that strapping assistant of yours will have to cover their spots tonight and possibly until Monday."

"That's going to be four shows tonight!"

"You're a big boy. If anyone can do it, it's you sweet cheeks."

Bertha punctuated her sentence by playfully slapping Lucien's firm, muscular buttocks and tottering off on her six-inch stilettos.

On one hand, Lucien was glad of the extra money, but on the other he knew that all the extra shows would be tiring and restrict his availability for his private clients.

I'll work something out.

Lucien hurried to his and Oliver's dressing room at the end of the hall – basically just an oversized broom closet with a bathroom attached but it served their needs. When he opened the door he was treated to the most pleasant sight of Oliver's pert little white ass, framed by a red jockstrap, spread temptingly before him. His assistant was bent over doing up the clasps on his matching red PVC boots. Not wanting to waste any time,

Lucien closed the door, sank to his knees and shoved his face right in between the round cheeks.

"Damn, I need to fix my boots more often," exclaimed Oliver, making no effort to stand back up again.

Oliver had one of the finest asses Lucien had ever fucked and his cock was equally as fine – ten juicy uncut inches that had had many a man drooling for a taste…or a ride. Lucien keenly inhaled the pleasant musky scent of Oliver's ass, as his tongue explored inside the passage. After a minute or so of hungrily feasting, Lucien sat back on his heels.

"Wish I could eat this for longer but we've got to be on in fifteen minutes."

"Yeah, Bertha warned me. Best we don't get too excited if we're going to make it through all the spots."

"I know, but still…"

Lucien spat on Oliver's exposed hole and pushed two fingers roughly into the passage. Oliver cried out in obvious pleasure while he pushed his hips back in a natural response. The crotch of Lucien's jeans bulged as his rapidly hardening cock strained against the material. Lucien moved his fingers in slow, circular motions, stretching the tight hole and massaging the interior. With his free hand, Lucien reached between Oliver's legs and grasped the erect manhood dangling between them. The foreskin had drawn back slightly to reveal a trickle of precum escaping the engorged cockhead. Lucien ran his fingers along the shaft, and rubbed them over the tip, spreading the sticky liquid over the sensitive glans.

Oliver gasped in response, making Lucien smile devilishly.

"Keep that up and I'm going to blow," he warned.

Reluctantly, Lucien released Oliver's cock, removed his digits from the inviting passage and gave the buttocks a firm slap.

"Later," Lucien growled seductively.

"Can't wait!"

Lucien got to his feet and quickly stripped out of his jeans and t-shirt so he could put on his first outfit for the evening – black leather pants with blue piping and an asymmetrical harness. It was a look that had proved popular time and again, and was sure to get the crowd worked up, which in turn helped increase the tips.

The pair was soon ready to go but before they left the room Lucien grabbed Oliver, held him tight up against the door and gave him a fiery kiss. From the way they grabbed at each other it was clear that neither particularly wanted it to end. Once more Lucien's fingers searched out that tempting entrance and began to work their way inside. Their passionate embrace threatened to spill over into full-on penetration but a sudden knock on their door interrupted their play.

"It's time, gentlemen!" came Bertha's muffled voice through the door.

They grudgingly broke apart, erections clearly outlined by their outfits – although it was hardly as if the audience would mind.

"Yeah, we're coming!" answered Lucien, only mildly annoyed that work needed to take precedence over defiling his friend. "Ready, boy?"

"Yes, Sir!"

They exited the dressing room and went towards the sound of the boisterous crowd, who sounded even rowdier than normal.

They better be good tippers.

* * *

Lucien was feeling thoroughly exhausted as he walked through the city center on his way home. He and Oliver had spent the last week doing double their usual amount of shows – Chad and Sally weren't returning until tomorrow. While it had been enjoyable, not to mention profitable, Lucien was glad to have today off. He had spent the afternoon in Geek HQ, perusing the shelves for new titles and had found quite a few of interest – a supernatural detective story, in particular, had caught his eye. Lucien's recent influx of cash meant that the khaki-colored satchel slung over his shoulder was now full of new purchases that he fully intended to start reading when he got home.

Lost in his thoughts, Lucien was walking past the outdoor ice rink in front of the Town Hall, when he spied a familiar figure skillfully gliding along the ice with his long chestnut hair and bright blue scarf billowing out behind him. Lucien stood transfixed at the sight.

As if conscious of being watched, the ice-skater turned his head and warmly smiled. He then swiftly changed direction and glided towards the barricade where Lucien was standing.

"Hey Lucien," said Skye, a friendly smile upon his lips.

"Hi."

Lucien felt a surge of warmth flooding into his body.

Why does he have this effect on me?

"Do you want to come ice-skating with me?"

"What?"

"You know, put on skates and whiz around the rink like a Christmas fairy."

"I don't think so."

"Come on. It'll be fun."

"Another time."

"Don't tell me a big muscleman like you is scared of a little ice?"

"I…I just don't feel like it."

Lucien shifted uncomfortably in his place. He didn't like to be challenged. Truthfully, the real reason he didn't want to go on the ice was that he was embarrassed. He'd never learnt how to skate, as no one had cared enough to teach him.

Despite his discomfort, there was something so innocent and childlike in Skye's eyes that tugged at Lucien's resolve until it came crumbling apart. Before he knew it, Lucien was sitting on a wooden bench, just inside the rink entrance, putting black and blue skates on his size thirteen feet with a grinning Skye standing before him.

Once he was all laced up, Lucien gawkily clomped over to the edge of the rink and tentatively stepped onto the ice. He made it about two feet before his feet slipped from under him and he landed heavily on his ass. Lucien was immediately filled with fury, first at his own clumsiness, then at Skye for making him do it. He could feel the wetness of the ice seeping through his jeans and into his underwear.

Lucien was about to lose his temper completely when he heard Skye's melodic laugh behind him. The sound washed over him and he felt the anger gradually give way to amusement and he began to laugh at himself.

"You need a penguin?" teased Skye.

"No, I do not." Lucien replied firmly, while purposely not looking at the nearby row of penguin-shaped sleds for toddlers.

Skye offered his hand and helped Lucien to his feet.

"Use me, then."

"You better not drop me."

"Wouldn't dream of it."

The two then began to move around the rink slowly together, while the rest of the skaters easily passed by them. Lucien was concentrating hard on not falling over, not an easy feat given the constant threat of being knocked off balance by teenagers playing tag or the toddlers who flew past like they'd been born with skates on and a total lack of fear. Lucien held onto Skye with a vice-like grip, although that didn't stop him from having a few more tumbles. Despite the warmth he felt inside at being so close to the busker it seemed to Lucien that Skye's arm was strangely icy-cold.

Must just be from the rink.

As his confidence increased, Lucien loosened his hold a little but didn't release completely. After a little while, Lucien was surprised to find that he was genuinely enjoying himself. He was also a little sad that he'd been too afraid to give it a go before but he vowed to himself that he'd try it again soon.

Maybe with Skye?

Before he knew it three hours had passed and the rink was practically deserted. The pair skated over to the side, stepped back onto the light-green, carpeted area and sat down on the benches to take off their skates.

"Thanks…it's been fun."

"I know," replied Skye with a cheeky grin. "Just wait 'till next time."

"Next time?"

"You'll see."

With that Skye leapt up, his skates slung over his shoulders and sped off towards the exit. Within seconds he had disappeared into the night. Lucien wanted to follow him but he'd barely untied his laces and he knew there was little chance of catching up with his strange new friend.

Are we friends? I don't really have those…well, except for Oli.

Lucien was interrupted in his thoughts, by the approach of a hefty, harassed-looking woman in uniform, who'd obviously come over to hurry him up. He quickly untied his rental skates and swapped them for his heavy, black boots. Lucien then retrieved his satchel from the lockers and left the rink as the lights were shutting off.

As Lucien gingerly walked back home, a little sore from all his falls on the ice, his thoughts returned to the mysterious lad who had a strange hold over him. A little grin fixed itself to his lips and was only dislodged by another unexpected encounter half an hour later.

* * *

Lucien had just exited the metro by his apartment building when he noticed that the laces on his right boot had come undone. As he bent down to tie them back up – somewhat carefully seeing he was still sore from his numerous impacts with the ice – there was a sudden tugging and Lucien felt his satchel being yanked from his arm. The force knocked him to the ground and he saw a small figure running off down the street.

Quickly recovering his senses, Lucien scrambled to his feet and took off in hot pursuit of the thief. At that time of night there was hardly anybody about and Lucien could clearly hear the frantic footsteps of his attacker scurrying not too far up ahead. The chase only lasted a few blocks as Lucien's powerful legs propelled him rapidly through the deserted streets and closer to his prey – the exhilaration of the hunt obliterated any trace of the pain.

Lucien turned the corner and could see that the thief had run into a blind alley. His lips curved into a malevolent smile, as he contemplated exactly how he was going to punish the misguided mugger.

He moved into the entrance of the dimly lit alley and was hit by the acrid aroma of stale urine. There, up against the grimy back wall, was the thief, looking every bit the trapped animal.

"Nobody steals from me!" thundered Lucien.

"I'm sorry. I'm sorry, alright. Please, don't hurt me," pleaded the thief.

"I should wring your puny neck!"

As he got closer, Lucien saw that his attacker was much younger than he'd thought – only in his teens – and was trembling in fear. Lucien's rage faltered, dulled by the sight of the terrified boy. The boy's clothes were dirty and nowhere near warm enough for the wintery weather. He could see a desperation in the boy's eyes that he knew all too well from his own time on the streets.

"Give me back my satchel," demanded Lucien, his voice calmer than before.

The boy tossed the satchel to Lucien and cowered back against the wall.

"I should take you straight to the police."

"Please…I'm so sorry…just let me go."

Lucien could see that the boy was on the verge of tears and felt a stirring in his heart that had been absent for quite some time – it was sympathy. His mind flashed back to a time when he, too, had tried to steal from the wrong person. Sadly, he'd received a black eye, several stitches and the faded scar on the left side of his neck for his trouble – an experience he didn't wish to pass on to another troubled child. Lucien suddenly decided on a much different method of dealing with his would-be assailant.

"Are you hungry?" Lucien asked in the least threatening tone he could manage.

"What?"

"Do you want something to eat?"

"I…I don't…please, let me leave."

"Look, you can either come with me to the diner around the corner or I can take your skinny ass to the police station. What's it going to be?"

The boy seemed dazed by this unexpected turn of events. Apparently realizing he only had one true option he timidly answered Lucien's question.

"The diner."

The twosome walked in silence to Granny's – an old-fashioned diner at the corner of Lucien's street that never seemed to close. Lucien had often stopped by after a long shift at the club for a quick snack before bed. He liked the homey atmosphere of the place. The food was as cheap as it was deliciously fattening. Fortunately, Lucien's vigorous performances and loyalty to the gym meant that he was able to work off all of the excessive calories contained within just about everything on the menu.

Once they were seated in a booth, Lucien ordered two hamburgers with the works and sodas – the chase had given him an appetite and Lucien thought his companion looked in need of a good meal.

"What's your name?"

"Christopher…Topher."

The two sat in an awkward silence, which was thankfully broken by the arrival of the food, delivered by a heavy-set, buxom brunette with a kind face, who'd been quite a looker back in the day. Topher practically inhaled his burger while Lucien looked on thoughtfully.

When he cleared his plate and finished his drink, Topher looked at Lucien uneasily.

"Thanks, but I should go."

He made to get up but Lucien stuck out his arm, grabbed a hold of Topher and pulled him firmly back down to his seat. The lad looked terrified, so Lucien hastened to reassure him of his intent.

"Don't look so worried. Now, I've done you a favor. I just want a few answers. How old are you?"

Topher appeared nervous and more than a little mistrustful. He fidgeted with the balled up napkin on his plate, his eyes looking about furtively. Lucien well remembered feeling the exact same way whenever anyone had showed the slightest interest in his wellbeing.

"No need to be scared, just tell me the truth."

"Fifteen, Sir."

He has good manners for a thief.

"Call me Lucien. What are you doing on the streets?"

Evidently coming to a decision to trust Lucien, Topher took a deep breath and began his tale of woe. Unfortunately, it was one Lucien had heard far too often before.

"My parents kicked me out because…because they found out that I'm gay."

In the harsh fluorescent lighting of the diner, Lucien noticed that Topher had faded bruises on both arms and had a good idea where they'd come from. Not for the first time, Lucien thought that people should be forced to take rigorous exams before being allowed to have children

After seeing that Lucien hadn't gotten up in disgust at the revelation of his sexuality, Topher continued.

"My friends abandoned me and I had nowhere else to go, so I left my hometown and hitchhiked here. I got into the city a few days ago. I only had a backpack with me but it was stolen the first night when I fell asleep at the bus station. I'm so sorry about trying to steal your bag but I hadn't eaten since yesterday morning and…"

"It's OK," interrupted Lucien. "You got somewhere to sleep tonight?"

"No…not really."

A look of concern crossed Lucien's face, for the second time that night his thoughts whisked back into his own past and ran through the likely possibilities of what would happen to the teenager if he stayed on the streets – forced prostitution, drug addiction, illness…or a nasty combination of all three. Lucien had certainly had his share of misfortune and regrettable experiences, and was lucky to have made any sort of life for himself afterwards.

This is none of my concern! But, maybe if someone had been kind to me? Who am I kidding? He'll probably rob me blind. What can I really offer him?

Suddenly, his eyes focused back onto Topher, as he came to a decision that he hoped he wouldn't regret in the morning.

"OK, you're coming with me."

"You said you wouldn't take me to the cops."

"I'm not. You're staying at my place tonight."

"No…I don't think so. Thanks for the food but I'm not going to put out or anything."

Topher was obviously worried that Lucien had something untoward in mind.

"Don't worry, I've got a spare couch and you're far too young for my tastes."

"Why are you doing this? You don't even know me and I tried to steal from you."

"Let's just say I know what it's like to do it tough."

Lucien paid for the meal and led Topher around the corner, back to his building. Thankfully, the elevator was working again, although Lucien wouldn't have minded having another round with the repairman. Once inside the apartment, Topher still seemed quite tense and afraid of what might happen to him.

"As long you don't try to steal from me, you'll be safe here tonight. Understand?"

"Yes, Sir...I mean, Lucien."

Lucien gave him a towel and showed him to the bathroom, while he went to find some spare clothes for Topher to change into – the ones he had on weren't the freshest. He didn't know what he was going to do with the boy but there was a surprisingly strong protective instinct inside him that wouldn't let him turf the kid back out on the street.

When Topher emerged from the bathroom, freshly clean and dressed in one of Lucien's large t-shirts and track pants, he looked even smaller and more vulnerable than before. His floppy brown hair was slicked back and his warm brown eyes were brimming with gratitude.

"I don't know how I'll repay you."

"Don't worry about it. Get some sleep and we'll work out something more permanent for you tomorrow."

"Goodnight, Lucien."

A flicker of emotion crossed Lucien's heart but he promptly pushed it aside.

I'm turning into a bleeding heart!

* * *

The following Saturday, Lucien awoke to the heavenly aromas of sizzling bacon and freshly brewed coffee wafting down the hallway and into his bedroom. He groggily exited the bed – the previous evening's drinking had taken its toll – threw on his robe and padded down to the hallway and into the kitchen, where Topher was busily at work preparing breakfast.

Lucien had only planned on letting the boy spend the night but when the morning had come he just couldn't find the words to tell him to leave. It was uncharacteristically generous of him. Lucien didn't know where this sudden bout of charity had come from but he wasn't so sure he liked the change in himself. He had gotten along just fine without forming emotional attachments to people and having to deal with their problems.

That aside, Lucien was surprised to find that he didn't altogether hate the companionship. Topher was quiet and hadn't interfered with his life at all, so Lucien was reluctant to turn his back on the boy. Besides, his apartment had never looked cleaner although he felt a little guilt over rescuing the boy from the street only to become a slave.

"That smells great! But you really don't have to do that every morning."

"I know. I just…I just want to show my appreciation. And I like cooking."

"This can't be permanent you know."

It was something Lucien had said on a daily basis since Topher's arrival, but seemed to be more and more an empty threat.

"I know, I know."

Suddenly, there was a light knocking on the door.

Dammit!

Lucien had completely forgotten that Oliver was coming over for their usual Saturday morning breakfast of donuts and coffee. He hadn't told Oliver about the unexpected houseguest and was unsure of how his assistant would react.

"Fuck it," he muttered to himself and went to open the door.

Oliver breezed through the door and straight into the lounge room. His right hand clutched a big white paper bag with circular grease stains starting to form around the base. Emblazoned on the side was the logo for Fallen Angel Cakes – a black-winged donut – and their slogan printed beneath – "sinfully delicious". It was something with which Lucien and Oliver wholeheartedly agreed.

"They were out of the Frosted Maple, so I got extra Apple Crumble and Coconut Cream. Hope that's…." Oliver's train of thought was derailed by the sight of Topher, peering into the lounge room from the kitchen doorway. "Sorry, I didn't realize you had company."

"This is Topher…he's staying here for a while. Topher this is Oliver."

Lucien saw several looks flicker across Oliver's face as he took in the information before seeming to come to a conclusion.

"Can we talk, privately?" asked Oliver

"Come with me."

Topher retreated to the kitchen as Lucien led Oliver to the bedroom and closed the door behind them.

"Tell me you're not fucking him!" demanded Oliver.

"What? No! He's just a kid!"

"Then what's he doing here. He's underage. It doesn't look good."

Lucien bristled at the interrogation.

"You're acting like a jealous housewife! Not that it's any of your business but he was abandoned by his family and he was living on the streets."

"How did get you involved then?"

"He tried to rob me but…"

"What?"

"Look it doesn't matter. He's just a young kid who got in trouble all because his worthless parents couldn't deal with the fact that he's gay. I know a little something about fucked up families and I thought I could help."

"That doesn't sound like you."

"I know."

Lucien was only marginally offended, as he knew Oliver's words were true.

"He can't stay here indefinitely."

"Well I'm not sending him back out there, he can't fend for himself."

Oliver looked like he was about to continue the argument but obviously thought better of it.

"What are you going to do with him then? He should be in school."

"I know. I know. I haven't decided yet."

"Will you let me help you then?"

Sensing that he'd won the battle, Lucien agreed.

"OK. That would be good." Feeling magnanimous in victory, Lucien offered an olive branch, or rather a helping of crispy bacon. "Have breakfast with us. You'll see he's a sweet kid."

"Damn, you've changed. It's almost like you've got a heart. What's happened to you, Tin Man?" teased Oliver.

"You're fucking hilarious and I don't know. Maybe I've been infected with the spirit of the season."

"Doubtful, Scrooge."

"What's that make you? Tiny Tim?"

"Well, I do have a big…crutch."

"That you do."

Lucien reached over and gave the aforementioned crutch a firm squeeze before giving Oliver a quick, hungry kiss up against the door. Things may have become more heated if there hadn't been for the sudden loud crash of a plate being dropped onto the tiled kitchen floor.

"Sorry!" Topher sheepishly called out down the hallway.

"Breakfast...right!" said Lucien, as they broke apart and regained their composure.

The twosome returned to the lounge room to find that Topher had filled the mahogany dining table in the corner with a veritable feast, combining his original breakfast with the copious donuts that Oliver had brought.

"Hope you're hungry. I'm really sorry about the plate," said Topher nervously. He was apparently worried about the outcome of the bedroom conversation.

"Thanks, Topher. It looks great and I've got plenty more plates." Noting Topher's worried look he hastened to reassure his houseguest. "Don't worry kid, you aren't being kicked out."

Topher visibly relaxed and sat down at the table. The others followed suit and the threesome dug into the delicious breakfast before them.

"What's going to happen to me?" asked Topher tentatively.

"I haven't worked that out yet, but Oli is going to help."

"Actually, I think I already have an idea but I need to make a few phone calls before I..."

"No cops!" interrupted a clearly terrified Topher.

"No, no cops. I promise."

Both Lucien and Topher looked thoroughly relieved. Given Lucien's past interactions with them he had no desire to go back on their radar – there were one or two charges from his delinquent days that he still hadn't answered for.

"Are you boyfriends?" asked Topher, sounding just a tinge jealous.

"No. He's just a friend," replied Lucien.

Lucien glanced over to Oliver and saw a sad expression flutter over his friend's features and then it was gone.

What's that about?

To change the mood Lucien steered the conversation to the much safer topic of their favorite TV shows. When it was revealed that Oliver and Topher shared a love of Doctor Who the tension eased and they passed the rest of the breakfast in agreeable company.

* * *

Over the next few weeks Lucien found himself thinking more and more about his mysterious new friend, Skye. Lucien hadn't seen the busker since that night at the ice rink and was still perplexed by the strange effect he seemed to have on him.

Lucien had kept his eye out for the handsome singer whenever he was walking through the city center, but to no avail. Well, that wasn't strictly true. He had caught one or two glimpses of him, or thought he did, but whenever Lucien turned to follow it was as if the man had disappeared into thin air. He had a sneaking, and thoroughly unsettling, suspicion that perhaps Skye had been a figment of his imagination. He wasn't sure what was more worrying, an imaginary friend or a real one who seemed to have almost supernatural powers of persuasion.

He couldn't help but wonder if Skye had something to do with his recent bursts of emotion. Lucien hadn't been bothered with anyone's feelings, excepting Oliver's, until Skye had come into his life and he'd been happy enough – for the most part.

Topher was still his houseguest and Lucien's protectiveness over the boy, and concern for his welfare, seemed to grow by the day. It wasn't as if Lucien was gaining anything in return for sheltering him. Granted, he had a free live-in housekeeper, which wasn't without its benefits, but that wasn't what stopped him from simply depositing Topher at the nearest orphanage and wishing him the best. Rather, he felt a brotherly affection for the lad, which was a surprising new sensation that he'd never experienced before – his relationship with Oliver had never really been familial.

It was, however, a living situation that needed to change. It would be fair to say that Topher had developed a little crush on his savior. Occasionally, Lucien had caught his young houseguest gazing at him with barely disguised interest in his eyes. Not that Lucien would ever act upon it. As a teenager, he had been taken advantage of enough times not to wish it upon another.

Lucien tried to reassure himself that is was only a coincidence that his out of character behavior had commenced with meeting the busker, but there was a niggling doubt in the back of his mind that Skye was important somehow.

Maybe he's my fairy godfather?

* * *

The heat of the spotlights was causing both Lucien and Oliver to perspire, sending beads of sweat down their straining bodies. It was Saturday night and they were on the main stage, midway through their first show of the evening. This routine was one they did about once a month and was always a crowd favorite.

Oliver was secured to the chain link spider web – a most useful piece of equipment – spread eagle, wearing only a skimpy navy-blue jockstrap that bulged obscenely in the pouch. Lucien, clad in skin-tight black leather pants and matching vest, put down the cat o' nine tails on the small table by the side of the stage and moved onto the next portion of the show – candles. He picked up a thin red candle, lit it and moved over to Oliver.

Lifting the candle, Lucien let the flame hover over Oliver's chest, enough to warm the skin but not enough to burn – he was a professional, after all. When he saw the wax begin to melt in earnest, Lucien slowly tipped the candle to the side to allow it to drip down onto his captive assistant. Ever the showman, Lucien was positioned so the crowd could see every tantalizing moment.

Oliver gasped as the first drop of hot wax hit his chest, narrowly missing his right nipple. Lucien moved his hand towards the center so that the next few drops fell right between Oliver's compact and firm pecs. He continued slowly waving the candle over Oliver until his chest was sufficiently splattered in red, then Lucien moved his hand down letting the wax fall over the wonderfully chiseled six-pack, careful not to spill any on the jockstrap. Oliver strained against his bonds as each new drop hit his exposed skin, the ever-growing bulge in his jockstrap indicating his enjoyment of the proceedings.

Lucien continued in his play, dripping the molten wax over Oliver's arms and legs, taking time to decorate the writhing body in splashes of vibrant red. He took care not to cover any of Oliver's numerous tattoos – six in total – as he liked the look of them outlined in dripping red. By the end, Oliver resembled a piece of thoroughly modern art – one which quite a few members of the audience would have liked to display in their homes.

To finish off the show, Lucien turned to the audience and blew the candle out slowly, his lips forming an enticing pout. He turned back to his partner and used the candle to trace along the outline of Oliver's massive erection, which was struggling to be contained by the stretched pouch. Lucien took the candle and slid it inside the elastic band of the jockstrap. He pulled it towards him creating space to slip his hand inside and grab a hold of the stiff, fleshy rod. Oliver whimpered softly as Lucien began to slowly pump the cock with his fist inside the underwear. It had the effect of delightfully teasing the audience, as they could only imagine the glorious sight of Oliver's manhood being so expertly manhandled and dream that they were the ones doing it.

Lucien looked Oliver directly in the eyes, the chemistry between them undeniable, as increased his pace, tugging forcefully on the erection, while a steady stream of precum leaked over his hand. Suddenly, he stopped and turned back to look at the audience once more.

"Should I put the poor boy out of his misery?"

This received a multitude of cheers and shouts for the affirmative.

"What do you think, boy? Do you deserve release?"

"Only if you think so, Sir!" shouted Oliver, loud enough to be heard at the back of the club – he clearly knew how to stir up the crowd as well as Lucien.

The spectators cheered even louder, all evidently eager to see Oliver meet a happy ending. Lucien smiled wickedly and resumed his good work. He pumped his fist hard and fast, and within mere moments Oliver's breathing became labored, his body tensed in preparation for the imminent orgasm. Oliver's head pressed back into the web and he let out a series of short loud grunts as he came in shuddering bursts, all still hidden by the flimsy material of the underwear.

Lucien continued to milk the cock until every last drop had been expelled, at which he point he lifted his hand up to Oliver's mouth and made his captive lick it clean. The audience applauded and called out, and tips soon filled the big, glass jar at the front of the stage.

"Good, boy," Lucien whispered to Oliver, who smiled back. "Thank you, Ladies and Gentlemen. We'll be back just after midnight!"

Lucien undid Oliver's bonds and helped him off the stage, through the curtain and to their dressing room – his circulation had yet to return, making it a little difficult to walk unaided.

When he'd recovered, Oliver hopped in the shower to wash off all the wax.

"Need some help?" offered Lucien, who was standing naked in the doorway.

"Why thank you, kind Sir."

Lucien squeezed in behind Oliver; the shower was barely big enough for one grown man, let alone two. They stood together as the hot water beat down on their bodies. Lucien held Oliver in a tight grip, enjoying the feel of the slippery skin pressed up against his. As much as he would have liked nothing more than to pound Oliver senseless, Lucien preferred not to cum until after he'd finished all his shows. Instead, he settled for nibbling Oliver's neck and running his hands all over the toned body before him, while Oliver wriggled contentedly in his arms.

They stayed there until the heat began to leave the water and they reluctantly left the comforting embrace of the steamy shower and dried off.

Oliver was dressed again first, so he offered out to the bar to grab them some drinks before it was time to get ready for the next show.

"Hurry back, boy."

"Of course, Daddy."

Lucien threw his towel at his cheeky companion but he was already out the door. He grinned to himself and began to rifle through the clothes rack in search of his next outfit.

Time for the leather chaps, I think.

* * *

Much later that evening, the duo was roaming the club floor, mingling with the patrons – it never hurt to be friendly with those who gave you tips. The crowd was usually fairly alcohol-infused by this point in the evening but they were generally well behaved – apart from the occasional grope from an overenthusiastic fan or two.

They had done a few circuits of the room and were on opposite sides of the main room when Lucien saw one such admirer grab a handful of Oliver's ass and give it a firm squeeze. The man in question was late middle-aged and not the most attractive of specimens, with thinning sandy blond hair, dark pig-like eyes and a potbelly. Lucien noticed that he appeared rather inebriated but didn't think any more of it until a few minutes later when the guy started grabbing at Oliver far more aggressively.

Lucien quickly made his way over to the pair just in time to catch the man's uninspired attempt at seduction.

"Yeah, you're a real dirty cocksucker aren't you? Bet you want it bad."

Even though the man sounded like a bad eighties porno, Lucien thought it best to shut him down before he became a problem.

"Hey! Calm down a bit." Lucien said firmly. "We're all here for a bit of fun."

"It's OK," said Oliver, obviously trying to downplay the situation.

"He's a little whore and he likes it, so why don't you just fuck off!"

The man pushed Lucien away and turned back to continue his assault on Oliver. Lucien felt a rage bubbling inside him and grabbed the man by the back of the neck and spun him back around to face him.

"Listen, buddy. I think you've had enough to drink tonight. Maybe you should think about going home and sobering up."

The man struggled free of Lucien's grasp and stumbled backwards into Oliver, who in turn fell against a table, spilling drinks and smashing a glass.

"Don't tell me what to do, you black bastard!"

He charged at Lucien, his arm raised in attack and his face twisted in fury. It was a rage shared by Lucien who didn't take kindly to racial abuse at the best of times. Lucien raised his own arms, ready to punch his would-be opponent when Sid suddenly appeared from nowhere and quickly frog-marched the guy outside. He moved rather fleetly for such a big wall of muscle.

Bertha was up on the stage as quick as a flash, in an apparent effort to restore the festive ambiance of before.

"Well, wasn't that exciting boys and girls! To help us all forget about this little unpleasantness, free shots for the next ten minutes!"

The crowd cheered its appreciation and a great many of the patrons made their way to the bar.

Lucien moved over to Oliver who was busy drying himself from the splashed drinks with napkins.

"You, OK?" asked Lucien.

"Yeah, I'm fine, just a little soggy. My hero," he teased.

"Well you're nobody's whore but mine."

"Damn straight."

Oliver kissed him for his chivalry, to the great enjoyment of the nearby patrons, who undoubtedly would have happily swapped places with either of the pair. The revelers soon forgot the confrontation and the night continued on without any further incident.

* * *

Topher had been living with Lucien for nearly a month when Oliver presented them with an alternative solution over lunch. They were sitting at a corner booth of Granny's and had just finished eating an enormous shared plate of spicy chicken nachos.

"So, what do you think?" asked Oliver expectantly.

"I'm not sure," replied Topher, looking to Lucien for reassurance.

Lucien hesitated. In theory, there was nothing wrong with Oliver's plan but he had reservations. Oliver's parents had agreed to apply for temporary custody of Topher. They had been foster parents for nearly fifteen years and had helped many children in their time of need. Unluckily, they had been on holidays in Europe until the previous week, so Oliver hadn't been able to present it as an option for Topher until now.

Lucien's reluctance was more due to his own prejudices than any practical considerations. Indeed, he had nothing against the Walkers personally, but his own experience with the foster system had been traumatic to say the least.

"They seem to have done an OK job raising Oli…for the most part."

"Gee, thanks." Oliver said while punching Lucien playfully on the arm.

"But do I really have to tell people about my family?" asked Topher.

"Unfortunately, yes. Social services won't agree to place you in the foster system until they can verify your story. I've already made an appointment for tomorrow with the social worker who's overseen most of my parents' foster kids. His name is Murray and he's a decent, understanding guy. What do you say?"

"Will you come with me," Topher asked Lucien with a pleading look in his eyes.

Lucien felt a protective urge course through his body. He had come to care for Topher far more than he'd like to admit. Their similar backgrounds undoubtedly had forged a bond between the pair and Lucien found he was quite invested in what happened to Topher. He still wasn't sure what had started this change in his personality and had yet to decide if it was a good thing or not. Lucien certainly liked having Topher in his life but was wary of opening his heart any more than was strictly necessary. He had been guarded for so long it was difficult to accept that there may be people worth caring for who cared about him in return. The same could be said about his relationship with Oliver, which seemed to contain ever-increasing levels of emotion that Lucien didn't know if he was ready for.

"Sure, if you need me to."

"I'll be there too," added Oliver. "After all, we'll practically be brothers."

Topher smiled and his eyes shimmered with a hint of tears. "I'd like that."

Just then the waitress, a homely blonde girl with a crooked, but friendly smile, politely interrupted their conversation.

"Can I get you boys any dessert?"

Lucien took charge, feeling a sudden need to cheer himself up in the face of Topher's probable near departure.

"We'll have the Jumbo Sundae Platter, thanks."

"Oki doki!"

"Trust me kids, it's a delicious sugar coma waiting to happen."

Lucien was proved right when twenty minutes later, with the plate scraped clean, the trio sluggishly left the diner and headed up to Lucien's apartment to recover from their gluttony.

* * *

The next week passed by in a blur of formalities and paperwork, and Topher was soon living with Oliver's parents. Lucien understood it had been rough on Topher having to go over his sad story multiple times and the feelings of shame and regret that undoubtedly accompanied it. He knew firsthand what it was like to admit that your own parents found you unworthy of love. It wasn't something he'd wish upon anyone, let alone someone he cared for.

Lucien was feeling his absence. He was plagued with a sense of loneliness that hadn't been present before he'd taken Topher in from the cold.

No good deed goes unpunished.

Truthfully, Lucien was still a little annoyed at Oliver for interfering. Even though rationally Lucien knew that living with the Walkers was in Topher's best interests, he missed the companionship.

In order to combat this strange new feeling of emptiness, Lucien had been spending an inordinate amount of time at the gym – not that he needed it. He had just finished his sixth session for the week and it was only Thursday.

His overworked muscles ached as he walked through the white cityscape. The first snow of the season had started that very morning and kept up all day, with more predicted in the days to follow. It was shaping up to be one of the coldest winters in recent memory. Despite being wrapped up in his heavy coat, thick scarf and several layers underneath, Lucien was still feeling the winter chill.

Up ahead, Lucien saw a Christmas market set up just outside the main entrance to Janeway Park. The stall that attracted his attention was the one selling the mulled wine. The delicious sugary aroma wafted across the street and filled his nostrils. His mouth watered in response and his mind was made up.

That'll hit the spot.

Lucien was almost to the front of the line when he felt a warmth creeping up his back and into his chest just before he heard a melodic voice behind him.

"Do you want to build a snowman?"

Lucien turned around to face Skye.

"Do I look like a fucking Disney princess?"

"Well, with a blonde wig and a green dress I think you'd make a passable Elsa."

"Hilarious."

"Excuse me, Sir. What can I get for you?" asked the portly man behind the counter.

Lucien turned back to the stall and ordered two large cups of mulled wine.

"Thanks," said Skye, happily accepting the drink. "So, how about that snowman?"

"You're serious?"

"Sure. There's plenty of material!"

"That's only for kids."

"Come on, live a little, you big scaredy-cat!"

For some reason he had yet to fathom, Lucien seemed unable to resist Skye's suggestions, no matter how alien they felt to him. The pair headed through the wrought iron gates at the park's entrance and walked through the snow-dusted scenery. Lucien sipped his drink, relishing the taste of the warm sugar-spiced wine as it filled his mouth and trickled down the back of his throat.

They kept walking seemingly all alone, the city sounds muffled by the surrounding trees. Given the late hour and chilly temperature it was unlikely they'd encounter many others out for a stroll. Their breath fogged out before them as they chatted while they walked. They had traversed nearly the full length of the park when they came upon a pristine open clearing.

"It's all ours!" exclaimed Skye.

He downed the rest of his wine and then ran into the middle of the clearing to begin rolling snow for the construction of their snowman. Once more, Lucien became infected with Skye's childlike glee and quickly finished his own wine before running out to join his new friend.

Fifteen minutes later, there were three balls, of decreasing size, placed on top of one another – a base for a fine snowman indeed.

"I'll go get some branches for his arms," said Skye, before racing off to the tree line.

Lucien stood alone in the field staring at the snowman. It was the first one he'd ever built and while he felt a sense of accomplishment there was also an underlying sense of loss. He had missed out on so much during his childhood and while he had since done a reasonable job convincing himself that such things didn't matter, the occasional sliver of regret made it through to his consciousness. As much as he derided the notion of needing friends and family, Lucien couldn't help but become a little maudlin.

Why didn't I deserve this?

He was disrupted from his unanticipated introspection by a snowball smashing into his left shoulder.

"Got, ya!" yelled Skye from a few meters away.

The remains of the snowball fell from Lucien's coat and a small smile crept across his lips.

"You're going down!"

Lucien dropped to his knees, his hands a flurry of movement as he made several snowballs in quick succession. He stood up and launched his assault, sending the small, white projectiles flying through the air.

Skye was nimbler than Lucien had thought possible, easily darting out of the way. It was almost like he was flying through the air at times.

But that's not possible.

"You've gotta do better than that," Skye teased.

Taking up the challenge, Lucien speedily made more snowballs and dove back into battle. No matter how hard he tried he couldn't seem to hit Skye, although his opponent appeared to have no trouble at all hitting his target. Their laughter rang out through the clearing as they chased and attacked one another.

After ten minutes of frantic play, Lucien begrudgingly accepted defeat.

"OK, OK, you win. I surrender."

"Bout time."

"How can you move so fast?"

"Genetics." Skye said with a smug look. "Told you next time would be fun."

"Yeah, it was. Thanks."

"My pleasure, but now I gotta run. See you Lucien!"

"Wait! Why don't you give me your…" Lucien trailed off as Skye had already disappeared into the darkness. "…number?"

Why does he always do that?

Lucien brushed off the snow from his numerous hits and trudged back out of the park. As he reached the main entrance again his phone rang. It was Oliver.

"Hey cockhound, what's up?"

"Feel like some company tonight?" offered Oliver. "I've got an itch that needs scratching."

Lucien's crotch swelled involuntarily at the thought.

"Sure, I'll be home in about twenty."

"See you there!"

Lucien picked up his pace and hurried to the metro, an impish smile on his handsome face at the thought of the hours of tawdry sex ahead of him.

At least he doesn't disappear off into the night.

* * *

The following Saturday, Seventh Circle was packed. It was the club's thirtieth anniversary and in honor of the momentous event, performers past and present had gathered to celebrate. Among the guest artists was Oliver's former Dom – Master Vic. He was back in Port Davinica on vacation and Oliver had talked about him incessantly in the week leading up to the party – much to Lucien's growing annoyance.

Lucien took an instant dislike to the man as soon as Oliver had introduced them earlier that day. It wasn't that he didn't find the man attractive, far from it. In his mid-thirties, with cropped blond hair, handsome features and a tall muscular build, Vic was eye-catching to say the least. Ordinarily, Lucien would have been more than happy to play with such a magnificent specimen of manhood, but every time he looked at Vic he felt an overwhelming urge to punch him in his smug face. If he didn't know better, Lucien would have thought he was suffering from jealousy.

Further drawing Lucien's ire was the way that Oliver seemed to hang off of Vic's every word, laughing at his jokes and repeatedly touching his arm.

He's just like a groupie!

Lucien managed to avoid them most of the evening, spending time mingling with the other performers and invited guests. It was near midnight when they caught up with Lucien again.

"Hey Luc. I've got something to ask you," slurred Oliver.

He'd obviously been indulging in quite a lot of the festive cheer and was slightly unsteady on his feet.

"Yeah, what?"

Lucien's brusqueness was apparently lost on Oliver, but not on Vic if the quizzical expression he gave Lucien was any indication.

"Vic has asked me to do a few shows with him while he's back. You don't mind do you?"

Lucien struggled to keep his anger in check but his heart began to beat faster, fueled by a smoldering sense of betrayal.

"Why would I care?" he responded through gritted teeth.

"Thanks, Luc! You're the best!"

"Yeah, thanks, buddy!" added Vic, as he pulled Oliver in close to him.

"I told you he wouldn't mind."

Resisting the urge to bitch slap both of them, Lucien took himself off to the bar and attracted the attention of the head barmaid, Merida.

"What can I get you, honeybear?" she asked.

The heavily made-up, peroxide blonde behind the bar had a world-weary look about her that belied her twenty-six years.

"Line 'em up!"

She promptly set out six shot glasses and filled them with Bison Grass Vodka, Lucien's usual poison of choice.

Lucien downed them in quick succession. Unsurprisingly, they did nothing to improve his mood. Every time he caught sight of the pair his annoyance grew.

"Again!"

"As you wish, my liege."

Merida dutifully lined them up again and Lucien dispatched with them just as speedily.

"Hey Soldier, you might want to slow it down. No need to drain the bar dry this early." Bertha had miraculously materialized beside him – she could be quite stealthy when she wanted.

"I'm fine," grumbled Lucien in response, not bothering to look at his boss.

"Really? Vic and Oli look pretty cozy over there."

"So what? It's not like I own him."

"No, you don't. Although I'm not so sure that he doesn't own you."

Jerked out of his pity party, Lucien spun around to face Bertha.

"What do you mean?"

"Nothing, my dear. Just the mutterings of an old woman."

Bertha patted his hand in a motherly fashion that seemed rather incongruous given the revealing, red PVC outfit she'd squeezed herself into, which had in turn produced a gravity-defying cleavage.

"Try and have a good evening."

And with that she tottered off towards the stage to announce the next show.

Lucien looked to the spot where he'd left Oliver and Vic but could no longer see them. He scanned the crowd but couldn't find any sign of them.

Fuck them!

His head cloudy from all the shots, Lucien headed backstage to relieve himself in the toilet attached to his dressing room. He lurched along the hallway and flung open the door and there before him was Oliver on his knees orally serving Vic.

"What the fuck are you doing?"

"Someone's had a bit to drink," joked Vic, who continued to pump himself into Oliver's face.

Oliver himself hadn't seemed to notice the interruption, too preoccupied with Vic's impressive manhood. Enraged Lucien yanked Oliver to his feet.

"You can't do that in our dressing room!"

Oliver appeared to be quite bewildered at first but quickly came to his senses.

"Where do you get off? Why do you care who I fuck? You're not my boyfriend!"

"Hey guys, I'm going let you sort this out between you," said Vic, excusing himself.

He strode out of the dressing room while buckling back up his pants; clearly wanting to be away from whatever messy situation was about to unfold.

"Vic, wait!" Oliver cried out to the retreating man's back.

Oliver turned back to Lucien with his face full of fury.

"What the fuck is your problem?"

Oliver was near screaming. Lucien had never seen him in such an angry state and felt immediately chastened about his behavior.

"I'm sorry, I've drunk too much," explained Lucien, his tone full of remorse.

"I don't care how many you've had, you have no right to act like this."

"Look, Oli I…"

"No I don't want to hear it! You've crossed the line. I'm not your fucking property!"

Oliver stormed out of the dressing room; slamming the door so hard behind him it lifted off the top hinge and hung awkwardly in the doorway. Lucien was absolutely dumbfounded. The fight had had a sobering effect and he was left alone in the dressing room to ponder his actions.

Why am I acting like a jealous harpy?

* * *

Lucien was dripping with sweat. The room was humid and lit by the red bulbs along the ceiling. His arms burned from the exertion but he brought the whip down again and again. The fight with Oliver had been three days ago and they hadn't spoken since. Oliver had organized to take the week off for his end of year exams so the pair hadn't had a chance to resolve their issues. Lucien had texted a few times but had received only radio silence in return.

Lucien was venting his frustration by torturing the naked, muscular man locked in the sturdy, wooden stocks before him.

Fortunately, the gent had a predilection for pain and was paying Lucien handsomely for such treatment.

The fellow in question was Bartholomew Kingsley III, a golden-haired Adonis with a nasty streak. He was a bully of a man in public but thoroughly enjoyed being humiliated and punished in private. They were in one of the special rooms in the basement of Seventh Circle that were reserved for client sessions. The floor was littered with all manner of delightful paraphernalia, including three dildos, a wooden paddle and a riding crop – all of which had been used on Bartholomew over the past hour. His pale skin was a mess of marks that showed up even in the dim lighting.

"Who's a worthless little worm?"

"I am, Sir!"

Lucien brought the whip down again and again, enjoying the sound as the leather snapped at the abused buttocks. After a while, he reached down and gave Bartholomew's balls a sharp tug downwards, causing his captive to yell out. Not that he appeared to mind his treatment given the fact his beer-can-thick cock jutted out between his legs and was dripping a veritable puddle of precum onto the increasingly sticky floor.

"You been punished enough yet, boy?"

"Never, Sir!"

"Good answer, boy."

Lucien gave one last crack of the whip and released Bartholomew.

"That was the best session yet!" panted Bartholomew.

"Thanks. Now get that red ass of yours back home to your wife."

Bartholomew quickly dressed and headed out. Lucien gathered up all the used accessories and took them to the small laundry area at the back of the club, where he proceeded to thoroughly wash them – cleanliness is next to godliness, after all. When he was done, Lucien took them back to the over-sized toolbox in his dressing room and carefully arranged them back into their proper positions – he could be anally retentive in more ways than one.

Lucien closed and locked the toolbox and turned around to go to the bathroom so he could shower off. He started to move forward but was distracted by a shiny piece of yellow material on the floor – it was one Oliver's jockstraps. Lucien picked it up and held it affectionately. A wave of shame flooded through him as he relived the fight – for about the thousandth time.

What's wrong with me? I'm not supposed to care! He's not my boyfriend!

He hated the maelstrom of emotion that whirled within him. Lucien stomped to the shower, angry with himself and the world in general. He quickly rinsed off and switched back into his street clothes before he headed out into the cold.

* * *

After having worked out more of his aggression on his client, Lucien returned home feeling slightly better, but he was still troubled by his fight with Oliver. The elevator doors opened and Lucien turned to find Topher sitting outside his front door, reading one of Lucien's Blue Hunter novels.

He must have snuck it out last time he was here, little bugger!

Topher's face lit up when he saw Lucien and he jumped to his feet.

"Hey, what are you doing here?" Lucien said more gruffly than he intended.

"I…I just wanted to talk. I'll go."

"No. Sorry, I've had a rough day."

Lucien unlocked the front door and they filed inside. Lucien grabbed a couple of cans of soda from the fridge and they made themselves comfortable on the sofa. Lucien noticed that Topher had a nervous air about him.

"So, what's going on? Everything alright at the Walkers?"

"Yeah, it's all good. I just wanted to ask your advice. I didn't have anyone else to talk to."

"What about?"

"It's…it's about…sex."

Lucien smiled. It was good to have a distraction from his worry over Oliver and he felt glad that Topher felt comfortable coming to him.

"What do you want to know?"

"Well…I haven't really done anything. There's porn and stuff but I really don't know what to do."

"Yes, I saw that you pilfered one of my books."

Lucien wasn't truly annoyed but he liked teasing his young friend and Topher managed to look a mortified combination of embarrassed and guilty.

"I'm sorry, I know I should have asked."

"It's OK, just ask next time."

"I will!" he answered, sounding relieved.

"Is there someone you want to have sex with?"

"No!"

Lucien thought he was protesting a little too violently but he let it slide.

"I just wanted to be prepared is all. It's not like I want you to show me or anything but I just wanted to talk to someone who would tell me the truth and not baby me."

"OK. Ask away."

Topher started a little nervously at first but as they chatted he seemed to grow more comfortable, asking Lucien all manner of things. For his part, Lucien enjoyed helping Topher, he certainly could've used such advice when he was starting out in the big scary world of man-on-man sex and was happy to share some helpful tips.

"Gag reflexes diminish with practice…spit isn't a good enough substitute for lubricant…and perhaps most importantly, spicy food and bottoming don't mix!"

They'd been chatting for a few hours when Lucien realized that it was starting to get rather late.

"You should get home before the Walkers miss you."

"Yeah, I guess. Thanks so much, Lucien."

"If you have any more questions, you know where to find me."

"Thanks. I knew I could count on you."

Topher jumped up and gave him a big bear hug. It made Lucien's heart flutter with a fraternal affection that warmed his soul. Lucien soon saw him out and then retreated to his bedroom to sleep. As he lay there, his mind was filled with a series of conflicting thoughts. He had gone this long without family and attachments and now the world seemed to be intent on throwing emotional entanglements at him left, right and center.

He's such a sweet kid. I don't need complications. Why do I have to push everyone away? You're better off alone!

* * *

Things had been frosty between Lucien and Oliver for over a week and showed no signs of thawing. They had only performed together once since the fight and a chainsaw would've have found it tough going to cut through the tension. Neither of them seemed willing to address the big, angry, pink elephant that was crashing about the room.

Lucien didn't want to things to continue on like this but he was at a loss for what to do. He was far too proud to admit he was wrong but the prospect of losing Oliver from his life was weighing heavily on his mind. It was his night off from the club and Lucien was restless at home, with not even the mind-numbing banality of his favorite reality show – The Real Housewives of Kansas – able to soothe his disposition. He switched off the TV, grabbed his thick navy-blue coat and headed out to find a distraction.

Half an hour later he was wandering around the city center. It was just after midnight so the area was fairly deserted. The preponderance of festive decorations about the place annoyed him and he was glad it would all be packed away in just over a month.

Lucien was toying with going to ManHole – a nearby cruising club – to relieve his restlessness in the arms of a few random strangers when he saw something in the distance that immediately arrested his attention. It was a man wearing a bright, blue scarf walking towards him.

Skye!

Lucien increased his pace and the two ended up meeting right in front of the Santa's village. Despite the cold night air, Lucien felt the familiar warmness beginning to fill his chest.

"You wanna go see Santa?" asked Skye by way of greeting.

"No…and anyway it's closed."

"So? I know a way inside," Skye countered with a mischievous grin.

He grabbed Lucien by the hand and together they walked around the back of the structure where there was a small gap in the chain link fence. They squatted down and crawled through the space and soon found themselves in the middle of a mini winter wonderland, with colorful presents and candy canes strewn about the place in a haphazard fashion. The security lighting from outside was diffused through the artificial trees and gave the place an eerie quality.

"Wait here for a second," said Skye before disappearing into the gloom of the grotto.

Lucien felt a little silly standing in the middle of the deserted Santa's village, seeing he was a grown man – not that he'd visited such things a lot during his childhood. Christmas was for happy families and his certainly hadn't fit the bill.

"OK, you can come in."

Lucien entered the grotto and saw that Skye had turned on a bunch of fairy lights that covered the ceiling, making them appear to be a sea of twinkling stars. In the middle of the room on Santa's big white and gold throne sat Skye in a red suit that was far too big for him.

"Ho, ho, ho! Come sit on Santa's lap, young man."

"I don't think so."

"Don't worry, even naughty boys are allowed time with Santa."

Lucien was hesitant by there was something magnetic about Skye that he still couldn't manage to resist – not that he was trying particularly hard. After a moment, Lucien dutifully trooped over to the throne and sat on Skye's lap.

"What do you want for Christmas, young man?"

"I've got no idea."

"Perhaps an electric blue, ten-speed mountain bike with white stripes and silver tires?"

Lucien was gobsmacked and felt tears prick his eyes. That had been exactly the present he'd wanted when he was ten.

"How did you know that?"

"Lucky guess."

Lucien tried to stand up but Skye kept him in place; he was stronger than he looked.

"I never told anyone that. Who are you?"

"Well, the truth is…"

Skye's explanation was cut short when a bright flash of light passed over them.

"Who's in there?" demanded a deep, stern voice.

The pair jumped up from the throne.

"Quick, let's go," said Skye, grabbing Lucien's hand once more.

They raced through the back of the grotto with the sound of heavy footsteps following close behind them. They made it back to the hole in fence and scurried through, and then kept running until they were a few blocks away, laughing like lunatics.

"We lost him!" exclaimed Skye, his eyes shining with excitement.

"Yeah, he was a probably an overweight rent-a-cop."

"Time to go. You be a good boy, now."

And with that Skye ran off into the night, still fully decked out in the Santa suit. Lucien just shook his head in disbelief and amusement.

Who the hell is he?

* * *

Lucien was sitting with Topher in window table at Dom's Delights, the café next to his gym, enjoying two exceptionally moist cupcakes – butterscotch and blue velvet. They had met up a several times since their little talk about the stallions and the bulls and their brotherly bond continued to grow.

"How's Oli? I haven't seen him much lately," asked Topher.

"He's OK, I guess."

"Is everything alright with you guys?"

Lucien could see that Topher's eyes were burning with a mixture of curiosity and concern.

"Yeah, sure."

"Doesn't seem like it."

Observant little bugger.

"We had a fight."

"Did you break up?"

"No, we didn't break…I told you he's not my boyfriend."

"Why not?"

"What?"

"I mean you seem to really like each other and I know that you play around together. So why aren't you together?"

"It's complicated."

"Adults are weird."

"You got that right. Enough matchmaking."

"OK, OK."

Topher was much more confident than the boy he'd first met nearly two months beforehand in the dingy alley. The friendship they'd developed warmed his heart in a way he never thought possible and he liked their easy camaraderie.

"So found any boys to practice on yet?"

"Nah," said Topher shyly. "Well, there is one guy I kinda like but I'm pretty sure he doesn't know I exist."

"You gotta make him notice you then."

"How? Go up and kiss him?"

"Or give him a lap dance, your choice."

Topher gave a half-embarrassed laugh and playfully pushed Lucien's chest. It was a sound Lucien liked to hear. He was glad to have the focus shifted away from him and his turbulent feelings. He wasn't used to thinking so much about his relationship with Oliver. It had been casual and fun but now there was obviously something deeper going on but Lucien was too scared to explore it further.

Can I open myself up to be hurt again?

* * *

The next day, Lucien finally swallowed his pride and called Oliver to ask him to come over so they could talk things out. It wasn't something Lucien was comfortable doing but he wasn't prepared to lose his closest friend over a stupid drunken mistake. Lucien didn't like the messiness of feelings within him but was beginning to realize that all the years he'd spent denying them hadn't worked out that well either. They had always been there, bubbling away behind his stoic veneer waiting for their chance to burst forth and complicate his life. Lucien had repressed them for so long he was almost incapable of dealing with them in an adult fashion.

Thirty minutes later there was a knock in the door. Lucien opened it to find Oliver holding up a large bagful of donuts from Fallen Angel Cakes.

"Truce?"

Evidently he was as eager as Lucien, to end their recent cold war.

"Sure, come in. I'll put on some coffee."

"Irish, please. It's freezing outside."

"No problem."

When they'd settled on the lounge, with their alcoholic coffees in hand, there was an awkward silence. They quietly munched on donuts, subtly avoiding eye contact, as neither of them seemed to know how to begin.

Lucien turned towards Oliver who looked up at him expectantly, so he took a deep breath and began to talk.

"I'm sorry I acted like a dick."

"It's OK."

"No, it's not. I can blame the alcohol but, to be perfectly honest, I was just being a complete idiot. I had no right to say the things I did. You were right. You're not my property and you're free to do what you want without my approval."

"Wow, who are you and what have you done with Lucien?" joked Oliver.

"Very amusing."

"I mean you look like him, but I'm pretty sure you're a body snatcher."

"Alright, alright. I know I was a jerk. I don't want to lose you…I mean you're a great assistant." Lucien was still reluctant to admit the true depth of his feelings, even to himself. "And I value your friendship."

"Damn straight. I must say I kinda like this side of you. Apologetic and nearly human-like with emotions."

"You're sooo funny." Lucien knew he deserved a harsher rebuke than such gentle teasing.

"I need to apologize too."

"No, you don't. It was all my…"

"Yeah, I do. I was all wrapped up in Vic being back and I overreacted in the dressing room too. So, I guess we're both idiots."

Lucien smiled, feeling much better than he had in weeks.

"We're good then?"

"Mmm…almost."

"How can I make it up to you, boy?"

"I'm sure you can think of a few things."

Lucien suddenly jumped up off the couch, roughly grabbed a hold of Oliver and heaved him over his shoulder.

"That's more like it!" Oliver said dangling over Lucien's back, being carried down the hallway.

Once they reached the bedroom Lucien threw Oliver onto the bed and jumped on top of him. They rolled around together frantically pulling at each other's clothes, which were hastily cast to the floor – t-shirts, jeans and underwear all went flying through the air – in their haste to be naked with one another.

Mere moments later, they were bare-ass naked grappling together like voracious beasts. Their tongues wrestled between their mouths, each battling for supremacy, as their bodies writhed around the bed. Lucien's smooth, mocha-colored skin slid and rubbed up against the pale white of his companion's.

Lucien pressed Oliver down and began the enjoyable task of biting and licking all the way down the body beneath him. He took his time to lick all the tattoos along the way. Lucien knew them well, his hands and tongue having run over them many, many times before – the barcode on the back of his neck, the small tree on his left shoulder, the matching stars on both wrists, the Tardis on his right ankle, and Lucien's favorite, a flock of birds flying in a V formation that curved around the left side of Oliver's torso. He had toyed with getting inked himself but had never found a design that he wanted to be permanent.

When he finished the scenic tour of Oliver's body, Lucien moved back to the center to claim his prize. Lucien teased all around Oliver's crotch, running his tongue along the creases on each side, around under the heavy ball sack and up and down the length of the shaft, pausing briefly to pull back the foreskin and suckle several drops of sweet precum out of the engorged cockhead.

Above him, Oliver moaned his appreciation and ran his hands along the back of Lucien's head in an obvious effort to draw him in closer. Lucien eagerly breathed in the sweet scent of Oliver – a pleasant mixture of perspiration and the coconut body wash he favored. Suddenly, Lucien dove onto the cock, swallowing it whole – quite an achievement given the width and length of the member, but he did have years of experience in which to perfect his technique. The manhood filled his throat to bursting, throbbing in response to the rapid movements of Lucien's tongue.

Oliver's nails dug into Lucien's shoulders as he clasped Lucien in even closer to him. Lucien slowly came back up off the enormous erection, and then began to steadily corkscrew up and down, as his tongue lazily circled around the thick shaft. He adored this cock probably more than any other he had encountered. It was perfectly proportioned and always tasted divine – something he'd told Oliver on more than one occasion.

Lucien gently swung his lower half around, so that his own cock was positioned near Oliver's face, all the while diligently worshiping the juicy meat he still had in his mouth. His companion didn't need any further hints and immediately impaled his face on Lucien's cock. His movements were faster and more frantic than Lucien's, seemingly far more ravenous. The room was filled with the erotic sounds of mouths engaged in delectable carnality.

After a while, Lucien broke away from the scrumptious sixty-nine – he had another meal in mind. Lucien flipped Oliver onto his back and then pulled him down to the end of the bed with his buttocks sitting right on the edge and his legs spread wide, ankles pointing at the ceiling.

Lucien sunk to the carpeted floor and dove face first into the exposed hole. He didn't take his time as he had with Oliver's manhood. He ate like a man possessed, his tongue probing as far into the musky recesses as it could reach. Oliver sighed and squirmed on the bed, clearly pleased with the expert tongue work being employed upon him.

Spreading the cheeks wide in an effort to penetrate even further, Lucien was desperate to taste as much of the fragrant passage as possible. It was a meal Lucien could happily eat on a daily basis, and had been known to feast on it for an hour or more at times, but today his pulsing erection and its near constant stream of precum took precedence.

Lucien leapt up and went to the top drawer of his bedside table, to grab the necessary supplies. The drawer held a nearly full packet of his favorite brand of condom – Wrapped. They were colored midnight-black and were opaque, which Lucien loved the look of and most importantly, they felt whisper thin. Lucien suited up and then squeezed out a large dollop of lubricant, which he spread over his latex encased member before returning to the bed. He placed his fingers at Oliver's entrance and lathered the excess lube around and just inside the hole. Lucien could see the look of absolute lust and need in Oliver's eyes and wanted to give him exactly what he wanted. He placed his cockhead at the center of the rosebud and pushed ever so gently, causing Oliver to moan in response to the pleasing pressure against his opening.

Instead of slamming straight in, as every fiber in his cock was demanding, Lucien kept his movements slow and measured. He used his cockhead to stretch the sphincter without penetrating far inside. With his hand firmly gripped around the shaft he made slow, circular motions that gradually increased in size, with each rotation widening Oliver's ring slightly further.

By the sounds emanating from Oliver, Lucien could tell that he was immensely enjoying being teased. Oliver grasped at Lucien's hips trying to pull him in closer but Lucien resisted, unwilling to stop the exquisite torture just yet.

"I need you in me now!" he begged.

Lucien kept up this technique, coming tantalizingly close to entering fully but shying away again. Eventually, Lucien succumbed to Oliver's pleas and decided to put the poor boy out of his misery. He changed his movements to small jabbing ones with each thrust taking him slightly deeper. Oliver's breathing became shallower as his body adjusted to the intruder slowly forcing its way inside. When Lucien felt his hips grazing up against Oliver's buttocks, he rested there briefly to let Oliver recover before beginning to fuck in earnest.

He leaned forward and gave Oliver a long, lingering kiss while he began unhurried gentle movements with his hips, prodding and poking at the velvety passage, stretching it to its limits. For some reason Lucien wasn't in the mood to violently pound Oliver, rather he felt like a far more slow and sensual session.

Oliver didn't seem to object to the more languid pace, making soft sounds of appreciation as Lucien slowly slid in and out. Lucien adored the sensation of Oliver contracting his ass around the intruder gently massaging it, as it went about its work.

The pair stayed in this tender mood for over an hour, swapping positions several times, with Lucien penetrating into Oliver from the side, from behind and beneath. Occasionally they just held still with Lucien buried to the hilt inside Oliver while they lovingly kissed, caressed and gazed deeply into each other's eyes. It felt slightly different to the other times they'd been together but Lucien couldn't pinpoint exactly what had changed between them.

As amazing and satisfying as their play had been, Lucien was in need of releasing the pressure in his aching balls. He flipped Oliver over to his back again and began to pound away roughly. Oliver adapted to the change of pace easily and was soon lifting his buttocks up meet the thrusts, sending the cock penetrating even deeper, to both their added pleasure.

Sensing that Oliver was close, Lucien wrapped a hand around his conjugal companion's bouncing manhood and jacked it furiously, in a rigorous effort to get his friend off. The pounding on his prostate and the firm hand on his member had the desired effect and soon ropes of white cream sprayed forth from Oliver's cock and splattered onto his chest and abs.

Lucien kept fucking him knowing full well that Oliver's passage was now ultra sensitive. At this point Oliver always begged for him to stop but Lucien never did. It wasn't out of sadistic intent; rather Lucien knew that it was highly doubtful that Oliver ever truly wanted him to stop pounding away. The main evidence being the huge smile that was usually spread over his face when they finished, much like the one on it now.

It wasn't possible to keep up his assault for too much longer, however, as the contractions of Oliver's passage during his orgasm had Lucien close to the brink. It only took several more hard thrusts before Lucien's body tensed and he filled the protective sheath with thick white cream. A loud groan escaped his lips as his body quivered in pleasure.

He collapsed forward on top of Oliver and kissed him gently as his full weight pressed down – not that Oliver seemed to mind in the slightest.

They stayed locked in this position, Oliver's legs wrapped around Lucien's torso, kissing and softly touching one another until their rehardened cocks demanded attention once more.

"My turn," said Oliver, as he rolled out from under Lucien and flipped him over onto his stomach with a sudden burst of strength – although Lucien was hardly resisting.

Oliver kissed the back of his playmate's neck, and then down the muscular back until he reached the wonderfully round globes of Lucien's ass. He gripped them tightly in each hand and pulled them wide apart. Oliver teased the area at first, working his mouth in closer and closer to the rosebud. He licked around the center and gently blew on the opening, causing Lucien to arch his back and spread himself even wider.

Normally, Lucien was an exclusive top. It wasn't that he didn't enjoy being pounded; in fact, he adored the feeling of a sizeable appendage stimulating his insides. It was more that he didn't trust anyone else enough to let them inside him physically – or emotionally for that matter. He feared the loss of control. Oliver, however, was his only exception to the rule.

Over the years, Lucien had come to trust Oliver and knew that his friend would never deliberately hurt him. In time, their play had come to reflect that with Lucien rather enjoying being plowed by Oliver's impressive manhood, as was about to be the case.

Once Oliver had suitably outfitted himself with latex and lube, he began his slow descent into the snug passage. Lucien clawed at the pillows and gasped and grunted as the manhood slid in inch by inch. Before he knew it, Lucien could feel the gentle rubbing of Oliver's dark pubic hair rubbing against his buttocks and the heavy balls against his own.

When he was sure that Lucien had adjusted to him, Oliver started to move his hips back and forth, pushing himself in just a little bit deeper with each thrust. He soon picked up the pace beginning to drive faster and faster until he was hammering away into the solid, muscular ass.

The sounds of their labored breathing and slapping of skin on skin filled the bedroom. Oliver pulled Lucien back up onto his hands and knees, and with a firm grip on his hips, slammed in repeatedly. Lucien roared in ecstasy as Oliver mercilessly plowed into him, hitting his prostate again and again. He knew that it wouldn't be long before their loads were freed from their erections.

Oliver reached underneath and jerked his friend, while continuing to pound away. His efforts were soon rewarded, when Lucien began to shake, his whole body contracting just before he exploded onto the cotton sheets beneath. Quickly, Oliver pulled out, ripped off the condom and with only a handful of strokes spurted his fresh load all over Lucien's broad, defined back. The splatters of white against the light brown skin made for a most arousing sight.

They both collapsed down back onto the bed, panting with exertion and huge grins plastered on their faces.

"That was pretty intense!" exclaimed Oliver.

"Yeah, I guess we should fight more often."

"I hope not."

As they lay together in the warm afterglow wrapped up in one another's arms, Lucien had never felt more content. He was on the verge of saying something that he hadn't said to anyone when Oliver spoke.

"So…I know I ask you every year…and you never come… but how would you like to come to dinner at my parents place next Friday?"

"For Christmas Eve?"

Oliver nodded, as his fingers gently traced around Lucien's dime-sized nipples.

"Yeah…I'm not sure. You know I'm not big on the family stuff."

"No pressure, but they'd love to see you, and so would Topher. He really looks up to you, you know."

Lucien felt a warm glow of happiness. Nobody had ever looked up to him before and he was slightly proud of the achievement.

Never thought I'd be a role model.

"He's a good kid."

"So you'll think about it?"

"Yeah." Lucien's tone was extremely non-committal.

"I'd really love to have you there as well."

"I said I'd think about it," grumbled Lucien, feeling pressured.

"OK, OK. No need to go back to your old grizzly self."

"I'll try."

It was late and their sexcapades had been marvelously exhausting. Oliver nuzzled into Lucien's chest and his breathing soon became deeper and slower. A minute or so later, Lucien realized that Oliver had drifted off. He rarely let Oliver sleep over – or anyone for that matter – but on this occasion Lucien wasn't keen to disturb him.

I could get used to this.

* * *

It was Christmas Eve and the streets were full of last minute shoppers, frantically racing from store to store in a desperate attempt to secure presents before the big day. Lucien, however, was oblivious to the forlorn plight of those around him, purely focused on the view before him. He had been standing outside the plate glass window of Geek HQ for the past ten minutes trying to decide what to do. In the centre of the crowded window display was the perfect gift for Oliver – a chair-sized Tardis with a door that opened, a flashing blue light, sound effects and about twenty figurines of various characters from the show. Lucien knew Oliver would go crazy for it but he worried that it was too big a gesture.

The snow fell gently around him but that wasn't what kept him frozen to the spot. Normally, he didn't bother with gifts until the sales were on and he could pick something up cheaply but this year was different. Not only was he contemplating buying a rather expensive present, but he was also toying with going to the Walkers and telling Oliver something that would change their relationship entirely.

What if he doesn't feel the same?

Just then, the cold around him seemed to evaporate as a comforting warmth spread throughout his body.

"Hi, Skye," he said, without turning around. He was almost complacent about the sudden appearances and sensations of his strange friend.

"You should buy it," replied Skye, coming to stand beside him. "You know he'll love it!"

"Yes, but how do *you* know all this?"

"I do have something of an advantage. I can read your heart. It comes with the territory of being a guardian angel."

Skye had said it as matter-of-factly as one would admit to being good at playing the piano or ten-pin bowling.

"You're a what?!?" said Lucien turning to face his companion.

"I can tell that you've sensed it…that I'm different. That warmth and lightness you feel around me. The way you find it impossible to say no to anything I ask."

"I don't know what to believe."

Lucien was slightly surprised to find that, as crazy as it sounded, it all suddenly made perfect sense. Once he'd accepted the news his mind whirled. Resentment and anger flooded through his body threatening to extinguish the warmth Skye had generated. His whole childhood, Lucien had longed for someone to come save him – a Prince on a white horse, ideally, but even a farmer on a cow would have done.

"If it's true why have you waited till now to come *guard* me? I could have done with your help a long time ago."

"I haven't always been assigned to you, only these past few years, and I'm sorry for what has been done to you. Nobody deserves to be treated that way."

"Then why bother *now*?"

"I couldn't stand to watch you deny your heart any longer. I've been doing my best to help you rediscover what had been so cruelly taken away from you but you have to take the last step by yourself. I can't push you any further."

All of Lucien's swirling, conflicting emotions seemed to fade away until there was only one left spinning inside his heart.

"I'm scared."

Lucien sounded very much like a wounded little boy; his usually deep baritone voice had an almost child-like treble to it.

"I know."

Skye's eyes were awash with sympathy.

"Can you see if it will all work out?"

"Nobody knows the future, not even our kind, but I can tell you that you're a good man and so is he."

Lucien still wasn't convinced. He felt that he had already had his share of heartbreak and couldn't bear the thought of any more.

"I don't want to be hurt again."

"Sometimes in life you have to make a leap of faith. Sorry to sound like a greeting card but it's true. If you don't risk anything then you'll never gain. I've thawed your heart as much as I can. The rest is up to you."

Skye moved forward and gave Lucien the lightest kiss on the lips. It felt like a gentle winter breeze.

"Don't worry. I'll be around if you need me."

And with that he shimmered and faded away into the falling snow. Lucien stood there trying to process the information and the improbability of what he'd just seen.

Maybe I'm having a breakdown?

After a few minutes, Lucien pulled himself together and made a decision. He turned right and walked straight through the wide glass doors at the entrance of the store.

* * *

An hour later, Lucien was standing in front of the Walkers two-storey house in the suburbs of Port Davinica, with a heavy, gift-wrapped box for Oliver tucked under one arm and a few smaller presents in his satchel, for the others. It had taken him ages to find a cab and the traffic heading out of the city had been so horrendous, Lucien thought he might not make it before the New Year.

He hadn't been to the house since he'd run away nearly eight years ago. A lot of memories flooded in and he regretted that he hadn't given the Walkers more of a chance, although given what he was about to do it was probably for the best.

At least Topher will have what I couldn't.

Lucien stood there with his hand hovering near the doorbell. Last minute doubts crept into his mind and he almost turned away but he began to think of how much he had changed in these past few months – even if it had been due to otherworldly influences. Remembering Skye's words he found the courage he was searching for and reassured himself.

I need to go for it. I deserve to be happy too.

He took a deep breath and pressed the button. Behind the door, Lucien could hear a tinny version of 'We Wish You A Merry Christmas' chiming away, followed by quick footsteps coming down the hall. The door opened to reveal Topher wearing a Santa hat and a multicolored woolen jumper with an oddly shaped reindeer knitted on the front.

"Hey, Lucien. I'm so glad you made it!"

"What the hell are you wearing?"

"Hideous, right? Mrs. Walker…I mean Abigail, likes them and they've been so generous to me I couldn't really refuse. Don't worry; I'm sure there's one in there for you too. You're just in time we haven't started dinner yet."

"I need to talk to Oliver first."

"But why can't you…oh," the realization dawning on his face, followed by a huge grin. "I'll just go get him."

I really hope I haven't made a mistake.

Topher rushed off leaving Lucien standing on the stoop, second-guessing himself and growing more nervous by the second. Oliver then popped into view and came down the hallway. He looked at Lucien with a puzzled expression.

"Why are you standing out there in the cold? Aren't you coming in?"

"I needed to say something to you first and then if you still want me to come inside I will."

"OK. What's up?"

Lucien's stomach was in knots and he felt like running away but he continued on regardless.

"This isn't easy for me to say. You know I don't like letting people in."

"That's an understatement," said Oliver with a smirk.

"Oli, I need to get this out."

Apparently, noting Lucien's unease, Oliver stopped joking and gave him a reassuring smile instead.

"OK. Please continue."

"You mean a lot to me. I've only just come to realize how much. I reacted the way I did about you flirting with Vic because I'm scared of losing more than just an assistant. I don't want to be friends, I need…I want more than that."

"What *do* you want then?" asked Oliver, his voice full of expectation.

Throwing caution to the wind, Lucien was finally ready to bare his heart. He understood that this was his chance to be truly happy.

"I want *you*…I need *you*…I love *you!*"

Now that the declaration was out Lucien felt liberated, although he wasn't sure whether to laugh or to cry.

"Will you be my boyfriend?" he asked tentatively.

Oliver didn't waste a second before responding.

"Of course I will, you big, dumb idiot. I love you too and I've been waiting for you to ask me ever since New York."

Lucien put down the gift, moved forward and wrapped Oliver up in his thick, muscular arms and into a most passionate embrace. They stood kissing on the stoop for a few minutes, oblivious to the cold and the snow.

When they eventually broke for air they were both grinning insanely like Cheshire cats.

"You better come in then. Don't want Mom to rouse on us."

Lucien picked up the box from the stoop and took Oliver's outstretched hand. Together they walked inside into the warmth of the family home and towards the delicious aroma of a festive feast.

* * *

It was the night before Christmas and there were quite a few creatures stirring – particularly the one in Lucien's pants as he stood under the mistletoe in the archway to the lounge room with a look of longing on his face. Sometimes Lucien could hardly believe he and Oliver had been together for a full year – definitely one for the record books.

"Can I help you with something?" teased Oliver.

"You know damn well what I want."

Lucien moved forward and dragged his boyfriend into a firm embrace.

"Dinner's ready!" Abigail called out from the dining room.

"We'll be there in a sec," replied Lucien.

Lucien moved his head forward and his lips lightly grazed Oliver's mouth before he increased the pressure and launched into a passionate kiss. Their bodies ground together, as they became lost in the kiss and promptly forgot their surroundings.

"Excuse me, gentlemen," said a nearby voice.

They broke apart to see Topher smirking at them.

"As hot as that was to watch, I think the parents might mind if you starting humping in the lounge room."

"Jealousy's a curse," teased Oliver, as he affectionately ruffled his foster brother's hair.

"Mom said if you don't get your butts to the table right now you won't get any dessert."

"Alright, we're coming."

As they dutifully trooped into the dining room, Lucien smiled at the cozy domesticity of it all.

"Finally, we can eat," said Oliver's father, Brent, in mock exasperation, but with a happy smile upon his face.

They took their places and started to serve themselves from the large steaming platters of food before them. Lucien looked around the table and back again to his boyfriend. He felt his heart swell. Lucien never imagined that he would find himself in such a Rockwellesque setting or that he would actually enjoy it.

As if on cue, Lucien then heard the sound of carolers in the distance. He thought it might have been his imagination, or perhaps too much eggnog, but the singing gradually became louder and louder. Lucien looked thorough the bay window of the dining room and saw a group of seasonal singers coming to a stop on the front lawn. They had just finished The Little Drummer Boy and began to launch into a beautiful rendition of Silent Night.

"Oh, how lovely," said Abigail.

"Could've waited until we'd finished dinner though," grumbled Brent.

"Shush, now. I'm trying to listen."

"Yes, dear."

Lucien gazed over at Oliver who rolled his eyes at his parents' lighthearted bickering. He grinned and wondered if that would be he and Oliver in about twenty years. Suddenly, a bright flash of blue in the midst of the carolers caught his eye. Lucien looked more carefully at the group and saw a very familiar face right in the middle.

Skye!

He hadn't seen his guardian angel since Christmas Eve last year but hadn't forgotten how Skye had magically changed his life for the better. Lucien wanted to get up from the table and run out onto the lawn to give him a huge hug, but thought it might be a tad difficult to explain. Instead, Lucien just gave a little wave, which Skye returned with a smile and a wink.

"Who are you waving to?" asked Topher.

"Just an old friend."

At that moment Oliver looked up, his eyes connecting with Lucien's, and gave him a wide smile. Lucien saw in his boyfriend's loving gaze the promise of many more Christmases together and he couldn't have been happier.

AIN'T NO SAINT

Valentine Goodness hated February with a passion usually only seen in the most disgruntled of soap opera villains. Not only was it the coldest and greyest month of the year – he was very much a sun worshiper – but it also happened to contain his birthday. Valentine wasn't an excessively vain man, mind you, and he wasn't particularly concerned about getting older either. Rather it was the fact that his special day fell on the fourteenth…it truly was Valentine's Day. Due to the highly commercialized nature of the day and the subsequent fuss people made over it, his birthday was often overlooked completely. If he ever tried to organize anything on the day itself, it would clash with the romantic plans of his coupled friends and his unattached friends would show up bitterly complaining about their singleton status.

It had gotten to the point where Valentine preferred to simply celebrate by himself. For his last birthday, he had celebrated in the least romantic fashion he could find – watching a show at a popular fetish club, Seventh Circle. When the muscular Master Noir had called for volunteers to help him punish his feisty, yet obedient, slave boy, Valentine had practically jumped from his seat. After the show the Master had invited him backstage for a much more intimate performance, just the three of them.

Best birthday ever!

Like any sensible child, Valentine blamed his parents entirely for his misfortune. Brian and Annette Goodness were a pair of proud, hopeless romantics, who had coincidentally met, married and then brought him into the world all on consecutive Saint Valentine's Days. If that hadn't been enough they had then had the audacity to name their son after the day itself – it practically bordered on abuse.

Valentine had been taunted and teased about his name and matching birthday all throughout his childhood and to a lesser extent as he entered adulthood. As a coping mechanism he had eschewed anything vaguely romantic, becoming quite cynical and closed-off about his feelings.

It wasn't that he couldn't get a man, far from it; in fact, he'd had more than a few of them. He was rather angelic in appearance with crystal-blue eyes framed by soft blond, curls and a heavenly, gym-honed physique but his nature was slightly pricklier. His striking good looks meant he had no shortage of suitors but never quite the perfect match. Since he'd turned thirty the previous year, his friends and family had seemingly conspired to send him upon a series of unsuccessful blind dates. None of the men had captured his interest for anything other than a quick, sweaty, naked session…and some hadn't even made it that far.

Throughout his twenties, Valentine had had a series of short-lived relationships, none lasting more than three months. It didn't help that he had the most appalling taste in men, always seeming to go after and attract the most unsuitable boys – possibly in subconscious rebellion against his parents who'd often told him that his 'Prince' would come. If they were ruggedly good-looking with a bad attitude and no prospects, Valentine was powerless to resist.

Despite the concerns of his nearest and dearest, Valentine was happy with his romantic life – or lack thereof. He was also content with his life in general. Valentine owned a vintage clothing store not far from the docks – Grandma's Closet – that did a brisk trade and kept him relatively busy. The store was actually named in tribute to his paternal grandmother, with whom he'd been exceptionally close. She had been something of a fashionista and he had inherited her sense of style as well as enough money to start the shop, where he loved helping his customers find their perfect outfit.

Over the course of a single week, however, Valentine's carefree, playboy existence was to be interrupted by the sudden, and altogether unexpected, arrival of not one, not two, but three handsome strangers into his life.

* * *

It was just after peak hour on Monday evening and Valentine was riding the subway home after an extremely busy day at his store, with the prospect of an even busier week to come. Port Davinica University was renowned for its costume parties celebrating the end of the scholastic year, most of which were being held on the coming weekend. Grandma's Closet stocked a wide range of clothing from uniforms to old theatre costumes and everything in between, and so was quite a popular destination with students at this time of year. There had been more than a few cute guys that Valentine wouldn't have minded giving a helping hand to during their fittings, but alas there had been far too many people for anything but a friendly perusal of their attributes. Regardless, Valentine had made a tidy sum and was pleased with the day's takings.

Valentine was feeling dead tired, even though he'd had the help of his sole employee, Sophinika. She was a confident, curvaceous lass in her late twenties, with wide brown eyes and dead straight brown hair that was highlighted with thick blond streaks. Valentine had hired her not long after he's opened the shop five years previously and the two had developed an almost marital relationship – friendly banter, occasional bickering and no sex.

Too tired for his usual gym workout, Valentine had decided to skip it and his usual walk home in favor of the metro. He wanted to get back to his apartment as soon as possible where a chilled bottle of rosé and a hot shower awaited. The carriage was empty except for Valentine and the strapping, ebony-skinned man seated opposite him. The man in question sat with his legs spread invitingly wide and seemed fairly engrossed by the philosophy textbook he was reading. To Valentine, the man's bodybuilder frame and broad, handsome features were somewhat incongruent with his reading material – although he generally knew better than to judge a book by its cover.

Unsurprisingly, Valentine's attention had been drawn slightly downwards from the book to the impressive bulge in the man's jeans. He must have been staring for some time because when Valentine eventually looked up the man was watching him with a suggestive grin upon his face. There was something familiar about him that Valentine couldn't quite place.

Valentine blushed and smiled back. It was then that he noticed the man's plump red lips and wondered what they'd be like to kiss…or look like wrapped around his cock.

"Good book?" asked Valentine, in an effort to start a conversation.

"It's alright, a little dry but it's required reading for my course."

"How much longer do you have to go?"

"Another year, then I'll see. Not sure if I want to bother going for my doctorate."

"Are you going to any of the campus parties this weekend?"

"Nah, I'm dancing every night."

At that moment, the lights began to flicker briefly in the carriage and it was then that Valentine realized why the man looked so familiar.

The main podium at Sanctuary!

"You're a gogo dancer, right?"

"Yeah," said the man with a winning smile.

"I've enjoyed your work." Valentine's tone was highly suggestive. "I'm Valentine."

"Abraham. Always pleased to meet a fan." He then looked up at the flashing panel indicating the stations. "Well this is my stop."

He got up to leave but then stopped and turned back to face Valentine.

"You wanna grab a coffee?"

A stirring in Valentine's groin had quickly put an end to his tiredness and he was suddenly feeling rather sociable.

"Yeah, sure. That'd be great."

They exited the station and after a brisk two-minute walk were soon standing outside Granny's diner.

"We could go here…or my place is right next door." Abraham indicated an adjacent apartment building.

His meaning was pointedly clear and Valentine was certainly not one for playing coy.

"Your place sounds good."

Abraham led the way upstairs to his second floor apartment while Valentine was practically entranced by the round, muscular buttocks straining against the jeans in front of him. The pair was barely inside the door before they were kissing each other with gay abandon and tugging at one another's clothes. Their kisses were urgent and hungry, the mutual need between them quite obvious. Valentine inhaled the strong, masculine scent of Abraham's aftershave, causing his manhood to grow ever harder. Before too long they had stumbled their way to the bedroom and fallen into a happy, naked coupling on the king-sized futon. Over the next hour their conversation consisted of a series of grunts, groans and sighs, which conveyed everything the other needed to know.

After they'd fully indulged their passions they lay resting on the bed sweaty, sticky and satisfied. When Valentine's breathing returned to normal he made moves to go.

"Thanks, that was…unexpected…but a lot of fun. I should probably get going, though."

Valentine wasn't one to linger once the deed was done. He got up and began to fetch his clothing from where it had been haphazardly thrown during their foreplay.

"You don't want a shower?"

"Nah, I can have one at home. Besides, I kinda like the feel of you still on me."

"Dirty boy." Abraham said with half a laugh. "Can I have your number?"

Valentine was a little taken aback, as he'd figured it would just be a one-off but the sex had been exceptionally good and he wasn't opposed to another session. Especially after Abraham had demonstrated his flexibility with a variety of positions during their play – surprisingly supple for such a muscular guy.

"Sure."

He fished out one of his business cards from his leather wallet and handed it to Abraham before he finished getting dressed.

"Hey, I think my buddies got their Halloween costumes from your place last year."

"Probably, it's one of our busier times."

They shared one more passionate kiss by the door with Abraham clad only in a towel, before Valentine went off on his merry way.

Even though Abraham had asked for his number, Valentine was still pleasantly surprised to see get a call from him the following day asking not only to see him again, but to have dinner with him too.

Someone's keen.

After deliberating for a few seconds – he wasn't particularly interested in dating anyone but figured it couldn't hurt to eat with the man before having him for dessert – Valentine said yes. He made plans to catch up with the gorgeous gogo dancer that weekend before Abraham's shift at the club. Valentine had then passed the rest of the afternoon with a small, contented smile on his face.

* * *

The next evening Valentine was wandering around his gym, Sweat Station, looking for a free piece of cardio equipment to do his warm up. The male-only gym was always rather busy around this time of day but with the imminent arrival of the summertime it was packed to bursting with men trying to get their bodies into flawless, beach-ready mode.

Valentine still had half an hour until his personal training session with James – a former marine with a no-nonsense attitude that kept his appointment book full of happy clients. James' chiseled features and matching physique undoubtedly added to his popularity.

There was only one machine available, a stationary bike off to the side of the main floor and facing another bike. Normally, Valentine didn't like to take either of these two, as he had no desire to be staring straight at a huffing and puffing stranger – well, not on the gym floor at any rate. Today, however, he was in luck and there was a rather attractive lad, with messy jet-black hair and dark almond shaped eyes, sitting opposite and working up quite a sweat. Valentine had noticed the man working out a few times before and he'd already admired the firm build, which strained wonderfully against the man's habitually tight and fairly revealing, workout attire.

As Valentine sat down he made eye contact with the man and they both gave a brief friendly smile. They both looked away but Valentine found himself looking up and stealing glances at the man. Valentine noticed that the man was doing the same, with their furtive peeks lasting a little longer each time. Eventually, the stranger broke the ice.

"You train with James, don't you?"

"Yeah. I've actually got him next."

"What's he like? I'm looking for a new trainer. Mine's moving away and he seems to get results…I mean just look at you!"

"Thanks." Valentine liked the man's brazen flirting. "He's hard but good."

"I'm Haruki by the way."

"Valentine."

"Don't go stealing my heart now."

It was a lame line he'd heard many times before but for some reason he didn't mind it coming from his new acquaintance's sensually full lips.

Valentine heard Haruki's bike start beeping indicating the end of the program.

"OK, that's me. Nice to meet you, catch you around."

"Yeah, I hope so."

Valentine enjoyed watching Haruki walk away, especially the way his bubble butt bulged against the thin material of his tight white shorts. He was so mesmerized that he nearly jumped off the bike when he felt a firm hand land on his shoulder.

"If you stare any harder your eyes will melt a hole in his shorts," teased James.

"Can you blame me?"

"No, not particularly. Wouldn't mind pounding it myself, but right now it's yours that needs to get whipped around the gym instead."

"Yeah, yeah."

"Don't sass me boy or it'll be extra crunches and pushups. Now, up you get, you're warm enough."

"Yes, Sir." Valentine said formally, as he gave James a mock salute.

"That's more like it, boy." James affectionately smacked him on the ass. "Get your sorry butt over to the Squat rack."

An hour later, Valentine was leaning up against the white tiled wall of the group showers, as the hot water beat down on his over-worked muscles. He caught a faint whiff of coconut from the man who'd started showering next to him.

"Tough session?"

Valentine turned and saw that Haruki had taken the shower beside his and was lathering himself up. He was decidedly impressed with what he saw, as the sweet smelling suds ran down over the darkly golden skin. Valentine did his very best to refrain from too obviously ogling the man. Fortunately, they weren't the only ones there, so Valentine was able to restrain his almost overwhelming urge to jump on his new acquaintance.

"Yeah, it was brutal."

"Beauty is pain," joked Haruki, as he turned to rinse the shampoo from his hair.

"Very true." It was then that Valentine's eyes were drawn to an intricate drawing on the back of Haruki's neck. "I like your tattoo."

"Thanks, it's my brother's name in Katakana." Haruki turned back to face Valentine. "It's a Japanese script. It's where we were born but we moved to the States when we were ten. He has my name on his neck too, we're really close."

They twosome continued to chat, spending quite a good deal more time in the showers than was strictly necessary, both seeming reluctant to end their conversation. In due course, Valentine's waterlogged, pruney skin forced him to finish up and he headed off to the lockers. Haruki followed closely behind and they happily found that their lockers were just across from one another. As they dried off their conversation began anew.

"I know this is forward but would you like to go for a drink some time?" asked Haruki.

He's so adorable.

"Sure, sounds good. Here's my card."

"Grandma's Closet? My ex loves that place."

"Does he just?"

"She."

"Sorry?"

"I was talking about my ex-*wife*." Apparently noticing the slight look of confusion on Valentine's face, Haruki explained further. "I'm bi…is that a problem? I know some guys don't like it."

Valentine hadn't had much experience with bisexual guys – well not that he knew about at any rate, although it was hardly like he discussed every guy's history before he messed around with them.

What could it hurt?

"As long as you don't bring her along, it's fine."

Haruki let out an infectious, hearty laugh that Valentine soon joined.

"Ah, no. I find exes tend to be a bit of mood-killer," said Haruki, seeming pleased.

The pair finished up and left the change room walking downstairs together. They stood a touch awkwardly outside the front of the gym. Valentine had an urge to kiss him right there and then, but thought it may be just a tad presumptuous. Then he did it anyway. It was a soft and gentle brushing of lips that had Valentine's manhood rapidly awakening.

When they broke apart both lads were wearing matching grins.

"I'll give you a call, Cupid Boy," said Haruki.

As he turned and walked away Valentine couldn't help but admire the view – it truly was a fabulous behind.

Can't wait to play with that!

Twenty minutes later, Valentine was walking in his front door, when his cell started to ring with an unknown number. He figured it was too late for telemarketers so took a chance and answered it.

"Hi."

"Sorry, I waited as long as I could. How about tomorrow night?" asked Haruki in a rush.

He sure is eager.

"Sure. How does Cockpit sound, around eight? It's one of my favorite bars."

"Sounds great. See you then, handsome."

Valentine was smiling to himself again.

It's going to be a busy week.

* * *

Valentine was in a particularly good mood that Friday, the drink with Haruki the previous night had predictably led back to his apartment and a very pleasant time rolling around naked, with the promise of another hookup in the near future. The day seemed to fly by with a steady stream of customers, mostly students getting their last-minute costumes, and it was nearly closing time before he knew it. Valentine began the process of packing up for the day when he was reminded of a thoroughly unpleasant chore.

"Don't forget to take the boxes with you," said Sophinika.

Her tone was that of a schoolmistress reminding an errant student about homework. Valentine knew full well that he couldn't have gotten by without her. She was far more business-minded and without her help the store would have folded years before – good file keeping wasn't one of his virtues.

"Boxes?"

"Don't play dumb. You promised you were going to sort out all the receipts so I could prepare the quarterly tax return. I'm not going through what we did last time."

"Alright, Mom!"

"That's a good boy. See you tomorrow, boss."

"Have a good night."

Despite an initial childish flare of annoyance, Valentine quickly shelved his plans of clubbing, as he knew that the task would take him well into the night, if not the weekend too.

I hate paperwork!

Half an hour later, Valentine was awkwardly struggling with three small boxes while trying to hail a cab. He saw one approaching and went to hail it, and promptly managed to drop one of the boxes sending receipts flying everywhere. Valentine sunk to his hands and knees, frantically scrambling after the papers that were fluttering about the sidewalk in the light, warm breeze. He became aware that someone had knelt down to help him but was too busy clutching at papers to see anything but a pair of strong, male hands.

It wasn't until they had collected all the papers that Valentine noticed just how handsome his helper was, especially in his fitted navy-blue suit that clung in all the right places. He also didn't fail to notice the man's piercing green eyes, strong jaw line and prominent nose.

"Thanks, so much. I'm such a klutz."

"Not at all. Do you need help carrying your boxes?"

"Nah, it's OK. I've just hailed a…" It was then that Valentine noticed that the cabbie must have driven off at some point during his frantic burst of paper grabbing.

"My car is just over there, I could give you a lift if you like?"

"Thanks, that's really generous…"

"Sean."

"Sean. I'm Valentine. But I wouldn't want to put you out. I live the other side of the city. Traffic might be a bit crappy."

"It's fine, I've just finished with my last client for the day so I'm headed that way anyway."

"Client?"

"I'm a lawyer. Don't worry I'm not a sleazy ambulance chaser, I'm a property lawyer." It seemed like a speech he'd had to give a few times before. "I was just inspecting the new premises of one of our clients around the corner. So, how about that ride?"

Valentine hesitated as he weighed up the pros and cons.

It'd be much easier than a cab. What if he's a nutter? He seems harmless enough.

Apparently sensing Valentine's discomfort Sean continued to try and allay his fears.

"It's no bother really. Besides, I quite like rescuing a dude in distress."

"Funny. Are you sure?"

"I get to be a good Samaritan and spend time with a handsome guy. Win, win."

He was still unsure of the offer; although it would hardly be the first time he accepted a stranger's friendly, helping hand. Ultimately, it was Sean's disarming smile and friendly demeanor that won Valentine over and he accepted.

They crossed the road to Sean's sky-blue convertible, which Valentine fell in love with straight away.

"Very nice ride."

"Thanks, it was my grandfather's. It was his baby and he kept it in mint condition."

"I have to at least give you some money for gas."

"I'm sure we can work something out." Sean gave Valentine a lascivious wink as he helped put the boxes in the back seat.

It was no surprise then that just over an hour later, with the boxes carelessly dropped on the floor, the pair was cavorting naked in Valentine's bed making all sorts of pleasure-filled noises. Thankfully, Valentine's flat mate, Prudence, was out for the evening, although it wouldn't have been the first time she'd heard such sounds of manly passion issuing forth from his bedroom.

When they were done Valentine thought that would be the last he'd see of his Good Samaritan seeing he'd more than repaid the favor.

"That was fucking hot. So, you free for a movie Sunday? They're showing Breakfast at Tiffany's at the Rex."

It was Valentine's favorite movie and his favorite cinema. It appeared they had more in common than just a mutual love of playing with men.

"Sure, why not."

Three dates in a week? Good to be popular, I guess. Although I'm sure they'll be done with me in a few weeks.

* * *

It appeared that Valentine had seriously underestimated his charms, as well over a month later, all three men were still very keen and making increasing demands on his time – although he was sensible enough to only see one of them per day. There had been a few close calls when he'd almost called out the wrong name during sex or nearly texted the wrong guy but he'd managed to stay on top of it…for the moment.

The juggling of the three suitors meant that he no longer had the time – or energy for that matter – for any random hookups. Not that he minded terribly, as all three of his companions were quite adept in the bedroom – and wherever else the mood took them – and easily satisfied any itch he needed scratching.

What had surprised Valentine, however, was how much he was enjoying spending time with them in a non-sexual way. Loath as he was to admit it, Valentine found that he actually liked being romanced. Each of the guys offered his own equally appealing qualities, which in turn made things more difficult for Valentine, as he had no clear favorite. He often found his thoughts drifting from one to another, pulling him in three different directions. Valentine adored the long philosophical conversations he had with Abraham, he could also happily watch hours and hours of classic films with Sean and he never tired of Haruki's amusing stories of the extraordinary things he'd removed from people in emergency rooms – not to mention the tall tales that they'd used to explain how said objects had become lodged there in the first place. To put it simply, they all felt like a perfect fit.

Even more astounding, was the fact that all three were decent guys and far from the type Valentine had spent his twenties pursuing. They all had jobs, treated him with respect and had yet to stand him up for any of their rendezvous. Given this taste of chivalry, Valentine had begun to question his long held cynicism towards love and relationships.

Maybe I did just need to meet the right guy…guys. I wonder how hard it would be to have three boyfriends.

Valentine couldn't help but feel slightly guilty about continuing to play the field, as he had the sense that each of the three was hoping for things to develop further. His commitment-phobic tendencies were undoubtedly to blame for his behavior and unwillingness to try and settle down with any of his playmates.

One drawback of this flurry of dating was that Valentine barely had time to see Prudence any more. The pair weren't just flat mates, they were exceedingly close and he valued her friendship deeply. They had met when she'd come into the shop on a quest to find the perfect vintage cocktail dress. Valentine had found the very thing for her in a matter of minutes – a shimmering emerald number that fit like a tailored glove – and a thoroughly grateful Prudence became a regular soon after. Their friendship had blossomed over a shared love of retro fashion and Mexican telenovelas – '*Las Pasiones de la Familia*' was their favorite by far. Prudence was unconventionally attractive with fine features, sharp hazel eyes, blonde dreadlocks and several lip piercings but it was a look that appealed to Valentine's particular sense of style.

They had been living together for about three years, ever since Prudence's last flat mate had moved out to be with her girlfriend. They had both been happily single at the time, often cynically mocking everything vaguely romance related – particularly smug couples who insisted on showing the world just how very content they were. This had lasted until Prudence had met Dirk at a concert and came dangerously close to becoming one of those dreaded couplings. Fortunately, Valentine was always there with a friendly, caustic remark to prevent her from becoming too sickeningly sweet. Not that he begrudged Prudence her happiness in the slightest. Indeed, Valentine actually rather liked Dirk, especially after Prudence had told him what her paramour was packing in his pants – he was amazed that she could walk properly after one of their nights together.

After yet another week of only seeing each other in passing, Valentine had made plans to catch up with Prudence during her lunch break. Prudence worked in a busy café, Perk Up, which was in the base of a huge apartment complex opposite Janeway Park. Valentine liked to eat there as the food was always good and Prudence was able to give him a discount. The fact that the manager also happened to be a part-time underwear model – whose ads Valentine had used for inspiration on more than one occasion of self-pleasuring – may have also played into his preference for eating there.

The café was almost deserted as she always took her break after the lunch rush had finished. The air was scented with the appetizing remnants of lunches, coffees and desserts. They were seated at one of the small tables by the glass windows that looked out upon the vast greenery of the park and the citizenry rushing about their business.

"You do know that you can't keep seeing all three, right?" Prudence said in a motherly tone.

"Don't see why not. They all seem rather happy to me."

Valentine gave a suggestive wink, to which Prudence merely rolled her eyes.

"Is your mind always in the gutter?"

"Pretty much."

"Do they know about each other?"

"Well none of them have asked." Seeing Prudence's exasperated look he continued. "We're all just having fun. It's not serious."

"Don't you want it to be? Wouldn't you like a regular boyfriend?"

"Nope."

"Why not? I mean they do all seem a big step up from your usual conquests."

"Thanks. I'm sure there's a compliment in there somewhere."

Valentine was far more amused than offended. Obviously realizing that her approach wasn't working, Prudence changed tacks.

"Honestly, you're acting just Maria did in *Las Pasiones* when she was dating her boss *and* her adopted brother. Just look how that turned out."

"Sure, she ended up kidnapped and forced to marry her doctor who turned out to be her long lost twin but my life isn't a soap opera."

"Could've fooled me."

"Ha! It'll be fine. Besides we're all guys, it's not like we have real feelings."

Valentine chuckled and ate a forkful of his pasta salad while Prudence sighed and took another sip of her cinnamon-spiced hot chocolate.

"You're a lost cause."

"Yup."

Prudence paused for a moment and focused a serious look upon her flat mate in an apparent last attempt to help him see reason.

"Val, somebody is going to get hurt."

"Only if we don't use enough lube," quipped Valentine.

"I give up!"

Valentine grinned and stuck out his tongue and they both fell about laughing, attracting the interested stares of the few remaining customers.

* * *

Around a week later, Valentine had a rare night off from his paramours to have dinner with his parents. It was his mother's birthday and his father had guilted him into it. It wasn't that he didn't want to see them but they usually badgered him about the state of his love life, which he found a little complicated to explain at present. It was also for this reason that he'd decided to come alone. Valentine was afraid that inviting one of his men to meet his parents would have definitely given the wrong signal.

Which one would I invite anyway?

They had met at his mother's favorite restaurant – Bombay Dreams – she simply adored their chicken Tandori. All three had dressed for the occasion and made quite the stylish trio. The family resemblance was quite strong, as Valentine had inherited his father's thick, wavy blond hair and his mother's striking eyes. Valentine's parents, still a very dashing couple even in their mid-fifties, had instilled in him from an early age the importance of looking one's best, particularly so for special occasions. Both Valentine and his father were dressed in charcoal-gray suits – although Valentine favored a more modern cut over his father's more classic three-piece – while his mother was wearing a flowing, ruby-red gown that he'd bought her for Christmas the year before. He was touched at the gesture and pleased that it very much suited her slight build as he'd imagined it would, also complimenting her sparkling blue eyes and raven black hair.

The trio was halfway through dinner before the expected interrogation began.

"So anyone special in your life, my angel?"

"No, Mom."

"We do worry about you."

Valentine did his best to keep his exasperation and growing annoyance under control. He began twirling the thick, silver ring he wore on his right hand. It had been a present from his beloved grandmother on his twenty-fifth birthday – she always had such good taste – and was one of the last things she had ever given him. He absolutely adored it and always fiddled with it when he was feeling uncomfortable. The thought of her never failed to have a calming effect on him.

"I know, but I'm fine. Not everyone needs the fairytale ending you know."

"Yes, but you're still our little boy and we want the best for you."

"I'm not the marrying kind."

"You'll meet the right boy eventually, then you'll know."

"Yes, Mom."

I have to be nice. It's her birthday. It's her birthday. It's her birthday.

It was now that Valentine's father decided to join back into the conversation.

"Leave the boy alone, Annette. He'll settle down when he's ready."

"Thanks, Dad."

"Although, there is a rather nice lad who just started in the accounting department at the firm if you'd like me to give him your number. I mean you never know, after all."

Valentine wasn't sure whether to cry or laugh. The latter instinct won through and he barely suppressed a snort of laughter. He understood that his parents wanted the best for him but they drove him up the wall sometimes. Given his past boyfriends he had to admit they might have had cause for concern.

If only they knew what I was up to now.

They hadn't batted an eyelid when he told them he was gay but considering he'd never shown the slightest interest in girls, except as friends, it was hardly a shocking admission. Not to mention that his bedroom walls had been plastered with posters of *4Hearts* – the most popular boy band of his adolescence – mostly featuring the lead singer Blaine. Valentine had had many a dream – both day and wet – about what they'd do together if they ever met. Strangely enough, Valentine had realized his fantasy several years later when he'd encountered Blaine on the dance floor at Sanctuary – the hottest gay club in the city – and the two had spent a torrid night together. The following morning, Valentine had briefly entertained the idea of their getting married and living in the suburbs, which all evaporated when Blaine's previously unmentioned boyfriend returned home unexpectedly from a business trip and had thrown Valentine out in a rage. At the time it had been even further proof to an impressionable Valentine that love was a source of misery and pain.

"Can we discuss something other than my love life, please?" asked Valentine, fighting his strong instinct to escape from their well-meaning meddling.

"Of course, dear," said Annette.

The family passed the rest of the evening in a mix of delicious spiciness and conversation, which thankfully revolved more about their future holiday plans on a Caribbean cruise rather than Valentine's potential soul mate.

* * *

Valentine had just hopped out of the shower when he heard a firm knocking echoing through the apartment from the front door.

Damn he's early.

"I'm coming," he called out while furiously drying himself.

He was expecting Abraham, as they were due to go out to dinner then clubbing at Sanctuary – the free entry and drinks were a happy bonus from dating one of the dancers.

Valentine decided he was dry enough and carefully exited the bathroom – slipping and breaking something wouldn't be helpful for the night's plans, after all – before rushing to the front door. He opened it with a wide smile of welcome, which quickly froze on his face. There standing on the rainbow-colored welcome mat was Haruki, not Abraham. Valentine was flustered. His pulse began to race and a sickly feeling rose in his stomach.

Did I double book them?

"Did we have plans?" asked Valentine; desperately trying to not show the panic he was feeling.

"No, I just thought I'd drop by."

Haruki moved forward and wrapped Valentine up in his muscular arms and into a hungry kiss. Valentine became caught up in the moment, eagerly kissing Haruki back, as his towel came undone and dropped to the floor. Valentine deeply inhaled the pleasant mixture of caramel, apple and coconut coming from Haruki – a pleasant side effect all of the various beauty products he used. Things were starting to get rather heated with Valentine's manhood at full mast and a complimentary bulge in Haruki's jeans. Suddenly, they were startled by a loud, angry voice.

"What the fuck, are you doing?"

There in the doorway stood Abraham, his face awash with anger and hurt.

"I would have thought that's obvious, buddy," said Haruki.

"But he's my boyfriend."

Then came a new voice from the hallway.

"No, he's my boyfriend!" Sean declared in his deep baritone.

Haruki stepped away from Valentine, leaving him standing there naked and shivering. The trio all looked at him with hostile eyes.

"So who are you dating?" they asked in unison.

Valentine sat up with a start in his bed, his heart beating wildly. The morning light seeped into the room around his heavy curtains. He was relieved it had only been a dream but looked down and saw that his raging erection had carried over into the real world.

Oh well, I might as well finish off.

Valentine pushed the feelings of guilt aside and took himself in hand. The thoughts of what his gentlemen callers could do to him all together soon pushed him over the edge. His thick, white seed spurted out forcefully all over his defined stomach. After he was spent, Valentine grabbed an old t-shirt that was lying by the side of the bed and promptly cleaned himself up. He wearily climbed out of bed and headed to the shower, for real this time.

Even though he was feeling quite content after his recent ejaculation, Valentine had a niggling sense of unease. He knew very well that it was caused by what he was doing with the boys, but it was a problem he was prepared to ignore as long as possible – despite the obvious intentions of his subconscious to deal with it more directly. It wasn't the first such dream he'd had but it had been the angriest – the others had ended far more happily…and stickily.

I probably should make up my mind.

* * *

A few days later, Valentine was covered in sweat and lightly grunting, surrounded by like-minded individuals.

"I can't," gasped Valentine.

"Yes, you can. Now, stop being a whiny little bitch and give me another twenty," came a booming, authoritative voice above him.

"I hate you," growled Valentine, before he started on the next set of diamond pushups.

"Good. Then I'm doing my job properly."

Despite the hardworking air-conditioning system, the air in the gym was thick with the heady musk of masculine toil. The warmer weather and heavy attendance during peak hour weren't helping matters. Valentine's clothes clung to him with perspiration as he pushed himself up and down. His chest and arms burned from the exercise and he cursed James with every repetition.

When he finished, Valentine collapsed exhausted onto the floor and rolled onto his back. Valentine gazed up at his trainer, looking very pitiful indeed. The one consolation was from that angle he was being treated to the pleasing sight of James' indecently short, bright blue shorts, which barely contained the monster sleeping within.

"So, which one are you going to pick?"

Valentine had spent most of the session discussing his latest dream and the need to choose one of his suitors before it became an awkward reality. He'd stopped discussing the matter with Prudence, as he couldn't bear the smugness she exuded about being right all along.

"I don't know. I much preferred the one the night before when the three of them each pounded me senseless and covered me in their loads."

"Of course you did, you dirty little fucker."

Over the years James had heard all sorts of stories from his client, although to be honest he'd been guilty of the same level of debauchery in his own past so was in no position to criticize.

"But you need to start thinking with your heart instead of your cock."

"I guess, but the other way is so much more fun," countered Valentine with a cheeky smile.

"Sure; for now, but you can't treat men like convenient toys forever."

"Speaking of toys. How is Theo?"

Valentine loved teasing James about his much younger boyfriend – by a good decade or so – whom Valentine had also had the pleasure of playing with a few years back. Theo's floppy brown hair, brown puppy-dog eyes and tall, defined build had been irresistible – the nine uncut inches between his legs hadn't hurt either...much.

"He's well, and just for that give me another twenty."

"I'm sorry, I didn't mean it."

By the look of malicious glee in James' eyes, Valentine knew his plea was falling on deaf ears.

"Don't care, get to it!"

As he pushed through the pain, his arms shaky with exertion, Valentine thought about what James had said. He knew the sensible thing would be to settle down with one of the guys but Valentine was hesitant of making a mistake. His judgment in such matters had hardly been reliable in the past – as people seemingly loved to keep pointing out to him.

Which one is the right one?

* * *

After his session, Valentine was feeling fatigued so he showered off and went to laze in the steam room for a spell to soothe his well-used body. It was newly renovated with several small frescoes and columns, which gave it more of a Romanesque vibe. The space had also doubled in size meaning there were plenty of spots to stretch out even during the busier times. Valentine found himself a cozy, dimly-lit corner, leaned his head back against the light blue and white tiles and closed his eyes. The workout and the warmth of the steam soon caused all of his aches and cares to simply melt away and lulled him into a half-slumber.

He awoke with a start ten minutes later upon hearing the unmistakable sounds of men at play. Even before the renovation it had been a favored location for the more amorous gym members to find their post-workout release. Valentine looked to his left and saw Avery – the Stretch class instructor – helping a good-looking muscle bear to achieve just that. As much as he would have liked to watch the full show, Valentine had other plans. He slowly stood up and made his way to the showers to quickly wash up and get ready.

Thankfully, the short rest had given him enough energy to continue on with his evening. Valentine dressed and headed over to a nearby bar – The Cat's Meow – to meet up with Prudence for Dirk's birthday drinks.

The bar was quite crowded, filled with a mix of hip young things of varying proclivities – it was quite a popular spot for gentlemen of a certain persuasion and their admirers. It wasn't a particularly surprising choice for Dirk given his great number of gay friends, even if he was most assuredly of the heterosexual inclination himself.

Valentine scanned the crowd and soon saw Prudence waving from a corner booth up the back of the bar. He determinedly made his way through the throng; encountering several gents he wouldn't have minded getting to know better along the way…although Valentine gently rebuked himself for such longings.

I already have too many!

When he reached their booth, Valentine received a rather enthusiastic greeting from the birthday boy, who'd obviously already had a celebratory cocktail or several. Dirk jumped up and gave Valentine a big sloppy kiss on the lips. Not that Valentine minded terribly. Dirk was athletic-looking with cropped chestnut brown hair and deep, dark bedroom eyes. Plus after what Prudence had told him about Dirk's mammoth manhood, Valentine would be lying if he said he hadn't fantasized about him once or twice after they first met…and quite a few times since. If Dirk hadn't been so unwaveringly straight – and dating his best friend – he would have happily given him a present to remember.

"So glad you made it, pretty boy!" exclaimed Dirk, slurring his words ever so slightly.

"Wouldn't miss it! Can I get you a drink?"

"A cocksucking cowboy! Will you have one with me?"

At the table, Valentine could see Prudence rolling her eyes in her habitual, theatrical manner.

Ah, drunken straight boys are hilarious.

"Sure, anything for the birthday boy."

"Thanks, man! You're the best. No wonder you have all those guys in love with you!"

Valentine shot Prudence a dark look and she looked away a tad guiltily. Valentine made his way to the bar. He shouldn't have been surprised that Prudence had told Dirk but he couldn't help feeling a little annoyed, even though it was hardly as if he had sworn her to secrecy. Valentine had hoped to forget about his dilemma for at least one evening but it didn't seem as if it would be the case.

He returned with the drinks and soon found his worries start to fade away as the warmth of the alcohol overtook his body and made his mind feel pleasantly fuzzy. Throughout the evening numerous guys caught Valentine's eye – and he theirs – but he didn't feel like particularly approaching any.

Not tonight.

As the evening wore on, a wonderfully diverse and friendly parade of people joined their merry band. Valentine didn't really know many of Dirk's friends so he spent most of the evening meeting an array of cheerful strangers. They were pleasant enough company and Valentine enjoyed himself immensely.

A few hours later, their group had all but dwindled away and a call went out for last drinks. Valentine hopped up to get one last round. As he approached the bar, he saw a couple of men kissing by the far end. The one he could only see from behind looked awfully familiar.

It couldn't be. Haruki?

Valentine felt a surge of jealousy course through his chest, which abruptly disappeared when the lads stopped kissing and the man in question turned around only to reveal that it was a complete stranger. Feeling embarrassed and a tad confused, Valentine ordered his drinks.

Why did I react like that? It's not like we're exclusive, so why do I care?

Discomforted, Valentine downed an extra shot before returning to the booth. Jealousy was a relatively new emotion for him, he was used to being on the receiving end of it, having had more than a few mistrustful men in his past.

Fortunately, Prudence and Dirk were far too inebriated to notice his sudden change of mood. He put on a brave face, which almost masked his inner turmoil and continued to smile until he was left alone in the privacy of his bedroom a short time later.

As he climbed into bed, Valentine's mind was still troubled.

Am I really turning into one of those sappy romantics? Maybe I do want a commitment? But who with, though?

* * *

A week later, Valentine had just hopped out of the shower when he heard a knock at the door.

Damn he's early!

This time it was Sean he was expecting. He scampered to the door and opened it to find a smiling Haruki standing in the doorway.

"Ready for the movies?" He moved forward, closed the door behind him and kissed Valentine deeply. "Or we can just stay here."

Valentine heart raced just as it always did in the dreams. All of a sudden, Valentine remembered that he had indeed made plans with Haruki and forgotten to write it down in his agenda, after becoming distracted by a particularly pushy customer at the store.

Damn it to hell! Serves me right. Now, I'll probably lose them all! Stop being so melodramatic.

"Hold that thought. Just give me a sec."

He practically ran to the bedroom and went for his phone hoping that he could cancel with Sean in time and avoid an uncomfortable confrontation. As Valentine picked up his cell, he noticed that there was already a missed call from Sean flashing on the screen. He quickly listened to the voicemail, his heartbeat pounded in his ears and a cold sweat started to bead on his forehead.

"Heya Val, I'm so sorry but it looks like I'll have to cancel, my boss dumped a huge load of work on me earlier and I was hoping to get it done, but realistically I won't be leaving here till *really* late. I feel bad about the last-minute notice, but I promise that I'll make it up to you soon, gorgeous man. Have a good night."

Thank the gods!

Valentine felt a sickly combination of relief and guilt. He knew that he couldn't keep on this like this. He wasn't being fair to the guys or himself for that matter. For the first time in his life Valentine had three amazing guys interested in him and he seemed to be doing his very best to sabotage things for himself.

What the fuck is wrong with me? I need to make a decision.

"Everything all right in there? Need some help?"

Still standing there only clad in a towel, Valentine could hear the suggestiveness in Haruki's tone and his manhood began to respond in kind.

"Sure, come on in."

Haruki was within the door and had Valentine pinned down on the bed a mere ten seconds later. Haruki's jeans and t-shirt we're quickly discarded and the pair wrestled together on the bed, moaning and attacking one another with their mouths. They then proceeded to have wonderfully hot and noisy sex, which helped Valentine forget about his problem... temporarily at least.

A delicious, ecstasy-filled hour later, when they lay snuggled up together in the sweaty afterglow, Valentine's guilt gradually returned, slinking back into his thoughts as a very unwanted guest. The sex had been as satisfying as always, but as Valentine watched Haruki's chest slowly rise and fall, his mind was troubled. He had truly come to care for all three guys and didn't like the thought of being without any of them. That being said, the situation wasn't one that was sustainable in the long term.

I feel like I'm cheating, which is ridiculous because none of them are officially my boyfriend. Who am I kidding? I'm being an asshole and I need to cut it out before I'm left all alone and have no one to blame but my indecisive, greedy self!

* * *

After a restless night, Valentine was as conflicted as ever. Haruki had left just after breakfast for his weekly rowing practice so it gave Valentine a chance to turn to Prudence for advice once more.

"I thought you didn't need my…how did you put it? 'Smug know-it-all opinion.' Hmmm?"

Valentine had the decency to look sheepish and apologetic.

"I know, I know. I'm sorry I said that but in my defense…" Valentine caught the darkening look on Prudence's face and changed his tack. "I'm sorry. You were right. I was wrong. Now, can you *please* help me?"

"I don't know. You were pretty mean. I should just let you get yourself out of your own mess." Prudence was obviously enjoying toying with Valentine.

"Pretty please! I promise I'll do *all* the housework for a month!"

"Deal." Prudence said with a self-satisfied grin playing on her lips. "The solution is easy. Write their names on pieces of paper and put them into a hat, and then I'll draw one out."

"Even I think that's a tad cynical."

"Got a better idea?"

Valentine ruefully shook his head and reluctantly went to work. He took a page from the notepad by the phone and tore it into three equal parts before he scrawled a name onto each one and popped them in the hat. Prudence picked one out while Valentine looked on uncomfortably. He was no great romantic but choosing a boyfriend through the luck of the draw seemed a little callous. Plus he was also sure the men involved wouldn't be particularly pleased if they ever learned that they were involved in the romantic equivalent of a lucky dip for his affections.

Prudence looked up at Valentine with the seriousness of a reality game show host about to announce that week's winner. Valentine's stomach was churning with anticipation – and possibly the mushroom omelet he'd eaten earlier.

Maybe the eggs were off?

"Come on, just tell me."

"OK, now just before I do. I have a question for you."

Valentine groaned and barely resisted the urge to snatch the piece of paper from her hand.

"First, close your eyes."

"Are you kidding me?"

His voice had become slightly shrill with the tension of waiting for the answer to his situation.

"You said you needed my help. Do as I say or I'll screw all the paper up and you do it by yourself."

"Fine. Fine," grumbled Valentine.

Valentine knew he wasn't in any position to bargain. Feeling foolish, he closed his eyes and wondered what his flat mate was playing at exactly.

"Now, just sit still and try to relax. Take a few deep breaths, it'll help clear your mind."

I'm doing all the housework for this?

"I don't know how this…"

"Hush up! Just do as I say. Now, breathe in, breathe out."

Chastened by Prudence's harsh tone, Valentine acquiesced. The room was soon silent apart from the sounds of Valentine's heavy breathing, although he still felt awfully silly. Apparently satisfied that Valentine was finally following her instructions properly, Prudence continued.

"I want you to answer me without thinking. Just go with your first instinct and blurt out your answer. Who will be the most difficult to leave?"

Valentine replied without a moment's hesitation.

"Haruki."

"I think we have your decision."

Valentine's eyes flew open.

"But who's on the paper?"

"It doesn't matter."

Valentine lurched forward trying to see who had won the draw but Prudence was quicker and swiftly grabbed all the pieces of paper, tore them into tiny pieces and went to the kitchen to throw them into the trash. Valentine followed closely behind, doubting his decision.

"But, how do I know I made the right choice? And it's not just because he was the last one I was with."

"Who was *always* the first guy to turn up in those dreams you had about them?"

"Haruki, but…"

"Your subconscious obviously knows what you want. I rest my case."

"But, I…"

"Valentine. I don't think you're really worried about making the wrong choice."

"Oh really? Then what am I *really worried* about Dr. Pru?"

Condescension dripped off of every word.

"Scoff all you like, but I think the real reason you put off deciding, and are totally freaking out now, is because you're scared."

"Of what?"

"Being a grown up and having an adult relationship with a decent guy who isn't completely wrong for you."

"I…That's…I mean…"

Valentine was frustrated and flustered. He knew she was right but he was still reluctant to give in entirely.

"Yes?"

"Fine. Maybe…maybe you're right. But there's no guarantee that it'll work out with Haruki."

"No, my pretty boy, but that's love. Sometimes you just have to run the risk. Take it from a reformed cynic."

"I guess."

Valentine's mind and heart were still turbulent with emotion – a swirling mixture of fear, excitement and hope.

"And if it all comes crashing down, I'll be here to get drunk, eat ice cream and mercilessly pick on his faults for as long as you need."

"Thanks."

Valentine smiled and gave Prudence a big bear hug. He knew what he had to do but wasn't looking forward to telling Sean and Abraham about his decision.

Time to man up!

* * *

Sean and Abraham had acted quite differently when he broke the news to them that he'd been seeing other guys and had fallen for someone else. He'd decided it was best to do it in a public place, figuring it was unlikely that they'd cause a scene if they were really upset, so he chose Prudence's café in order to have her immediate support if things didn't go according to plan – an idea she hadn't been particularly keen on.

"You've been what? So this has just all been a game to you? I thought you were better than that!" Sean had exclaimed angrily before he'd stormed out, leaving Valentine sitting awkwardly at the café table with the other customers looking on with a combination of amusement and pity.

Valentine had looked over to Prudence who had her left eyebrow cocked in her all too familiar 'I told you so' expression.

Happily, the meeting with Abraham had gone much better.

"Dude, it's fine. To be honest, I've been sleeping with my ex since before we met," said Abraham, his voice calm and friendly.

Irrationally, the revelation had made Valentine jealous but he knew it was ridiculous and incredibly hypocritical so chose to silently berate himself instead of saying anything. Even so, as soon he'd told them both, Valentine knew in his heart that he'd made the right decision.

It had been Haruki, however, that Valentine had been most nervous about speaking with, as he couldn't bear to lose him if things went badly. He briefly toyed with the idea of not telling him, but, in the end, Valentine decided that he needed to be entirely honest with Haruki if they were going to start a serious relationship. They had met at Haruki's spacious loft, which was located in the heart of the gayborhood, not too far from their gym. Valentine wanted to keep their conversation as private as possible.

Haruki had reacted with a simple 'Oh', but the look of disappointment on his face made Valentine feel very small indeed.

Why did I wait so long? I'm such an idiot!

Fortunately for Valentine, Haruki had been pragmatic in his following response.

"I guess we never agreed to be exclusive…and I do appreciate the fact that you've been honest about it now."

"So, I haven't lost you?" asked Valentine timidly.

"No handsome, you haven't. But, if we're going to do this, I want to be completely monogamous."

"Of course!"

Valentine felt lighter than he had in weeks. They ended up consummating their new relationship status, right there on the plush carpeting of the living room floor. It was a very happy day for them both.

That had been a few weeks ago and Valentine was currently cutting through Janeway Park on his way to the gym. It had been a beautiful summer's day and the park was still full of people enjoying the warm twilight. Valentine was in a very good mood. The shop was doing a roaring trade and his relationship with Haruki was in full honeymoon phase, although he still felt slightly guilty about how he'd treated the other two boys.

Valentine was beginning to think he may have misjudged this whole relationship thing and had a rather disturbing realization that his parents had been right – not that he'd ever tell them as much.

Wrapped up in his thoughts, Valentine didn't see a large stone lying in the middle of the path. As he was approaching the wrought iron gates at the main entrance, his left foot caught on the edge of the stone and nearly sent him sprawling into the dirt. He managed to right himself in time but when he looked up, Valentine saw a guy and a girl sitting on a nearby bench, kissing. The guy looked like Haruki from the back but he'd made that mistake before.

Not again, I don't. It's not him.

Valentine was just turning away when the couple broke apart and stood up to leave. To his horror, Valentine saw that it was indeed his boyfriend. Disbelief, followed rather quickly by rage flowed through his body. He stormed over to the pair, consumed with a green fury.

"What the fuck?" Valentine demanded, glaring at Haruki, as his heart pumped faster in anger.

"Excuse me?"

"What the hell do you think you're doing?"

"I'm sorry, do I know you?"

Valentine's rage grew even further as his boyfriend stared at him blankly.

"Why are you doing this? At least have the balls to be honest."

"Babe, who is he?" asked the girl, looking slightly afraid of the apparent crazy person yelling at them.

The couple looked dazed and stared at Valentine, as if he really was a ranting madman. In all fairness this is exactly what he looked like to those observing the situation.

"I think you have me confused with someone else."

Valentine couldn't understand why Haruki would do this to him.

Is it revenge for the other guys? Has he been toying with me this whole time?

"I don't know what game you're playing but I'm out. Fuck you, Haruki!"

"But, I'm…"

No longer able to deal with the situation, Valentine left the park in a rush, tears pricking at his eyes.

This is what I get for trying to have a relationship. I knew it was a mistake to trust a bi guy…sneaky, indecisive fuckers the lot of them!

Valentine was too upset to continue on to the gym so hopped on the metro and retreated back to his apartment, trying his best to cover his increasingly red, watery eyes from curious fellow commuters.

Prudence was out with Dirk so Valentine found that he had the place to himself, which was perfect because he felt like wallowing. Now that the anger had faded, all Valentine felt was an overwhelming sense of betrayal and hurt. Grabbing a king-sized tub of cookies and cream, choc chip ice cream from the freezer, Valentine shucked off his clothes and took to his bed to hide from the world and generally feel sorry for himself.

I hate men!

* * *

A few hours later, Valentine was half-heartedly scraping the last of the ice cream from the tub when there was a knock at the door. He wasn't expecting any one but had a pretty good idea of who it was. Haruki had been calling and messaging for the past hour but Valentine had refused to respond. He was tempted to not answer the door either but figured it was best to finish things properly, now rather than later.

Valentine stomped over to the door, his anger returning with every step. He flung open the door to see a bemused looking Haruki.

"Why the hell do you look so happy?"

"You have chocolate all around your mouth."

"How fucking dare you? You cheat on me and then come around to my place to insult me."

"I didn't cheat on you."

Valentine couldn't believe that Haruki had the audacity to stand there and blatantly lie to his face.

"I *saw* you! It wasn't just my imagination!"

"It wasn't me in the park."

Is he fucking kidding?

"Who then? Your evil twin?"

"Kinda."

The response momentarily stumped Valentine. It was the last thing he'd expected Haruki to say but at the same time there was a faint memory stirring at the edge of his mind that seemed to be vying for his attention.

"What?"

"It was my twin brother, Masaki. Although he's not evil… not really."

The memory of Haruki mentioning his twin brother on their first date broke through fully into Valentine's consciousness. He hadn't really given it a second thought - apart from that brief fantasy of taking on both brothers at once. Valentine was absolutely mortified. It hadn't even crossed his mind that it wasn't Haruki in the park. If he was being completely honest with himself the fact that Haruki was bisexual unsettled him more than he cared to admit.

"I…I…"

Valentine searched for the appropriate words to apologize for his atrocious behavior but none were forthcoming.

"Masaki called me not long after you ran off."

"Oh my god…he must think I'm a total psycho! And his poor girlfriend."

"Laura thought it was hilarious, so did Masaki, after they worked out what had happened and who you were."

I'm such a moron! I really am too stupid to live. Why can't a meteor crash down and take me now?

"I'm *so, so* sorry. Can you ever forgive me? I'd be furious if the situation was reversed. I can't believe I was such an idiot. You must think that…"

Haruki leaned forward and silenced his rambling boyfriend with a forceful kiss.

"Mmm, chocolaty. Yes, you're an idiot but you're *my* idiot."

"Gee, thanks."

Despite the teasing, Valentine was feeling incredibly happy and grateful that his buffoonery hadn't completely derailed his relationship.

"Besides, this isn't the first time it's happened…to either of us. So, can I come in?"

"Yes, yes of course."

He grabbed Haruki by the hand and dragged him inside, shutting the door behind him. They went to the comfy, overstuffed sofa in the living room and sat down closely together.

"So, is your brother straight then?"

"No, he's bi like me."

"Is there anything the two of you don't do the same?"

"Yeah, I'm a much better kisser."

"Oh really?"

"Yeah, I'll show you."

Haruki leaned forward and his full lips lightly grazed against Valentine's. The kiss started softly but within moments had become much more fiery, their tongues battling between their mouths, as their hands grasped at one another.

I love make-up sex!

The misunderstanding behind them, their passionate embrace moved from the sofa to the bedroom, where they happily rolled around for a few delightfully sweaty hours.

* * *

The rest of the summer passed by in a blur of beach days, romantic dates and much laughter – Valentine couldn't remember ever being happier. Even though they had only been properly together for three months it felt far longer.

The couple had also become gym buddies, as they were keen to spend as much time together as possible. Valentine loved to take the cross trainer next to Haruki on the treadmill during their warm up so he could stare at his boyfriend's beautiful behind as it strained and bounced inside his shorts or track pants…it looked good no matter what he wore. The view gave Valentine all sorts of mischievous thoughts that he usually put into practice after their sessions, sometimes they didn't even make it home, relieving their lust in whatever semi-secluded spot they could find. The back stairwell, car park and steam room had all borne witness to their passion.

It was the first time that Valentine had vaguely entertained a long-term future with someone and it both scared and excited him. The pair had even taken the serious step of forgoing condoms, taking their trust in one another to a much deeper level. The hard cynical shell around Valentine's heart had been slowly crumbling as the contentment of being in a healthy relationship gradually eroded his doubts and fears.

His happiness was evident to those around him.

"It's good to always see a smile on your face." Sophinika had commented on more than one occasion.

"You're actually much more pleasant to be around these days." Prudence had teased.

"The sex must be good to keep a stray dog like you faithful," quipped James.

It was the end of the weekend and the weather threatened to be less than clement for the following week so the boys made the most of the opportunity and spent the afternoon at Murdoch Beach. They went there on Haruki's scooter, which Valentine adored riding on. It had surprised Valentine originally that a surgeon would prefer a scooter to a flashy car but it actually seemed better suited to his boyfriend's carefree nature.

Valentine liked the feeling of freedom as the wind blew over them while they zipped through the traffic. It also helped that Valentine was forced to hold tightly onto Haruki's hips for balance, his crotch rubbing right up against his boyfriend's delectable derriere.

After a fun afternoon soaking up the sun and splashing about in the waves and the rock pool, they packed up and headed back to the scooter. They then rode it from the main car park to the smaller one up on the bluff overlooking the beach. The area was named The Head and was also a popular parking spot of an evening for couples wishing to become a bit amorous. They parked the scooter in the far right corner of the car park, close to a small grouping of trees and bushes, and wandered onto the grassy section of the bluff to watch the sun set over the ocean. Due to the heat of the day, they were only clad in their board shorts and flip-flops. As they sat cuddled up in one another's arms, the skin of their naked torsos stuck together from the remnants of the sun lotion, salt and sweat.

The car park slowly emptied out leaving the pair alone as the sunlight steadily faded around them.

"Time to head home?" Valentine murmured softly into Haruki's ear.

"Fine with me, I'm starting to get hungry anyway."

They picked up their belongings and headed across to the scooter. The car park itself had no lighting – the main reason it was such a preferred nighttime spot – so the corner where they'd parked was now shrouded in semi-darkness. Valentine decided to take advantage of their seclusion when they reached the scooter. Without saying a word he ripped Haruki's board shorts down around his ankles – the joys of Velcro – and pushed him back onto a seated position on the scooter, before sinking to his knees and burying his face in his boyfriend's crotch.

Unsurprisingly, Haruki didn't resist in the slightest and ran his hands gently over Valentine's head and shoulders, evidently enjoying the experienced mouth going about its work. Haruki's strong legs were spread wide and he openly offered himself to his boyfriend.

Valentine corkscrewed up and down the thick, uncut manhood, savoring every last bit of the juicy eight inches. He nibbled on the foreskin, playing with it, pulling lightly with his teeth while his right hand massaged Haruki's smooth, round balls. His other hand had undone his own shorts and Valentine leisurely wanked himself as he fellated his boyfriend. The trimmed black hair tickled at Valentine's nose as he took the member deep into his throat and held it there while Haruki groaned above him. He liked the feeling of pressure as Haruki's strong hands kept him firmly in place. By the way the fingers were flexing against his scalp, Valentine knew that Haruki was close. Valentine, however, wasn't ready for things to end just yet.

Standing up, Valentine pulled Haruki to his feet and pulled him into a hard embrace. The pair stood kissing together as the warm summer breeze caressed their nearly naked forms and filled the air with the salty scent of the ocean. They could hear the crashing of the waves on the beach below which only added to the excitement of playing outside in the beauty of nature. Their manhoods rubbed together, leaking precum and coating each other in a thin film of stickiness.

"Fuck me," whispered Haruki.

"Yes, Sir!"

They quickly both cast aside their board shorts to give them greater mobility. Haruki straddled the bike and leant forward, which had the pleasing effect of lifting his buttocks up in a thoroughly inviting manner. Valentine spat on his fingers and then moved them down to the puckered hole, gently running them around the entrance as he lightly kissed Haruki's darkly golden, muscular back. He slowly applied pressure and his ring finger breeched the sphincter and traced inside the passage in strong circular movements, causing Haruki to squirm in pleasure. A second digit soon joined in the fun, the two fingers working in tandem to stretch the hole and prepare it for the imminent invasion.

Haruki gasped and moaned as the fingers skillfully manipulated his prostate, sending waves of pleasure through his writhing body. He pushed backwards; obviously eager to have the thick digits penetrate deeper inside.

Valentine could have joyfully fingered his boyfriend's wonderfully tight ass for a much longer time but the aching in his cock took precedence. Plus, as the evening grew late the probability of being disturbed by other frisky couples grew stronger. Bending down, Valentine shoved his face deep inside the buttocks, his mouth lubricating the entrance with saliva, much to Haruki's apparent enjoyment, given his groans of pleasure. Valentine happily inhaled the pungent scent of Haruki's passage, causing his cock to grow even harder.

He reluctantly stood up away from the delicious, musky treat, grabbed the bottle of sun lotion from his satchel and squeezed a small pool of oil onto his hand, which he then used to lubricate his erection. Valentine admired Haruki's broad shoulders that narrowed down to a trim waist and the delicious curves of his bubble butt, which was spread enticingly on the scooter before him. He straddled the bike behind Haruki and nuzzled his slick cockhead against the moist entrance. Valentine pushed forward ever so gently as he lightly bit on the back of Haruki's neck and traced along the tattoo with his tongue. He felt the ring gently give way as his glans passed through the tight opening and moved inside. Glorious warmth immediately engulfed his cock as it slowly slid in, inch-by-inch. Haruki moaned and wriggled his hips as the intruder sank deeper and deeper inside.

After a minute or so of careful maneuvering, Valentine was buried to the hilt and had his arms wrapped around Haruki in a vice-like hold. He stayed perfectly still, letting his boyfriend adjust to the rigid member, gently licking and nibbling on Haruki's ears and the sides of his neck. Valentine adored the feeling of the plump ass resting up against his hips. Even though the risk of being caught was high, Valentine could have happily stayed locked in place like this forever.

In due course, Valentine started to tenderly move backwards and forwards, his manhood circling inside the snug silky passage, poking and stretching it. He then began to long-dick Haruki, drawing himself nearly all the way out with only the engorged cockhead remaining inside the tight hold of the entrance before sliding all the way back in to the base.

Perspiration began to form on both their bodies as the movements became more vigorous, with Valentine's erection rapidly sliding in and out. The pumping grew even more urgent as the load in his balls begged for release. His breathing got more ragged as Valentine approached his final release.

"I'm so close."

"I want your load in me!" demanded Haruki, in a voice hoarse with pleasure.

That was all the encouragement Valentine needed and a few thrusts later, his body tensed and shuddered as the seed exploded from his cock and into the velvety embrace of his boyfriend's ass. Valentine clung to Haruki as each spurt wracked his body with a burst of ecstasy. Even after he was fully spent, Valentine kept a firm hold of Haruki, feeling his heart hammering against his chest.

"Damn, you feel so good, Haru."

"Right back at you, Mister."

Valentine gently pulled out and gingerly hopped off the bike, his legs were a little weak after straining during their passionate fucking. He sank back to his knees as Haruki also climbed off the bike.

Haruki stood above his boyfriend, cock in hand, and started to furiously jack himself off with Valentine staring back up at him with a pure look of carnal lust. Within moments, his body began to tremble and Haruki grunted loudly as his load was released and sprayed up and back down, hitting Valentine's chest and face. Valentine swiftly moved forward to swallow the last few spurts, greedily suckling on his boyfriend's sensitive manhood.

When he was certain that he'd managed to suck out the last few remaining drops, Valentine climbed to his feet and kissed Haruki softly on the lips. He grabbed his beach towel from his bag and the pair wiped away the remnants of their play. They were just putting their clothes back on when the bright glare of headlights flashed over them.

"Good timing," smirked Valentine.

"I don't know…I wouldn't have minded an audience," replied Haruki, only half joking.

"Naughty boy."

"That's why you love me."

"Maybe."

Valentine moved forward and gave Haruki a long, languid kiss.

"Careful, Mister. You might get me started again."

"I'm willing to risk it," said Valentine before moving back in for another loving kiss.

Moments later, another set of headlights passed over them and they broke apart.

"Let's continue this back at my place," suggested Haruki with a mischievous glint in his eyes.

"Lead the way, Doc."

They climbed onto the bike and soon zoomed off into the night with Valentine holding onto Haruki in a tight clinch.

* * *

Two weeks later, Valentine was surprised to find himself in the heart of suburbia. Granted, the suburb in question, Lovedale, was only a twenty-minute journey from the city but he had rarely ventured into the world of family-friendly domesticity since leaving his parents' home more than a decade beforehand.

He was standing in the spacious home of one of Haruki's old school friends, Sarah, and her girlfriend, Catherine. It was Sarah's thirtieth birthday party and there was quite a crowd gathered to celebrate, including Haruki's brother and his girlfriend. Valentine had run smack bang into them roughly a minute after arriving and his face immediately turned an almost scarlet color. He hadn't seen the pair since the incident in the park, having been far too embarrassed by his unwarranted outburst to face them. Haruki had offered for them to catch up more than a few times since but each time Valentine had pleaded for mercy. This time, however, there was no escape. Even though he knew it was only a matter of time before their paths would cross again, Valentine had foolishly hoped that it wouldn't be for good long while…perhaps even years.

"I believe you've met my brother and Laura," said Haruki, evidently enjoying his boyfriend's discomfort.

"I'm so sorry. I was unbelievably rude. I didn't even think that it…"

Valentine's apology threatened to become an incoherent jabber as the shame of his actions overtook his brain. Thankfully, he was stopped mid-babble when Masaki clamped a firm hand on Valentine's shoulder and gave him a dark, penetrating look that Valentine well recognized. If he didn't know better Valentine would've sworn he was staring deep into his boyfriend's eyes.

God, they're identical!

His trepidation rising, Valentine braced himself for a harsh rebuke for his actions.

"It's OK, Haruki's had to deal with one of my psycho exes before."

"I'm not crazy," replied Valentine, feeling increasingly self-conscious.

"That's not what my brother tells me. Good thing you're so hot."

Suddenly, Masaki's stern face broke into a wide smile, leaving Valentine a little perplexed. Valentine turned to his boyfriend with an expression of hurt and confusion only to be greeted by peals of laughter from both brothers.

"He was kidding, Val."

"Oh, yeah, right."

Valentine tried to play along with the joke but was more embarrassed than before and wasn't sure where to look. Apparently sensing his boyfriend's discomfort Haruki moved forward and gave Valentine a good strong hug and whispered in his ear.

"It's all over now. I'll make it up to you tonight."

As they broke apart Masaki gave Valentine a friendly squeeze on the shoulder as well.

"No hard feelings, buddy."

"You have to admit, it was pretty funny," added Laura.

Feeling more reassured, Valentine relaxed and started to enjoy himself. The party had been going about two hours when Sarah called for everyone's attention.

"Excuse me, Ladies and Gentleman...and all the rest of you charming riffraff. I'd just like to thank you all for coming to celebrate the death of my youth."

This was met with a raucous response of laughs, whistles and cheers.

"However, this isn't the only reason you're all here. We've gathered all of you wonderful people here today for another special event."

A confused murmur went around the room, as the guests looked at each other with quizzical expressions until Sarah continued.

"We would be honored if you'd all like to gather in the back garden and watch us get hitched."

There were various cries of shock and congratulations as the crowd moved forward to congratulate the pre-newlyweds, before they were ushered outside while the soon-to-be-brides had a quick costume change.

"Did you know about this?" asked Valentine, as they were strolling out to the back lawn.

"I may have had a little inkling."

"Then why didn't you say anything?"

"Because it was a surprise, silly boy. Are you OK, you seem a little anxious? You're not still worried about my brother are you?"

"Yeah...I mean, no, I'm fine."

He wasn't being completely honest. Since the announcement, Valentine had a niggling feeling of unease. It wasn't that he was opposed to weddings per se; rather the fact that he was attending one with his first serious boyfriend had reawakened his commitment-phobic tendencies. The sensation of discomfort only continued to grow throughout the ceremony.

The soft light of the late afternoon filtered through the brilliant autumnal colors of the trees and bathed the backyard in a warm glow. Catherine and Sarah looked absolutely radiant in their simple, yet elegant, white gowns. Sarah's crystal blue eyes, flowing auburn tresses and willowy build made her appear rather like a fairytale princess, which was complimented perfectly by the more elfin look of Catherine's bright green eyes and cropped platinum blonde hair.

There were more than a few glistening eyes as the ladies exchanged vows and pledged their love to one another. When the celebrant, Margaret – a pleasantly, plump middle-aged woman with frizzy brown hair and twinkling blue eyes – pronounced the pair officially joined in wedlock the garden was filled with cheers and much clapping.

The party continued on well into the night with a great deal of drinking, dancing and merriment. Despite his earlier unease, Valentine was able to relax once more – no doubt helped by the numerous glasses of champagne he had gulped down. He even shared a few dances with both Masaki and Laura, all glad that the awkwardness was now well on the way to being behind them.

By the end of the evening, Valentine was in a much-improved mood, happily snuggled up with Haruki in a taxi ferrying them back to the city.

"That was a beautiful ceremony," said Haruki, as he gave Valentine a light peck on the cheek.

"Yeah, it was."

"Much simpler than my wedding was. Our parents insisted on a big formal wedding and it kinda turned into a bit of a circus. If I got married again I think I'd like something simple. What about you?"

The haze of alcohol evaporated rapidly and Valentine's pulse quickened at the unexpected talk of his future wedding plans.

"Huh?"

"If you got married, would you like something like Sarah and Catherine's or something more formal?"

Are we at that stage of the relationship already? I'm not ready!

"Don't know. Haven't thought about it."

"Really?"

"Yeah…anyway, do you want to go to the movies tomorrow? The new Star Trek film is supposed to be good."

Valentine hated sci-fi with a passion, but he was so keen to end this topic of conversation that desperate measures needed to be taken.

"Sure. We can get our inner geeks on. Maybe grab dinner at The Spicy Samurai afterwards?"

"Sounds good."

Valentine was relieved that talk had turned away from ceremonies but he was still left with an unsettling thought.

Are we moving too fast?

* * *

A feeling of disquiet stayed with Valentine all week. He admonished himself multiple times for overreacting but he couldn't quite shake the idea that he was trapping himself. Even as he sat with Haruki on the couch watching an old movie and eating Indian takeout – their regular Friday night date and one of his favorite parts of the week – Valentine had a strong sense of being tied down.

"You OK, you seem lost in your own little world?" asked Haruki, affectionately ruffling his boyfriend's hair.

"Yeah, just a little tired."

"There's a couple of things I wanted to ask you about but if you're too sleepy it can wait till tomorrow."

"Nah, it's fine. What's up?"

"You remember my buddies from the rowing club; you met them at that house party a few weeks back?"

"Yeah, they were fun."

"Well, they're renting a mountain cabin up in the Christie National Park over New Year's and they invited us along. I think it'd be great and said we'd be interested. What do you think?"

All of a sudden, Valentine's flight or fight response was activated, sending his brain and emotions spiraling.

He's making plans months in advance! What if I wanted to do something else? It's like we're not even separate people anymore.

"You should've asked first!"

"I didn't say we'd definitely go."

"That's not the point!" Valentine's voice was rising in volume and he felt helpless to stop himself from having a full-on meltdown. "You can't decide stuff for me. It's not like we're married."

Haruki's face was awash with confusion; his eyes stared intently at his boyfriend, apparently searching for an answer to the drastic change.

"Where is all this coming from?"

"I just think it's rude to speak for me. I'm my own person."

"You're being ridiculous. I don't understand why you're making such a big deal out of nothing at all." Haruki's tone was steadily darkening to match that of his boyfriend.

"So I'm ridiculous now? Sure, whatever." Valentine got up and roughly snatched up his satchel and jacket from the dining room table. "Look, I'm going to head home."

"I thought you were staying over?" Haruki's voice wavered slightly and his eyes showed his puzzlement and a touch of hurt. "Can't we talk about this?"

"No. I just feel like being by myself tonight. I'll give you a call tomorrow."

Valentine rushed out of the apartment without a goodbye kiss, his heart racing and tears threatening to spill from his eyes. He was angry, angry with Haruki and with himself.

Now I've gone and done it, he won't want to be with me after that.

* * *

Thirty minutes later, Valentine slunk in through his front door. His mind had been churning ever since he left Haruki's apartment, asking himself questions he was fearful of answering.

What if I'm in the wrong? Have I completely lost it? Will he still want to talk to me tomorrow?

"Val?" Prudence called out from the kitchen. "I thought you were crashing with Haruki tonight."

"Not any more."

Valentine flopped miserably down on the couch and flipped on the television. Prudence soon entered with two mugs of hot chocolate; each had tiny, pink and white marshmallows floating on the foamy top.

"I made you one too…I popped in a little Baileys to give them some kick." It was then that Prudence apparently noticed her flat mate's sullen demeanor. "Is something wrong?"

"We had a fight," grumbled Valentine.

"Oh no. What did you do?"

"Me? How do you know it was my fault?" Valentine said a tad too indignantly.

"OK, what was it over, then?"

"He was organizing a trip without asking me!"

"You're kidding, right?"

Prudence didn't even try and hide her incredulity, much to Valentine's chagrin.

"Nope."

"You're an idiot."

"What?"

Valentine was hurt by her lack of support.

She should be on my side!

"You picked a fight, *over nothing,* because you're a raging commitment-phobe."

"Tell me something I don't know."

"Listen up, pretty boy. I'm the first to admit that I've had trouble with relationships and am by no means any sort of expert."

"You got that right," agreed Valentine snarkily.

"My point is; you've got an amazing guy, if you'd stop being so scared to notice."

"I…it's just that…you don't…"

Every argument that Valentine could come up with seemed too silly to actually say aloud. He knew that he was in the wrong but was having trouble admitting it to himself, let alone anyone else.

"Maybe…*just* maybe, you have a point."

"I know I do. So, what are you going to do about it? Hmmm?"

"I don't know. He probably doesn't want to ever see me again. I think I've ruined everything. Yelling at his brother, overreacting over nothing, why would he want to be with a crazy man?"

Valentine's eyes felt hot at the imminent return of fresh tears. He turned away not wanting to show Prudence how overly emotional he had become.

"I think you should give him more credit than that. Besides you're cute as a button. How could he resist? Go apologize!"

Her kind words comforted him, but Valentine was still feeling a little unsure.

"I guess I could try," he began timidly.

"That's my boy!"

"OK, but I'll do it tomorrow. I can't face him again tonight."

"Fine, but if you come home tomorrow without having done it, I will personally kick your toned butt back down the stairs."

"Yes, Mom."

"That's enough cheek out of you!"

The pair sat together and settled in to watch an episode of *Las Pasiones de la Familia* they'd recorded. Due to their busy schedules they were about a week behind with their viewing. The next few hours whizzed by in a series of bitch fights, intense stares and two interrupted weddings. It was almost enough to take Valentine's mind away from his troubles…almost.

* * *

Summoning all his courage the following morning, Valentine called Haruki. It rang several times, each trill making his stomach churn a little more. Valentine anxiously fiddled with his silver ring as he waited. He thought – and was very much hoping – it might go to voicemail and was preparing to leave a message when Haruki answered, breathing heavily.

"Hi."

"Are you OK? You sound out of breath."

"Yes, I just left my phone at the other end of the ward and had to race back to grab it. What can I do for you?"

Valentine couldn't tell by Haruki's tone of voice whether he was just being professional or was angry with him. He very much hoped for the former but knew he most probably deserved the latter.

"Um, OK. I just called to…I need to…to say that I'm sorry. I'm an imbecile and you should totally disregard my stupidity from last night. Can we start over?"

There was a brief pause before Haruki responded and Valentine though his heart may very well burst from his chest in anticipation.

"You're adorable."

"So…that's a yes?" he asked tentatively, scared to jinks anything.

"Yes, you doofus."

Valentine was positive he could hear the smile in his boyfriend's voice.

"I can't tell you how glad I am. I really thought that I'm messed everything up and the last thing…"

"Hey Cupid Boy, sorry to interrupt but I really need to get back to work."

"Oh…yes, of course." Valentine somehow resisted the urge to slap his own forehead. "Can we meet tonight? I really want to make up *in person*."

The sexual intent in his voice was so obvious it would have even made Madonna look subtle.

"Certainly. My last appointment is around six so we can meet at mine around eight for dinner?"

"Sounds perfect."

"There's still something I need to talk to you about anyway."

"Nothing *too* serious I hope."

"No…well possibly, but it's not something I want to get into over the phone."

"Oh, OK."

Doubt crept back into Valentine's mind and his heart lurched ever so slightly.

Maybe he does want to dump me? But, then why invite me to dinner?

"Look I've really got to go, otherwise I'll fall behind with my patients. See you tonight."

"Sure, I'll see you then."

Fortunately, Valentine didn't have too much time to sit around torturing himself by obsessively trying to analyze the conversation, as he had to get to the store and open up for the day. A steady stream of customers kept Valentine busy during the day, but the odd worrying thought would still cross his mind.

What could be so serious he needs to talk about it in person?

After he closed, Valentine went to the gym to try and work out some of his nervous energy. Despite, pushing himself through a particularly grueling workout he was still in a slightly agitated state and was outside the front of Haruki's apartment building at exactly 8pm, buzzing the intercom.

As soon as Haruki opened his front door, Valentine attempted to apologize yet one more time for his behavior.

"I'm so sorry…"

Valentine was immediately cut off by an enthusiastic kiss hello from his boyfriend that moved from the front door, up the stairs and into the bedroom, where words were no longer needed.

Afterwards, when they were lying on the bed both sated and sticky, Valentine turned to Haruki determined to apologize and explain his overreaction.

"I guess I freaked out that we we're getting too serious."

"Why?"

"Well, you were planning a trip months in advance… and all that talk about weddings after we left Sarah and Catherine's."

Haruki laughed, his sexy baritone reverberating around the bedroom, sending a warm glow through Valentine's chest, although he couldn't see the humor of the situation.

"What's so funny?"

"Oh, my silly, silly, Cupid Boy. You're great, but marriage is the furthest thing from my mind. We've only been together a few months and I'm nowhere near ready for it either."

"Oh."

"Don't get me wrong, I do love you but I enjoy what we already have."

Relief flooded through Valentine's body. He felt so foolish getting worked up like a schoolboy over absolutely nothing.

"But, would it be so traumatic if I did want to spend the rest of my life with you?" teased Haruki.

"No, it's not that. It's just that I haven't been the best at picking good guys and I've been burned a lot. I guess, I just kept waiting for the other shoe to drop and when it didn't I had to sabotage myself instead. Still think I'm adorable?"

Haruki leaned forward and gave Valentine a gentle kiss.

"Even more so."

Valentine felt relieved and kissed him back. It was then that Valentine remembered the mysterious 'talk' that had been bothering him.

"Didn't you want to talk to me about something else before I went all crazy on you?"

"That I did…A few years ago I did a stint for Doctors Without Borders."

"Very humanitarian of you," said Valentine, as his fingers slowly traced circles on Haruki's chest and defined stomach.

"Yeah, it was an amazing opportunity."

"What does that have to do with us now, though?"

"A doctor friend of mine, Sergio, works with them all the time and he's approached me about possibly doing another tour. The only thing is that it would mean being away from Port Davinica for a little while."

A sharp shiver ran along Valentine's spine and his fingers froze mid-circle.

"How little?"

"That's the thing. Last time I went for a year, but as a surgeon I can go for shorter periods. I was considering going for around six months. It would also depend on where I get sent."

Valentine was reeling. He had just gotten used to the idea of a serious relationship and now he was being blindsided with the worry of a long distance one.

"Would I be able to visit you?"

"I'm not sure, but probably not. The areas they work in tend not to be that stable and I wouldn't want you to be in harm's way."

"But it's OK for you to be?"

His tone was sharper than he had intended but Valentine's emotions were making it difficult to keep from becoming too worked up.

"I know there's a risk but they're doing good work and really make a difference to people in need."

"When would you leave?"

"Well, if I accept then I'd be headed over in a month."

The admission both shocked and stunned Valentine. He barely knew what to say.

Is it all over?

"And what about us?"

"I was hoping we could do the long distance thing? If you're up to it?"

"I don't know what to say."

"I totally understand if you need time to think about it. I think you're an amazing guy and I believe we have something quite special together. I don't want to lose you but this is something that I feel I really need to do…Do you understand?"

"I think so."

Many thoughts were racing through Valentine's mind and jumbling together, as the implications of what his boyfriend was asking him slowly sunk in. There was, however, one concern more pressing than the others.

"Would you still want to be monogamous?" asked Valentine, fairly sure he already knew the answer.

"To be honest, the thought of you with anyone else would kill me. I know it's a long time, but I'm prepared to wait for you."

"Easier when you're in a warzone."

Valentine regretted the snarky words as soon as they were out of his mouth, even more so when he saw the hurt in Haruki's eyes.

"That's not fair."

"I know, I'm sorry. I shouldn't have said that. It's just a hell of a lot to process and I need to think about it."

"It's fine. I know that I've just dumped this on you so take your time."

"OK."

There was an awkward silence, as they both tried to pretend that everything hadn't completely changed for them.

"How about we just have dinner and then we can talk about it later?" suggested Haruki.

"Sounds good."

Valentine tried his best to make small talk as they ate but all he could think about was Haruki leaving. After they'd finished dinner, Haruki offered for Valentine to stay the night, an offer he eagerly accepted. They didn't discuss the potential separation again that evening, choosing to watch TV instead. As they lay cuddled together on the lounge, Valentine nervously spun his ring around and around, his mind abuzz with conflicting thoughts.

I don't want him to go. But it's a really good cause, stop being so selfish! Could I be faithful? What if he is the one?

* * *

Over the course of the week that followed, Valentine thought of very little else. He liked Haruki more than he had any guy and didn't want to lose him. Their relationship was the best that he'd ever had but he was still plagued with doubts.

Six months is practically forever! Maybe if we'd been together for longer?

Even though he truly cared for Haruki, Valentine was unsure of his ability to stay faithful in the face of an extended absence. He honestly couldn't decide what would be worse – to end things and part as friends or try the long distance path and hurt Haruki when he inevitably succumbed to temptation. In order to try and clear his thoughts, Valentine talked it out with his most trusted advisors.

Prudence had been less than reticent in expressing her opinion.

"Of course, you should wait for him, you oversexed cockhound. It shouldn't even be a question. Haruki is way better than you deserve. He's going off to help the tortured masses and all you can do is think about when you can get your rocks off."

227

James, however, had been far more sympathetic to Valentine's plight.

"Monogamy is tough at the best of times but when you're in different countries it just sucks. When I first enlisted, I was still with my college boyfriend and we pledged to stay faithful but within the first month we'd both cheated. What can I say? Men have needs. "

After more soul searching than Valentine thought he was even capable of, he came to a decision. Valentine decided to tell his boyfriend of his choice that night, as Haruki was cooking dinner for them again. Throughout the dinner, both of them tried their best to keep the conversation light and gay but there was an obvious undercurrent of tension during their meal. They had just finished their dessert of a most delicious pear crumble – one of Haruki's signature dishes – when Valentine could no longer contain himself.

"I don't think I can do it," he said in a rush, wanting to get through the bad news as quickly as possible.

"I figured that might be your answer."

Haruki's voice was edged with disappointment and a little sadness.

"I love you but I kept running things over and over in my head and I just don't think it'll work. Honestly, I know what I'm like and the thought of no sex for six months is insane and I don't trust myself not to cheat…I don't want to do that to you."

"There's always cyber sex?" suggested Haruki hopefully.

"I know…but I just don't think it'll be enough. I'm well aware that I sound like an absolute asshole and you're probably lucky to be escaping from me, but it's how I feel."

"I can't say that I'm not disappointed and as much as I don't like your answer I appreciate your honesty at least."

Valentine felt as small and nasty as he did the day he'd admitted to Haruki that he'd been seeing Sean and Abraham as well.

"I just think I'll end up hurting you and I care too much about you to risk it. I know that sounds dumb."

"No, I get it…Are you sure you won't reconsider?"

Shamed by the look of pleading and dying hope in Haruki's eyes, Valentine desperately wanted to say yes but knew it would end badly.

"No, I just don't think I can."

The pair sat there uncomfortably, both apparently trying not to become overly emotional. It was Haruki who eventually broke the silence.

"What do we do now? Break up or stay together until I go?"

There was a long pause as Valentine considered the options but he could only come to one heartbreaking conclusion.

"I think the longer we leave it the harder it'll be."

"You're probably right," agreed Haruki reluctantly.

"Can we stay friends? I don't want to lose you totally from my life, Haru."

"I'd like that. Well we should end thing properly then."

"What do you mean?"

Haruki took Valentine by the hand with a sad smile on his face and led him to the bedroom. They slowly undressed one another, both wanting to savor their last time together. They were soon kissing lovingly, gently running their hands over each other's exposed flesh. Falling to the bed, they tenderly made love one last time, losing themselves in the bittersweet moment.

An hour later they were holding one another in a close embrace, the evidence of their lovemaking drying on their skin.

"Are you sure you won't change your mind?" asked Haruki, obviously hoping for a last-minute reprieve.

"I wish I could, Doc. I do love you, you know."

"Right back at you, Cupid Boy."

Valentine got out of bed and slowly dressed. Even though he thought he was doing the right thing, Valentine started to cry as soon as he left the apartment. He was a blubbery mess all the way home at which point he locked himself in his room and didn't come out until the following day.

In spite of their amicable parting, the pair didn't see each other again during Haruki's remaining weeks, only keeping in touch through texts and the occasional call. Valentine didn't trust himself not to break down and change his mind even though he knew it was for the best, no matter how miserable it was making the both of them.

The day Haruki left, Valentine locked himself in his room with two tubs of Rocky Road ice cream and with only one thought circling continuously through his brain.

I hope I've done the right thing?

* * *

It was barely a week before Christmas and the city was a veritable winter wonderland, with the snow-covered cityscape and brightly colored decorations practically enforcing an aura of merriment and good will. Valentine, however, was far from being in a festive mood. In fact, he was downright miserable.

It had been two months since Haruki had left and not a day passed that Valentine hadn't dwelled on his absence. He had only had sporadic contact with Haruki since he'd left for Nepal. A week after they'd broken up a massive earthquake only forty miles from the densely populated Kathmandu had decimated the region and left thousands homeless and many more requiring medical aid.

Valentine had been glad that he'd been sent there instead of a warzone, although he knew that it was still a dangerous place to be.

For the first few weeks, Valentine had absorbed everything he could about the disaster, scouring the Internet, almost obsessively, for any mention of the place. He even set up Google alerts so he wouldn't miss anything, although that only made his heart race every time he received a notification. His fears lessened with the passing weeks but the ache in his heart from missing Haruki wasn't fading in the slightest.

Valentine realized that he should try and let go of his feelings for Haruki and move on but it was much easier said than done, as he continued to doubt his decision. In trying to keep such lovelorn thoughts at bay, Valentine had been doing his very best to lose himself in a sea of decadent carnality. He'd gone back to his previous hard-partying ways and seeking comfort between the legs of as many handsome strangers as he could find – and there had been a lot. While it was physically satisfying it left him emotionally empty.

Whenever he saw happy couples strolling around the city, or even shopping in his store, Valentine couldn't help but be reminded of Haruki and what he'd given up. In his darker moments, he wished that they'd never met but he knew such thoughts were unhelpful and ultimately false. There had been more than a few times when he'd been tempted to call Haruki, beg his forgiveness and ask for another chance but he'd always stopped himself.

Why would he take me back? I'm better off alone. I've blown my chance with him.

Despite Valentine's repeated assurances to his nearest and dearest that he was fine, Prudence wasn't so easily brushed off.

231

And had decided apparently to hold her own private intervention, just as Valentine was preparing to leave for the evening.

"OK, sit your butt down, pretty boy."

"But Mom, I'm headed out." Valentine had the angsty teenage whine down pat.

"Very funny. I just wanted to talk to you about how you're doing."

"Do we have to do this now?"

Reluctantly, Valentine sat down on the opposite end of the sofa. He knew that Prudence would only hassle him later.

"Yes, I think we do."

"Fine, you have five minutes? Go!"

"So, you're going out clubbing again?"

"What if I am?"

"Look, I've known you a long time and I know when you're not happy. These past few months you've been going out all the time…going through god only knows how many guys."

"Listen, Mother Teresa, you can stop your slutshaming. I'm just having fun."

"I don't care how many guys you fuck. You know me better than that." Taking a softer tone she continued. "It's OK to miss him you know."

"Who?"

"You know who."

"Actually, no, it's not OK. I ended things so I don't get to feel bad about it."

Valentine's jaw was clenched and it looked like he might bolt at any minute. It was easy to see that she'd hit a raw nerve.

"If you still want him back why don't you reach out? Call him."

"I can't."

"Why not?"

In a fit of anger, Valentine jumped to his feet.

"Because I don't deserve to be with him, alright! I couldn't even be bothered trying to keep it in my pants while he was away. He belongs with someone who would wait for him, not an idiot whose cock makes all the decisions. How could he love me after the way I acted? I was so selfish and now I've lost the best thing that ever happened to me. "

"Val, I didn't mean…"

"What? I know I fucked up and I'm doing the best I can to move on. So just mind your own fucking business!"

Prudence flinched at the harsh, aggressive timbre in Valentine's voice, but apparently wasn't going to give up so easily.

"Stop feeling so *damn* sorry for yourself. You're not the only one who's messed up with relationships."

"I can't deal with this any more. I'll see you later."

"Val, wait!"

Valentine paid no heed to Prudence's plea and stormed out of the apartment, slamming the door behind him. By the time he reached the street his fury hadn't abated and he was no longer in the mood for clubbing. Rather he needed an immediate release, the kind only a certain kind of establishment could provide. Valentine headed straight to a nearby cruising club, ManHole, where he spent the next three hours attempting to fuck away his emotions. All his encounters blurred into one steamy, sticky mess of debauched devilment but his only real desire was to forget.

After he had cum for the third time, Valentine felt both physically and emotionally drained. He slowly made his way back to the apartment, hoping that Prudence had long gone to bed or was away Dirk's for the night – he couldn't deal with another confrontation. Once home, Valentine went directly to the bathroom and turned the shower up to an almost scalding temperature, quickly filling the room with a thick haze of steam. He cast aside his clothes, which bore traces of his recent activities and hopped into the hot water to wash away the remaining evidence of his play.

In his previous life, such a busy night would have been a source of pride but all Valentine felt was regret. Not only had he ended a perfectly good relationship, but he'd also attacked his best friend for trying to help him. Their conversation had made him face all the emotions he'd been trying to repress and his heart felt as raw as if the break up had only been yesterday.

Why am I screwing everything up? I'll end up old and alone.

He started to lather himself up but found tears coming to his eyes and soon streaming down his face. Valentine sunk pitifully to the floor and his body was wracked with sobs.

Have I made the biggest mistake of my life?

* * *

Christmas arrived and departed in a blur of presents and food but the festivities had failed to alleviate Valentine's continuing dark mood. On the plus side Valentine had managed to make things right again in his relationship with Prudence. It had taken a long, tearful conversation, the morning after their fight, with much heartfelt apologizing and several long hugs but by the end of it they were even closer than before. Valentine had agreed to be more open with his feelings and mindful of his reckless behavior, but he was far from a happy man.

Thankfully, the store was closed for a few weeks over the holidays, giving Valentine some time away from dealing with the public and having to pretend he wasn't absolutely miserable. He spent his days trying to cheer himself up with the misery of others by binge-watching one reality series after another – who knew there were so many Desperate Housewives in need of media attention.

Things were so dire, that since that night at ManHole, Valentine hadn't had the desire to pleasure even himself, let alone any random strangers. He moped around the apartment and he moped around the gym. Prudence and James did their best to try and boost his mood but nothing they tried managed to lift Valentine's seemingly impenetrable cloud of depression.

New Year's Eve was only three days away and Valentine didn't plan on doing anything, despite the numerous offers he'd had from family and friends. It was almost as if he punishing himself with hermit-hood. Rationally, Valentine knew he shouldn't be pushing everyone away but his heart was overflowing with a clutter of messy emotions that he didn't know how to deal with properly.

Valentine had just finished a particularly brutal session with James – it was at his own request as it helped keep his mind focused off of himself – and was feeling exhausted. James had attempted to raise Valentine out of his maudlin state with a series of bawdy jokes all to no avail.

On the way home, Valentine called into The Spicy Samurai to grab some takeaway – he rarely felt like cooking of late. Haruki had introduced him to the Mexican Japanese fusion restaurant on their third date and Valentine had been a weekly customer ever since. The reminder of his ex didn't help his mood but the food was so damn good.

He had paid for his order of Wasabi Quesadillas – his favorite fiery treat – and was about to leave when he saw two familiar figures seated at the window and feeding each other in a sickeningly romantic fashion. The couple's intimate meal caused his heart to ache and had Valentine on the verge of tears. At first, he thought it was the overt display of romance that was troubling him, but after a moment he realized he knew the couple in question – Sean and Abraham.

What the fuck? They're dating now?

Valentine rushed out before they spotted him. His world was spinning and he felt slightly nauseous. It seemed that the universe was conspiring against him, rubbing his heart in all his mistakes. He hurried along the sidewalk, oblivious to all those around him, his head a confused jumble of thoughts.

Don't I deserve to be happy too?

He brooded all the way home as the snow gently fell down around him coating the world in white. Once inside, Valentine put down the takeaway on the kitchen counter, his appetite long gone. Suddenly, he came to a decision and riffled through his gym bag until he found his phone and dialed. He knew if he didn't call right this second he might never do it.

There was a terrible silence as the phone took its time connecting to its destination. Valentine gripped the phone so hard his knuckles turned white. Eventually, without ringing, his call connected to straight to voicemail.

"Hi, You've reached Dr. Haruki Ito. I'm obviously out saving the world or more probably having a nap. You know what to do."

As soon as Valentine heard the sound of his voice he knew that he'd made the right decision. He smiled at the familiar message, took a deep breath and opened his heart.

"Hey Doc, it's Valentine. Look, I know I'm an idiot and that I have no right to expect anything from you but I miss you so much. I've made the biggest mistake of my life. I should have never left you…I know it's a big ask but if you're keen I'd really like to give things another go. I don't deserve it and you can probably do much better than the likes of me but I'll do everything I can to make it up to you. OK… now that I've made a complete fool of myself, I'll go…I love you."

Valentine reluctantly hung up. Strangely, he felt better than he had in months.

Even if he doesn't want me, at least I tried.

He marched back into the kitchen and reheated his takeaway. His appetite had returned with a fierce tenacity. After he wolfed down his meal, Valentine plonked down on the sofa, throwing himself once more into the unreal world of reality TV, although he couldn't help furtively looking at his phone every five minutes.

* * *

The final three days of the dying year crept by, with Valentine practically jumping on his phone every time it made a sound. Valentine had twirled his silver ring around so many times it had left a sore, red mark. With each passing day, Valentine feared the worst and was beginning to believe that he had truly lost everything. Not only was the idea of a second chance with Haruki becoming more and more remote, but his desperate rambling message had probably shattered any hopes of maintaining a friendship.

Distraught by the lack of any response, Valentine was sitting alone on the couch, preparing to see the New Year in with only the television, a large meatlover's pizza and a bottle of red wine for company. Prudence had invited him to a party at Dirk's but Valentine hadn't felt the least bit sociable. She had left him to his tortured solitude about an hour beforehand.

Part of him desperately wanted to call again, afraid that Haruki hadn't received the message, although another part was fearful that he had and just didn't want to answer. Valentine was driving himself slightly mad, obsessing about it all but he couldn't seem to stop the dizzying merry-go-round of questions in his head.

What if he met someone else? What if he doesn't love me anymore? What if he truly was the love of my life?

Unexpectedly, his phone buzzed and Valentine leapt on it, absolutely certain of a New Year's Eve miracle. Sadly, his hopes were dashed when he saw by the screen that it was only Prudence.

"Hey, Val. Why don't you come over? I just found out that Dirk's cousin Mark is going to be here. He's single and really hot! I'm sure you'd have fun."

"Thanks, but I just don't feel up for meeting any one new."

"OK. Can't say I didn't try."

Valentine could hear the disappointment in her voice and felt bad for letting her down but he just couldn't muster the will to even leave the apartment, let alone go to a party.

"And I appreciate it but I just can't tonight. I'd be terrible company."

"Alright. I won't be home till tomorrow. Look after yourself."

"I will. Have a fun night."

"Happy Almost New Year."

"You too. Bye."

Valentine hung up and the phone immediately rang again.

"What now, Pru?"

"It's not Pru."

Valentine's heartbeat spiked at the sound of Haruki's voice and his body tensed, sitting on the very edge of the lounge.

"The answer is *Yes*."

"What?"

Valentine was genuinely unsure if Haruki had actually said the word he'd been longing to hear or if it had just been his wishful thinking.

"I said, *Yes*, you silly man. Of course I want to be with you."

Happiness flooded through Valentine's body and he thought he might very well burst from the pure strength of it.

"I can't tell you how much I've been wanting…" Valentine was struck by a sudden unpleasant thought. "Why in the hell did you wait so long to call me?"

"I'm sorry, but the cell towers have been out due to a storm and there was no signal for the last few days. I only just got your message."

I'm still such an idiot!

"I keep saying the wrong thing. Are you sure that you forgive me for being an idiot?"

"Well, I'm certainly used to it by now."

"Hey!" exclaimed Valentine, with mock offence.

"You know I love you."

The warmth Valentine felt at hearing those words simply swept away all the pain and doubt he'd been carrying these past few months.

"I love you too. I can't wait until you're back! I've missed you so much. I've been regretting my decision every day."

"I've missed you too. It's been so rewarding helping people here but I'm keen to come home."

"When are you coming back?"

Even though Valentine desperately wanted to hear the word 'tomorrow', he daren't hope for a second miracle.

"That's the tricky thing. There isn't a set date but probably not for another two months."

Valentine's elation quickly faded with the prospect of spending even more time away from the man he loved, but he decided that it was high time he became a grown up.

"I can wait," he said determinedly.

"You're sure?"

"You're worth it."

"That's how I've always felt about you. Hey, I've got to go. Happy New Year, Cupid Boy!"

"Happy New Year, Doc."

Valentine sat on the couch in a state of absolute bliss. When he recovered from the shock of the joyous news, Valentine sprinted to the bathroom. He had a shower, shave and was dressed in his party finery, in record time. It was time to celebrate and he had a party to get to.

Happy New Year to me!

* * *

January was filled with much messaging and the occasional Skype call when the patchy Internet signal allowed. It appeared that things were wrapping up in Nepal but Haruki still wasn't sure when he'd be home. Valentine's mood had improved beyond measure and everyone had noticed, as he walked around with a near constant smile on his face. Even though he still missed Haruki, Valentine felt far less lonely than he had the past few months.

Valentine, to his great amazement, wasn't even struggling with fidelity. It wasn't that he was so blinded by love that he failed to notice all other men – that was the stuff of fairytales. Rather he was able to appreciate the beauty of other men, particularly those straining away on the gym floor – and soaping themselves up in the shower afterwards – but for once his heart overruled his cock and all he wanted was Haruki. His hand, however, had been getting quite the workout…not to mention the frequent use of his extensive toy collection.

At the end of January, Valentine received the best news he'd had since Haruki had agreed to get back together. It turned out that his boyfriend would be home a month earlier than he thought, on Valentine's Day in fact. It was the first time in his adult life that Valentine could remember not hating the prospect of his birthday.

On the day itself Valentine arrived at the airport a full two hours in advance, such was his excitement at being reunited with his beloved. He sat by the gates, a huge bouquet of fragrant, brightly colored stargazer lilies – Haruki's favorite – gripped firmly in his hand as he waited.

Fortunately, the plane arrived at its allotted time and Valentine was eagerly waiting up against the barrier, his eyes fervently scanning the new arrivals for the familiar form of his long-lost boyfriend. After twenty minutes or so, Valentine began to fear that Haruki had missed his flight. He looked down to check if he'd missed any messages when he heard a familiar voice from beside him.

"Hey there, Mister. My boyfriend was supposed to pick me up but I'd happily go home with you."

Valentine turned to see a very tired-looking, and awfully scruffy, Haruki, with a cheeky smile on his lips.

"I don't know. My boyfriend would probably mind if I took a grubby stranger home from the airport," said Valentine, before he leaned forward and swept Haruki up into a vice-like grip and equally forceful kiss.

Their passionate embrace lasted quite a few minutes, oblivious to all those around them. When they finally broke apart, both their eyes were stained wet with tears of happiness.

"I'm so glad you're back," gushed Valentine.

"Happy Valentine's Birthday."

"You're so scruffy!"

"Well…I can go back if you like."

Haruki half-turned and Valentine latched onto him in a second.

"Don't even think about it! The only place you're going is home with me, Doc!"

They quickly made their way outside and jumped into the first available cab. Opportunely, there wasn't too big a queue at that time of day and the reunited lovebirds were soon zipping towards Valentine's apartment.

Haruki had rented out his apartment in his absence and the tenants still had another month on their lease, so Valentine had offered for Haruki to move in with him temporarily. Prudence had generously agreed to spend the weekend at Dirk's so they could have the apartment all to themselves for a few days.

As soon as they shut the apartment door behind them they came together with an urgent longing. Despite Haruki's tiredness from his long flight the sight of Valentine had apparently been enough to revive him. Unlike Valentine, he hadn't had the touch of another man in over five months so was rather keen to release some pent up tension. That being said, Valentine had been celibate for almost eight weeks himself…almost unheard of since he'd started having sex at the age of sixteen.

"Sure you don't need a sleep?" teased Valentine.

"Hell, no!"

To emphasize his point Haruki ripped off Valentine's coat, followed quickly by his t-shirt, jeans and underwear before hastily stripping himself and picking up his boyfriend and carrying him to the bathroom for a long, hot, steamy shower.

After stepping into the warm spray of water together, the pair began to kiss hungrily. The twosome them proceeded to make up for lost time, their hands exploring one another's bodies, becoming reacquainted with each other.

Valentine forcefully pushed Haruki up against the white tiled wall and kissed his way down his boyfriend's muscular body, which looked and tasted just as good as he remembered. Once on his knees, Valentine took Haruki's rock hard member in his right hand and the smooth heavy balls in his left. He licked the tip of the cockhead savoring the salty/sweet precum that was oozing from the tip. He teased it, swirling his tongue around the glans, all the while tugging gently on the very full balls. Without warning he swallowed it all in one go, his face pressed in tight against Haruki's crotch. He coughed and spluttered just a little – it had been a while, after all – but Valentine soon recovered and was bobbing up and down the shaft savoring the thickness and taste of the juicy manhood. Valentine had only been at it a minute or so before Haruki tensed up, gasping as his body shook and shot a very full load straight into Valentine's greedy mouth. In his desire, Valentine gulped down every last drop of the salty seed.

Slowly climbing to his feet, Valentine pulled Haruki in close for another long, languid kiss.

"Thanks, I needed that," whispered Haruki.

"Me too, but we're not done yet."

"I'm counting on it."

After washing each other very thoroughly – no nook or cranny left untouched – they hopped out and dried off, where a lot more kissing interrupted the process. Eventually, the lovebirds returned to the bedroom where Haruki took charge, throwing Valentine onto the bed face down.

"Beautiful," he murmured, just before he sank to his knees and shoved his face right into between the crease of Valentine's pert buttocks. He used his strong hands to spread the cheeks wide, wetting the sparse blonde hairs, as his tongue swirled around the entrance before burrowing inside the freshly cleaned passage.

Valentine's hands grasped at the pillows as his boyfriend's exploring tongue sent waves of pleasure all through his body. Haruki's stubble felt delightfully scratchy moving over his sensitive opening. It was all the more sensitive not having been penetrated by anything other than inanimate objects the past few months.

After he'd feasted for a good ten minutes, Haruki spun his boyfriend onto his back and dived forward to give him a deep, passionate kiss.

"Take me," begged Valentine.

Haruki reached for the top drawer of the bedside table, correctly assuming that Valentine still kept his supplies in the same place. He grabbed the lubricant and squirted a big dollop into his palm and used it to gently finger Valentine's hole, coating his cock at the same time. Haruki then lined up his weapon and slowly pushed his bare cock deep inside the warm, welcoming ass, all the while kissing Valentine and gazing deeply into his crystal blue eyes.

Once he was in to the hilt, Haruki sat up and grabbed hold of Valentine's muscular legs, keeping them spread nice and wide as he leisurely ground into his boyfriend's snug passage. His balls gently tapped against Valentine's buttocks, as hips moved in soft, slow circular motions, stretching out the slick, velvety tunnel.

Valentine wriggled on the bed, moaning in pleasure as he felt the manhood graze across his prostate with each gentle thrust. His hands reached down to Haruki's hips, in an attempt to pull his boyfriend in even closer inside him.

The room soon became heated with the warmth of their play, as Haruki increased his pace, starting to hammer into the moist hole before him. Their grunts and groans echoed throughout the bedroom, accompanied by the arousing sound of skin slapping together. Sweat trickled down Haruki's smooth, solid chest and dripped onto his boyfriend's writhing form.

Valentine's nails dug into the flesh of Haruki's buttocks, encouraging him to pound even harder. The frantic pace, coupled with the joy of finally being back with his beloved, soon had Valentine at the brink of orgasm without the need to touch himself. His body began to strain and shudder at the impending release. Valentine cried out as the first spurt exploded straight up into the air before splattering back down onto his tensed abs. He thrashed about the bed with each successive eruption, his head pushing back into the pillow.

The fierce contractions of Valentine's passage milked the manhood lodged deep inside, seemingly desperate to receive the creamy load within. Haruki gave one final thrust before pulling out. He arched his back as his body contracted in ecstasy and then sprayed his seed all over his boyfriend's slick torso, before collapsing forward and lying heavily down on top of Valentine. Heat radiated off the young lovers, making the room seem even more humid and sticky.

As their labored breathing gradually returned to normal, the spent semen mixed together between the two slippery bodies, becoming a deliciously messy testament to their lovemaking. The heady aroma of men at play hung in the air, as they lay kissing and stroking one another. The warmth of the bedroom and the strength of their exertions soon lulled the pair into a light doze, where they lay wrapped up tight in a tangle of sheets.

Some time later, Haruki reawakened with Valentine's rehardened manhood pressing into him. Apparently wanting to wake up his boyfriend in a most pleasurable manner, Haruki grabbed the bottle of lubricant once more, but this time used it to prepare his own hole for invasion. Haruki straddled his sleeping sweetheart and carefully maneuvered himself on top of Valentine's stiff erection. The head breached Haruki's tight sphincter and he slowly sat back, receiving each wonderfully thick inch.

Moments later, Valentine woke up to the magnificent sight of his boyfriend starting to ride his cock. To start with he was simply content to watch as Haruki leaned forward and back, gasping as the cock probed deep inside him. Valentine ran his hands along Haruki's sides, up to his chest, then across to the round, dark brown nipples. He lightly tweaked them causing Haruki to grunt his appreciation.

Wanting to control the motion, Valentine then slid his hands down to Haruki's slim hips and grasped them tightly. He used his strong grip to pull Haruki down as he thrust his own hips upwards, driving his manhood deeper and deeper inside. The lads were soon dripping with perspiration as their bodies slammed together in a frenzied need for one another.

Haruki jacked himself furiously, as Valentine's member repeatedly impaled him. A few feverish minutes later, the replenished load in Haruki's balls found its much needed release and sprayed all over Valentine. It splashed onto his heaving chest, neck and even his chin – not that Valentine minded in the slightest.

The sensation of the hot seed dripping down his body and the way the Haruki's muscles clamped down around his cock sent Valentine flying towards another ejaculation. Without even needing to thrust one more time, his manhood throbbed and began to paint Haruki's cozy passageway with his cream.

They repeated this pattern over the next few hours, taking turns sodomizing one another, and ejaculating until there was barely a drop left in either of their thoroughly drained sacks. Eventually, the exhausted pair fell into a deep slumber, awakening the following morning to restart their play once more. They spent the rest of the weekend in a glorious haze of fornicating, sleeping and eating. By the end they were both sore but sated and very much in love.

* * *

Their month of cohabitation seemed to be ending almost as soon as it started and Valentine couldn't imagine what he had been so scared of all these years. Granted, the joy of being reunited meant that they had spent that time in a virtual honeymoon, loved up and naked whenever they got the chance, but it had felt so right.

It was a few days before Haruki was due to move back into his own apartment and the pair were laying naked in bed together after yet another rousing session.

"It'll be weird not having you here all the time," said Valentine, as he snuggled in closer to Haruki.

"I've been thinking…"

"How unusual."

Haruki sat up and playfully smacked Valentine's exposed buttocks.

"Quiet, you. I was wondering how you would feel about making things more permanent?"

"What do you mean?"

"Would you like to move in with me…properly?"

"What?"

"I know we've only been back together for a few months but I never stopped loving you and I'm ready to take the next step with you."

Despite the suddenness of the suggestion, it didn't terrify Valentine as much as it once would have done. Valentine surprised himself by not endlessly questioning everything and just going with his heart.

"Yes, I'd love to!"

They kissed and celebrated in the best way they knew how.

In spite of his newfound domestic bliss, Valentine did have one concern, Prudence – his current flat mate. They had been living together for nearly three years now and were almost like a couple themselves. Fortuitously, it turned out that his concern was very much unwarranted, as Prudence had her own plans.

"Dirk's lease is finishing up and I was going to ask you if you minded him moving in here," explained Prudence when Valentine had mentioned his plans the following morning.

"Problem solved then!" Valentine had exclaimed happily, although there was a smidge of sadness. "I'll miss what we have though."

"Me too, pretty boy."

"We'll always have *Las Pasiones de la Familia*!"

The pair shared a warm, friendly hug before going off to tell their respective partners the joyous news.

The grand apartment swap happened over the next two weeks. After the couples had properly settled into their new lodgings, they held a grand housewarming extravaganza, featuring two housewarming parties in the same weekend to celebrate the new living arrangements, with much drinking and merriment to be had. Of course, come Sunday there were more than a few sore heads and tired bodies but all's fair in love and liquor.

* * *

Valentine was pottering about Grandma's Closet preparing to close up. He was in an exceptionally good mood, as he and Haruki were headed out for a romantic dinner to celebrate the anniversary of their first date. Valentine could scarcely believe the difference a year had made in his life. The promiscuous party boy had been tamed and was now living in unadulterated domestic delight. Not that he was a choir boy these days by any stretch of the imagination, with there still being rather a few rowdy nights about the town but the only bed hopping he was doing was in and out of his and Haruki's king-sized one.

Naturally, it hadn't been all smooth sailing for the lovebirds, with the occasional squabble and spat, but it wasn't anything that couldn't easily be fixed with a bunch of flowers and a heartfelt apology – and a good helping of make-up sex.

Normally, Sophinika would have been closing up but Valentine had sent her home earlier in the day. Her rather green complexion, from the flu she was doing her best to fight off, wasn't particularly conducive to garnering sales. Valentine had just finished tidying the racks up the back of the shop when he heard the small, silver bell jingle over the front door. He could see a big, brawny figure, wearing a black hoodie pulled up over his head, which shrouded the man's face in shadow.

"I'm sorry, we're just about to close."

As Valentine approached the man he saw that there seemed to be something wrong with his face. It took him a few seconds to realize that the man was wearing a mask and it quickly dawned on him what was about to happen.

From his waistband, the man pulled out a small handgun and moved forward in a menacing manner.

"Please…don't…don't shoot. I'll give anything you want," pleaded Valentine, his voice wavering in fear.

"Empty the till, now," demanded the man in a cold, emotionless voice.

"There isn't much money. We did the banking at lunchtime."

The man raised him arm and pistol-whipped Valentine, knocking him to the ground.

"Shut up, faggot! Just get up and give me all you have!"

Valentine climbed unsteadily to his feet and made his way to the counter. Due to the blow, his vision was a little blurry, so he moved carefully. The only thing keeping Valentine moving was the fear of what the man would do to if he didn't obey the commands.

"Hurry up or you'll get worse than just a little tap."

"OK, OK."

He hurried as best he could and opened the register. Luckily, as he'd told the robber, there wasn't a great deal of cash – barely a hundred in change. The afternoon had been relatively quiet and the transactions had been mostly electronic. He tentatively handed over the money.

"Is this IT?" the man screamed.

"I told you we already did the banking to…"

He was cut off by the man swinging his arm again, hitting Valentine square on the temple and sending him sprawling to the wooden floorboards.

"Now, stay down you little bitch or I'll fucking shoot you."

Valentine didn't dare say a word. His head was throbbing and the room was spinning around; the whole world appeared out of focus. Valentine felt hot tears rolling down his face, as he heard the heavy footsteps of his assailant quickly exiting the shop.

He lay there for what seemed like hours, but was in fact barely a few minutes, before he heard the bell above the door ring again. Valentine was petrified that the man had come back to kill him but it was a woman's voice that spoke next.

"Valentine…oh my goodness…are you alright?" She knelt down beside Valentine and helped him into a sitting position. She then handed him a wad of tissues from her purse. "Here put this against your head. Oh my, you're bleeding pretty badly."

Valentine was still somewhat dazed, he saw that his hands were stained red with blood but he hadn't made the connection that it was from his own head. To his dismay, Valentine saw that his silver ring was also coated in red.

"I'd just locked up when I saw that terrible man come running out and I called the police straight away. They should be here soon. Can I get you anything?"

Valentine couldn't yet form any words so shook his head slightly in response. He was just glad to have someone there by his side. When Valentine could see clearly again, he realized that it was Francine, the well-put together middle-aged woman who owned Fallen Angel Cakes just down the block. Usually, Valentine and Sophinika shared a thriving addiction for their donuts but presently he felt sick to his stomach and the thought of the sweet treats caused his stomach to lurch.

"I'm going to be sick."

Francine jumped up and grabbed the nearby trash can and held Valentine's hand. She then made soothing sounds as Valentine emptied his stomach.

"Don't worry, help will be here soon. You poor thing. Can I call someone for you?"

"Yes, Haruki, my boyfriend. His number is in my phone."

Valentine handed it over to Francine and let her call, as he wasn't yet confident in his ability to handle such a seemingly complex task.

"Voicemail…I'll leave a message." Francine said giving Valentine a reassuring pat on the hand.

The police and ambulance arrived simultaneously around fifteen minutes later. To Valentine, the next hour was pretty much a blur of people swarming around him, poking, prodding and asking questions. The one thing he did remember clearly, however, was one of the policemen – Officer Ford – whose ruggedly, handsome features and comforting presence calmed him down enough to make a brief statement.

"I can see that you're still in a bit of a state, so I'll give you my card and we'll chat when you've recovered," said Officer Ford, giving Valentine a hearty, warm smile and helping into the back of the ambulance.

* * *

Shortly afterwards, Valentine was patiently waiting in a cubicle to see a doctor. The paramedics had given him a little something for the pain and to help keep calm, so he was currently feeling a little floaty but still relatively in control of his faculties.

He'd been waiting about ten minutes when in walked one of the most stunning women Valentine had ever seen. Even with his firm male-centric leanings, Valentine could see that she was breathtakingly beautiful with piercing gray eyes, midnight black hair down to her waist and a lithe figure. She picked up the chart and quickly read through the report.

"Mr…Goodness. I'm Dr. Hastings. Let me have a look at you."

The name sounded vaguely familiar to Valentine but he couldn't place where he knew it. The blow to the head and the medication was undoubtedly not helping with his memory.

She examined the laceration to his left temple, and then had Valentine follow the light from her small torch with his eyes. Apparently satisfied with the results, she put down the torch and made a few more notes on the chart.

"Well, there doesn't seem to be any lasting damage. You will need stitches but that won't take too long and then we can get you home. Do you have someone to look after you tonight?"

"Yes, I think my boyfriend is on his way."

As if on cue, Haruki burst through the curtain of the cubicle, rushed to Valentine's side and gave him the gentlest of kisses on the forehead.

"Val! I'm so sorry. I was with in surgery when they called. I tell you, when they catch the guy I'm going to do some extremely creative procedures on him. Are you OK?"

"Yeah, the doctor is taking care of me.

Apparently only just noticing the doctor, Haruki turned to face her.

"Thanks, Dr…Maddie?"

"Hi, Haru."

"When did you get back in town?"

"Only last week. I've been meaning to call you."

It suddenly clicked for Valentine why he knew the doctor's name – he was being treated by Haruki's ex-wife! He cleared his throat to grab their attention.

"Sorry, Val," said Haruki, turning back to his boyfriend. "This is Madeline, my ex and Madeline this is Val."

"Nice to meet you," said Valentine offering his hand.

Valentine felt incredibly awkward. It was foolish but he was still a teensy bit jealous of Haruki's former spouse and now having seen her in the flesh he was more than a little intimidated. Valentine knew that the divorce had been rather amicable and he suddenly felt very inadequate in comparison.

"And you, although I wish it had been under more pleasant circumstances." Madeline turned to Haruki again. "Well, I see you still have impeccable taste. I must admit I'm a little jealous."

The compliment managed to filter through Valentine's fuzzy brain and he felt a small smile creep onto his face.

"Now, now you've had your share of comely companions too. There was that Sri Lankan photographer, the Brazilian soccer player, the…"

"Yes, yes." Madeline had a rich melodic laugh that Valentine warmed to straight away. "You better hush up, before your Valentine gets the wrong idea about me. Anyway, I should get back to work. Unless you wanted to do the honors?"

Haruki glanced down at his hands, which were shaking a little in an obvious reaction to the situation.

"No, I'm afraid my hands aren't the steadiest at the moment." Haruki gave Valentine a reassuring squeeze. "Don't worry, she's one of the best."

Haruki was proved correct as Madeline deftly went about her task, her nimble fingers working in a quick professional manner. In fact, it seemed to Valentine that she'd finished in only a few seconds – although the medication was quite strong.

"All done. Now you take care of this man of yours and let me know if there are any problems."

"Thanks, Maddie," said a clearly grateful Haruki.

"Yes, thanks very much," added Valentine.

"We should catch up when I'm settled in properly."

"I'd like that."

"Me too," agreed Valentine.

Much to his surprise, Valentine found that he actually meant it. It hadn't been the best of introductions but Valentine was glad that they had finally crossed paths.

The pair then caught a cab home, Haruki's scooter not being the best choice of transport for someone in Valentine's condition. Before too long, they were firmly ensconced in the comfort of home. Haruki took Valentine straight to bed and tucked him in, with all carnal thoughts being put to the side – for the moment, at least.

Understandably tired after his ordeal, Valentine soon drifted off to sleep with a watchful Haruki gently stroking his head.

* * *

Around two months later, the wonderfully long summer was coming to a close. Valentine's bruises had faded away and his stitches had fortunately only left the faintest hint of a scar. Thanks to the surveillance footage of nearby shops, the police had apprehended the thief a few days after the robbery – he'd stupidly taken off his mask a block away. The man, Ethan Jones, was a small time felon who had been in and out of jail over the last few years, which was where he was residing currently.

Officer Ford, who was even more handsome than Valentine remembered, had delivered the news to him personally. Had he been single, Valentine would have gladly given the strapping officer a thank you he wouldn't soon forget. Instead, Valentine settled for showing his appreciation with a huge hug and the offer of a fifty per cent discount if he ever wanted to purchase anything from Grandma's Closet.

"I might just take you up on that." Officer Ford had replied with his big, warm smile.

Valentine and Haruki had also taken Francine out to dinner to thank her for all her help.

"There's no need for all that." Francine had protested briefly before letting the boys invite her to Horizon, the five-star restaurant on the terrace of the Grand Babylon Hotel.

While Valentine had been rather rattled by the incident, several sessions with Dr. Waters – a therapist recommended by

Sophinika – had helped Valentine to put the trauma behind him, although he'd since invested in a more modern security system for the shop with an alarm buzzer for emergencies.

The robbery had also caused Valentine to evaluate his life and come to a very important decision. To that end, he had planned with Haruki to go to their spot on The Head for a sunset picnic. Valentine had carefully packed the hamper with all the essential supplies to make the moment perfect.

The loved up lads were sitting on a big red and blue checkered blanket, the warm summer breeze blowing gently as they ate. Valentine was exceedingly nervous but trying not to show it.

"Everything, OK?" asked Haruki.

"Couldn't be better."

The fading sunlight bathed Haruki's darkly golden skin in a most becoming glow and Valentine's heart couldn't help but flutter a little every time he glanced over at his beau.

I love him so much. No time like present.

"I've actually got something to ask you?" said Valentine timidly.

"Sure I'd love to mess around in the bushes again."

"No…I mean I'd love that too, but that's not what I was going to ask."

"Oooh, I'm intrigued now."

Valentine's stomach felt like it was doing cartwheels. He just hoped he could get his question out before doing something embarrassing like throwing up the chocolate covered strawberries they'd just been feeding each other.

"I've been doing a lot of thinking since the robbery, about what's truly important in my life. Haruki, you've made me so happy over these past months and I can't imagine my life without you. I never want to lose you."

Valentine took off his silver ring and held it out to Haruki.

"Dr. Haruki Ito, will you marry me?"

Haruki broke into great peals of laughter, hardly the reaction that Valentine was expecting.

"You could have just said no," said Valentine, starting to become an unpleasant mixture of cross and disappointed.

"Oh Val. I'm sorry. It's just that you beat me to it." He dug into his satchel and brought out a ring box. He opened it to show a finely crafted platinum ring. "I'll answer your question if you answer mine."

"OK," agreed Valentine, with a huge grin plastered on his face.

"Valentine Goodness, will you please do me the honor of being my husband?"

"Yes, of course I will!"

"Good, then of course I'll marry you too, my beautiful Cupid Boy."

After eagerly slipping the rings on each other's fingers, the newly engaged couple came together in a passionate embrace, rolling around on the ground in a state of unabashed bliss. Their celebration threatened to become rather indecent until the sound of a nearby car starting up reminded them of their surroundings. The pair sheepishly sat up on the picnic blanket.

Valentine rummaged in the hamper for the bottle of champagne that he'd secreted in the bottom, which he then presented with a flourish.

"Ta-dah!"

"So you were pretty confident I'd say yes, then?" asked a bemused Haruki.

"How could you refuse?"

Haruki leaned forward and gave Valentine a soft peck, as he gazed deeply into his fiancé's eyes and lovingly stroked his face.

"That's true…and I wouldn't have it any other way."

"Just as well," teased Valentine, as he started to undo the foil around the cork.

The bottle opened with a loud pop, sending the cork flying several feet and a releasing a gush of champagne, which the newly-engaged couple did their best to catch in their glasses, all the while giggling like schoolboys.

After they'd drunk a few celebratory glasses, Valentine crawled in between Haruki's legs, so that his boyfriend was cuddling him from behind. Looking out to sea, Valentine had a vision of their future spreading out before them with nothing but clear skies and sunshine for many years to come.

Maybe I'm a hopeless romantic, after all?

ABOUT THE AUTHOR

Jimi could be considered to be something of a refined blend of Australian/Polish heritage – given his passion for the arts, vodka and BBQs. He now lives in Paris with his wonderfully understanding French husband and cats.

For other of his raunchy ramblings and published work, feel free to browse http://www.jimify.me follow him on Twitter & Instagram @jimifyme or show your devotion at facebook.com/JIMIFY.ME

DIGITAL TITLES BY JIMI GONINAN

DOM'S DELIGHTS 1:

DOM'S DELIGHTS 2: BACHELOR PARTY BLOWOUT

DOM'S DELIGHTS 3: HUSBANDLY DUTIES

MILE HIGH CUB

LOVE THE SINNER

UNDERWEAR MAKETH THE MAN

BEST SERVED HOT

LUST AFTER DEATH

ON THE NAUGHTY LIST

AIN'T NO SAINT

For all Jimi's titles please visit his page at lydianpress.com

IN PRINT FROM LYDIAN PRESS

DOM'S DELIGHTS

Come on in and taste the love!

Dom has worked hard pursuing his dreams of delighting the masses with his tasty treats - indeed his cream has been eagerly eaten all about the town. Now he has almost everything he ever dreamed of – a successful business, loving friends and a beautiful beau. There's just one more thing he needs to make his life complete...to finally marry the man of his dreams!

There's so much to do before the big day but luckily, they encounter more than a few friendly helping hands along the way. Follow the adventures of Dom and his merry band of lusty lads as they help him overcome pesky obstacles and prepare for the most important day of his life. Everyone deserves a good old-fashioned happy ending, after all.

BEST SERVED HOT

Revenge has never been sweeter.

When Jameson loses everything he holds dear, he almost drowns in a sea of despair. Bitter and broken, he shuns his friends and retreats from the world. Then a chance encounter with a handsome young man offers him a glimmer of hope, and he slowly begins to piece his life back together. Will he be given the second chance at the love he so desperately deserves?

Lydian Press is dedicated to bringing you the finest
GLBTQ erotic literature on the web.

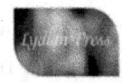

Visit us on the web at:

http://lydianpress.com

* 9 7 8 1 9 0 9 9 3 4 9 2 4 *